A Bride's

ROGUE

IN ROMA, TEXAS

A Bride's ROGUE

IN ROMA, TEXAS

DARLENE FRANKLIN

BARBOUR
PUBLISHING

Print ISBN 978-1-61626-739-1

eBook Editions:
Adobe Digital Edition (.epub) 978-1-62029-066-8
Kindle and MobiPocket Edition (.prc) 978-1-62029-067-5

Cover design: Faceout Studio, www.faceoutstudio.com

Published by Barbour Publishing, Inc., P.O. Box 719, Uhrichsville, Ohio 44683, www.barbourbooks.com

Our mission is to publish and distribute inspirational products offering exceptional value and biblical encouragement to the masses.

 Member of the
Evangelical Christian
Publishers Association

Printed in the United States of America.

Dedication

This book is dedicated with many grateful thanks to Julie Jarnagin for helping me make changes to the copyedit while I was in the hospital and for allowing me to be a grandmother to her son. (Because a boy can never have too many grandmothers.)

Chapter 1

Roma, Texas, 1897

Salt residue marked the trail of Blanche Lamar's tears down the front of her black twill suit. "At least I didn't need to buy new clothes for the funeral." A hiccup interrupted her sobs.

Dipping a washcloth in a basin of cool water, she blotted away the evidence of tears from her face and dress. She raised her face to look in the mirror. Mama always said that a lady should present a neat appearance, no matter what.

Hollow brown eyes stared out of her pale face, whiter than usual beneath her always bright auburn hair. Her black hat would cover the chignon, hiding the riot of color that had irritated Mama so.

"Oh, Mama." Blanche rubbed her eyes, but nothing stemmed the flood of tears.

A gentle knock fell on the door, and Mrs. Davenport, the pastor's wife, slipped in. "It's time." Clucking, she put her arms around Blanche's shoulders. Mama would be mortified by Blanche's puffy eyes. She sniffed the tears. . .and grief. . .inside.

"Take this, dear." Mrs. Davenport handed her a lace-edged handkerchief. "Are you ready?"

Nodding, Blanche followed her down the hall to the sanctuary. If only she had some other family member to accompany her—a father, brother, sister, aunt, grandparent—but she and Mama had been a tight family of two. Did one person constitute a family? *I'm alone.* Reverend Davenport and his wife were kind, but they couldn't tuck her in at night or tell her stories about the past. Tell her about the father Blanche had never known and now never would.

Organ music streamed through the open door of the sanctuary. "Rock of Ages." Mama loved that hymn. Blanche bit on her bottom lip against renewed tears.

"There's a good turnout. People admired your mother. You're not alone." Mrs. Davenport gestured at the sanctuary, three-quarters full of people, men and women, dressed in the same somber black as Blanche.

Except for one blot of color. A lone man, his hair nearly as red as her own, sat by himself on the back pew. His dove-gray suit glowed in the sea of black that made up the congregation. She searched her memory but couldn't place him. What was a stranger doing at her mother's funeral?

Pushing the man to the back of her mind, she took a seat on the front pew. After Mrs. Davenport sat beside her, her husband began his remarks.

Blanche struggled to pay attention to the pastor's words of comfort, about the promise of eternal life, his words of praise for her mother's good works among widows and orphans. Mrs. Davenport sang "The Old Rugged Cross," another one of Mama's favorite hymns.

At the end of the service, the pastor motioned Blanche forward. She forced herself to look down into her mother's face, prematurely white hair pulled back in a neat bun, wearing her favorite mauve silk dress, Bible placed between her hands. The mortician's blush on her cheeks looked unnatural. Mama didn't approve of cosmetics of any kind.

"Are you ready? Come, let's go." Mrs. Davenport whispered in her ear. At Blanche's nod, she cupped her elbow and led her to the church's fellowship hall. The scents of ham, beans, and potato salad greeted them, cloying her nose.

A long line of deacons and church matrons filed past Blanche, each one with a kind word to share about her mother. Their comments fell into a predictable pattern. With every repetition of "she's in a better place now," a silent scream built in Blanche's throat.

What would Mama make of the mansion God had prepared for her? She might insist it was much too fancy, that she only needed a room or two. God would have to change her mind; no one else had ever been able to.

No one acknowledged Blanche's pain, an almost physical ache. Not that she wished her mother back, not now that she had entered a place of peace and joy. No, Blanche's grief was for herself, her loneliness, and her final loss of any ties to her past.

Ruth Fairfax, Mama's best friend, came toward the end of her line. "You know you have a home with me, as long as you need it."

Blanche's heart swelled, and once again she blinked back tears. "Thank you, Ruth."

"I'll wait until you are ready to leave, so I can take you home."

"I appreciate that." Truth was, Blanche didn't know what the future held for her. Mama left a little money, enough to keep her going for a few weeks but not much more.

The man in the dove-gray suit came last in line. Upon a closer inspection, Blanche confirmed her first impression that she had never seen him before. What a dandy, with his three-piece suit, stiff collar and shirt studs, and curling mustache. What this man was doing at her mother's funeral, she couldn't guess.

Despite his fancy suit, the man's features settled in somber lines, his blue eyes solemn and serious. "Miss Lamar, I know we haven't met before, but first let me express my condolences on the loss of your mother."

"Umm. . .thank you." The appearance of this stranger troubled her in ways no one should have to endure at her mother's funeral.

"I know this must be a difficult time for you, but if I could have a few words with you in private either today or tomorrow, I would be most appreciative. Whatever time is convenient for you."

Blanche blinked. "I'm not in the habit of meeting gentlemen alone." She heard the asperity in her tone and chided herself for it.

"Of course not. But. . .away from all these people. Perhaps with the pastor?" The solid muscles beneath the well-fitting suit testified to his familiarity with getting his own way. Perhaps he was an attorney of some kind, with news of an unexpected will dispersing Mama's few worldly goods?

Blanche's pulse raced as another possibility occurred to her. Perhaps he knew something about her father. Perhaps Mama had broken her silence from the grave and arranged for the truth to be revealed in the event of her death. Her heart sped. "Tomorrow, here, at the same time?"

"I'll be here. Oh, and my name is Ike Gallagher." He reached into his breast pocket and handed her a card. *Ike Gallagher, purser, Lamar Industries, Ltd.*

Lamar Industries. Blanche's hopes rose another notch.

Ike Gallagher gazed across the church hall, filled with well-meaning people and tables laden with food. From his spot at the door, he had sensed at least half a dozen glances flick over him and dismiss him as not their kind.

Give them the benefit of the doubt, Captain Lamar had urged him. *They mean well.* Even if they only wanted to protect young Miss Lamar, why didn't they practice the love Christ preached? He'd rather grab a bite to eat at the saloon down the street.

Thinking of Blanche Lamar, he couldn't believe that straight-laced woman could be the offspring of Captain J.O. Lamar. Until last week, when the captain had pointed out the obituary of Cordelia Lamar, Ike didn't even know the captain had ever married. In the ten years Ike had known him, he had never mentioned one word about family.

The captain flirted with female passengers but never entertained any serious relationships. Ike attributed that to the captain's desire to avoid attachments—one of the ways they were alike.

The captain never would have revealed his secret, if not for the death of his wife. "Cordelia and me, we knew pretty quick that we weren't suited to each other. I didn't discover the news about the baby until after I had gone back to the River. And when I sent her money, she said she wouldn't accept money from me if she had to beg on the streets. I respected her wishes and stayed away. But now that she's gone. . .my girl. She's all alone in the world. I've got to be sure she's provided for."

After the study he'd made of Miss Blanche Marie Lamar during the funeral, Ike suspected she wouldn't be any more agreeable to Lamar's lifestyle than her mother had been all those years ago. The young lady might have only lived nineteen years, from what the captain had told Ike, but she dressed like an old maid already. He doubted she would agree to the offer he would make on behalf of the captain.

But then again. . .there was the set of her features, the flash in her eyes, the tilt to her chin when she'd challenged him about meeting men alone. Oh, he'd seen that tilt before, many times—when the captain wanted to make a point. Blanche Lamar might follow the rules, but she knew how to fight for what she wanted. For the sake of the captain, he would make his best effort to carry out his wishes.

Whistling, Ike flipped a coin. Heads, he'd go to the saloon. Tails, he'd go back to the hotel for the evening. Performing somersaults in the air, the quarter landed tails up. He'd see what action he could find at the hotel. He was good at ferreting it out.

After all, Captain Lamar would expect no less.

Ike headed straight for the bar until the bartender had chased him and his companions out shortly after midnight. A few hands in Ike's suite turned into an all-night affair, leaving him about a hundred dollars richer. Pale streaks of gray relieved the black sky when the last of Ike's guests left his room. He hefted the bag of coins and cash in his hand. No matter what Miss Blanche Lamar had to say later today, he'd had a successful trip.

A quick glance at the bedside clock reminded him that only four hours remained until his meeting with Miss Lamar. He would sleep while he could, he decided. After stripping down, he stretched out on top of the sheets, set his mind to wake up in a couple of hours, and closed his eyes.

When he awoke, he put on a fresh shirt—this one deep blue with mother-of-pearl studs. He reached for a red bow tie but decided against it. After all, they were meeting at a church; he should show proper restraint. Comb and pomade restored his hair to its usual perfection. Tugging on the lapels of his suit, he grinned at his image. Blanche Lamar didn't stand a chance against his charm.

Whistling "Oh Promise Me," he ventured down the stairs and into the bright sunshine of a summer day. With money in his pocket, time away from the river, and a pretty girl to see, he looked forward to the day. Even with her dull mourning clothes and grief-stricken face, the captain's daughter couldn't hide her beauty or the sparks that flew from her fiery hair.

Pausing by the hotel's dining room, Ike inhaled the aromas coming from the kitchen. He resisted the temptation to stop for a few minutes; Blanche didn't look like the kind of person who would take tardiness lightly. If he didn't show up at the church on time, she might decide he wasn't coming and disappear.

If that happened, he'd never hear the end of it. Thinking of that, he hastened his steps for Christ the King Church. Even when quiet and empty, the sanctuary didn't feel deserted. The air hummed with expectancy. God's house—the house where God dwells. A shiver ran down Ike's arms. He wasn't a superstitious man, but he didn't like to think of God looking over his shoulder at some of the mischief he got into. Goose bumps raced up his arms, and he shook himself. Put the same furnishings of plush pews and stained glass in a different setting, and he'd think *theater*. No need to get the whim-whams.

Shoes scuffled on the polished floor, and Ike turned to watch the approach of Blanche with the pastor. She wore the same somber black suit as at the funeral; maybe she was one of these people who thought she needed to adhere to strict rules of mourning. If anything, she looked paler than she had the previous day.

"Mr. Gallagher, I presume?" Reverend Davenport extended a hand.

Ike nodded.

"Let's retire to my study." The man, so thin he could almost have served as a model for Ichabod Crane, led the way to a room with two hardwood chairs in front of a walnut desk, surrounded by an ocean of musty-smelling books. Give Ike his purser's quarters any day, with sextant and telescope and logs. . .freedom this room didn't even afford a glimpse.

Two hard-backed chairs sat in front of a fearsome desk; no one would stay here long. The setting neither inspired confidence nor invited intimacy—something he excelled at creating, even in the dullest of back parlors. He reminded himself that this errand wasn't about him but about the captain's wishes.

He smiled to turn on the charm. "Thank you for agreeing to meet with me."

Blanche reached into her reticule and pulled out the ivory calling card he had left with her yesterday. "This says you're from Lamar Industries. Did my. . .father. . .send you?"

Chapter 2

Blanche held her breath for his answer.

"Captain Lamar gave me specific instructions in the event of your mother's death. As soon as I read her obituary, I headed here." A sad smile curved Mr. Gallagher's lips. "I wish we could have met under different circumstances."

Captain Lamar? Blanche snuck a glance at Mr. Gallagher. He was no more military than she was; his suit hailed more from Broadway than West Point. "Captain? He's a captain of. . .what?"

Ike tilted his head to the side, a soft chuckle escaping him. "You don't know anything about your father, do you?"

Tears sprang to her eyes as she shook her head. This stranger knew more about her father than she did.

"Your father regretted the circumstances that caused the distance between you. He's the captain of a boat."

Boat? The ocean lay scores of miles away to the south and east.

How he had come to meet Mama, Blanche didn't know. Perhaps Mama had met him on a once-in-a-lifetime vacation. Maybe her father had been lost at sea, and circumstances forced Mama to return to her hometown. A dozen possibilities suggested themselves.

She turned Ike Gallagher's card over in her hand. Lamar Industries had offices in Brownsville as well as right in Roma. The body of water connecting the two towns was no ocean, but the Rio Grande. The explanation that pushed into her mind was troubling. "A boat captain. . .on the Rio Grande? A steamboat?"

Ike smiled and nodded like a prize pupil. "J.O. Lamar was captain of the steamboat *Cordelia*. It's been traveling up and down the Rio Grande for two decades."

The *Cordelia*? He named his boat after her mother? The mother Blanche knew would never have married a riverboat captain, but only a man in love would name his boat after a woman. For a brief point in time, her parents had met, fallen in love, married, and had a child. The thought cheered her spirits.

Blanche examined Ike's words. "You said my father *was* captain? Has something happened? Is he dead?" Surely God wouldn't be so cruel, to bring her father so close only to deny her the opportunity to meet him.

"Now, Blanche. Don't make assumptions." Reverend Davenport planted his elbows on his desk and leaned forward. "Mr. Gallagher, you said you had a message for Miss Lamar from her father. May I ask what the nature of that message is?"

Blanche's stomach contracted. This was the heart of the matter.

"The captain regretted the differences that separated him from his only child."

So he did think about me.

"He respected his wife's wishes in the matter, as long as she was alive. But with her passing, he wanted to make Miss Lamar an offer." Ike turned a warm smile on Blanche again, a smile that could melt an iceberg. "You have a unique opportunity before you, Miss Lamar. The captain didn't know how you might be settled, financially. . ."

The question dangled in the air, unanswered. Her back stiffened. She and her mother had survived without her father's support for almost twenty years; she didn't need him now.

Liar.

"You will always have a home aboard the *Cordelia*. Especially since—" This time he covered his smile with a cough. "—the boat is your inheritance."

Her heart dropped. "So my father *is* dead."

"His fondest hope was that you would spend time aboard the *Cordelia*. He felt the best way for you to get to know him was to spend time aboard his boat."

"Are you saying that Miss Lamar is the owner of the boat?" Reverend Davenport frowned. Blanche wondered what her pastor would make of today's story.

"Not exactly. Not yet." Ike stared at his hands before looking up, his eyes sparkling. "For Miss Lamar to claim her inheritance, she must travel by boat to the final stop, down in Brownsville."

I might have known—a gift with conditions attached. "My father didn't leave a letter or any kind of written instructions?"

"He left lengthy instructions in Brownsville. He hoped you would accept his invitation. His dearest wish was for you to get to know him by traveling on the boat he loved so well." Ike withdrew an envelope from inside his vest. "Here is proof of my claims. Your parents' wedding certificate. Legal papers regarding Lamar Industries. I am authorized to provide whatever proof you might require."

"Miss Lamar?" Reverend Davenport turned the request back to her, but she knew what his advice would be. *Trust the Lord. Avoid the appearance of evil.* And riverboats had an evil reputation.

Blanche allowed herself to fantasize about breaking the rules this one time. Reverend Davenport meant well, but he couldn't understand the longing in her heart for family. He had a home for as long as he pastored Christ the King Church. His parents were respectable citizens here in town. He didn't face the necessity of finding a job. . .and a home. . .within the next month. He couldn't comprehend her hunger for a greater understanding of her parents.

"I'll have to think about it. . .pray about it. If Mr. Gallagher offered me assurance that my father is alive—"

Mr. Gallagher started forward, and she paused, giving him a chance to speak. He settled back in his chair.

"Since he hasn't, I prefer to consider my options. You understand, I am sure."

His smile faltered for a moment before returning to its full beaming splendor. "I have rooms at the Bells & Whistles hotel for the remainder of the week. Will you do me the honor of your company for dinner tomorrow evening?"

"Mr. Gallagher, you ask too much. Her mother was only laid in the ground yesterday."

"I'm afraid that's not possible. I will be at church tomorrow evening."

"Thursday night, then?"

The second rejection froze in her throat when she looked into blue eyes livened with flecks of green. What harm could one meal do? "Thursday night." She nodded. "That will help me make a decision before Friday."

Standing, Ike lifted Blanche's hand to his lips, and flame licked at nerve endings all the way to her shoulder. When he let it go, she almost expected it to be sunburn red, but it remained its usual pale color. She covered her confusion by asking one additional question. "Mr. Gallagher, you never did confirm whether my father is dead or alive."

"All of your questions will be answered when we reach Brownsville." With a brief press of her hand, he headed for the open door. "We'll talk more about it over dinner Thursday night."

The rest of the week stumbled by for Ike. After the meeting at the church, he had indulged in a sumptuous luncheon before spending the afternoon in bed. The nature of his work required him to be a creature of the night. That evening, he lost everything he had won the day before, plus a little more. Up in his room, he turned his pockets out. He still had a few coins, enough to start another game. He never dipped into his employer's money to play and he wouldn't start now. He might be a gambler, but he was an honest man. No one ever accused him of cheating without answering for the slander.

On Wednesday, he arose from bed early enough to walk through the town. Even though Roma was the *Cordelia*'s home port, Ike rarely spent much time exploring. Not much had changed. Prosperous as small towns went, a single bank closed its doors promptly at three in the afternoons. He caught sight of a general store, lending library, newspaper and printing office, two churches, one-room schoolhouse. A gentleman such as himself would have to special order clothing from catalogs at the general store given the lack of a tailor or haberdasher. Even the cotton grown locally was shipped elsewhere for fabrication.

A half-dozen horses were tethered to the hitching post outside of the saloon. Glancing over the doors, Ike discovered they belonged to rough-and-tumble cowboys, not the quality of men who favored the riverboat trade. The men he had met at the hotel represented the best action in town. The place looked as boring as Blanche Lamar's life must have been to this point. His mouth twisted in a smile; she wouldn't appreciate the comparison. Even so, as long as he didn't take her to any saloons, something in her haunted expression suggested she would relish the opportunity for more excitement.

Thursday dragged by as Ike waited for dinner with Miss Lamar. He had turned in earlier than usual on Wednesday night, his companions calling it quits after he'd won a tidy sum. A smile sprang to his face as soon as he awoke late in the morning.

The maid had returned all his shirts, freshly pressed, while he was sleeping. He settled on the dove-gray suit, blue shirt, and red bow tie, almost patriotic. He speculated on Miss Lamar's attire for a minute. As pretty as she would look in spring lilac or even a soft mauve chiffon, she would wear the same black-and-white suit.

He called for the bellhop. "I am taking a lady to dinner tonight.

Where can I find flowers? Or perhaps some special chocolates?" He winked.

"I will arrange for red roses and a box of chocolates." The man pocketed the coin Ike handed to him. "If I may." The man bent forward and straightened Ike's tie.

"Make those yellow roses." Red might send the wrong message. For a moment Ike felt like he had acquired a personal valet and grinned at the thought. "Thanks."

A quarter of an hour later, Ike stared at the items in his hand. He only meant to flatter Miss Lamar, to offer her some small luxuries he suspected she had seldom experienced. But would she misinterpret the gesture? He lifted the roses to his nose and sniffed. That was her problem, not his, he decided. He brought her gifts with the best of intentions.

He strolled down the street in the direction of the parsonage located next to Christ the King Church. The door opened as he climbed the steps and Reverend Davenport joined him on the porch. The pastor acted as protective as a father, a thought that tickled Ike's sense of humor given the circumstances.

"Miss Lamar will be down in a few minutes. Shall we take a seat?"

"Certainly." Ike placed the flowers and chocolate on the table between them and waited for the lecture he was certain was coming.

The pastor drew himself to his imposing height, emphasized by his thin frame. Fierce eyes regarded Ike from behind thin-rimmed glasses. "Miss Lamar has lived a sheltered life here in Roma."

"I am aware of that, sir, and here she comes. Shall we go inside?" He followed the pastor in rising and reached for the flowers and chocolates.

They settled in the pastor's study. "What assurances do you offer that you are who you say you are, and that Blanche will travel safely in your care?"

Ike shared his bona fides with the man. "As for Miss Lamar's safety, my own sister travels aboard the *Cordelia* with me. Captain Lamar took us in when we lost our parents, and we've lived there ever since."

That statement left Reverend Davenport discomposed. Ike pulled another trick from his pocket. "I am prepared to offer second berth for a companion, if you feel it is necessary, but I will warn you that space is limited."

At that statement, the pastor's shoulders relaxed, and he settled back in his chair, tapping his fingers on his desk blotter. He leaned forward and ran his right index finger through an address book, glasses perched on the end of the nose and his lips pursed in a slight scowl.

Out of the corner of his eye, Ike caught sight of Blanche. She had softened her mourning dress with a touch of gold, a locket around her throat, and her fiery hair blazed without the black boater hat. Ike relaxed.

Blanche had to clear her throat twice to get Reverend Davenport's attention. Ike stood as soon as her feet crossed the threshold to the study, his eyes lighting with pleasure at her appearance. His expression suggested he saw her as a woman, not as his employer's daughter, or a distraught orphaned daughter.

"Whom would you prefer as a traveling companion, Blanche? I'm sure Ruth would be happy to accompany you for a short trip, or perhaps you would prefer the company of a younger woman, perhaps Miss Trenton."

Miss Trenton was closer to Blanche's age than her mother's good friend by perhaps ten years, but she had spent so many years around her mother's friends that she fit right in with the older matrons. "I said nothing about a traveling companion."

"I told Reverend Davenport that we'd be happy to provide accommodations for someone to accompany you, if you feel it is prudent. But my sister is also traveling with us, and she is hoping you will share her cabin."

Blanche took courage from Ike's statement. "Then I don't think we need to bother either Miss Fairfax or Miss Trenton. *If* I decide to take the trip, I'm sure Miss Gallagher will be an adequate chaperone."

Was that admiration she spotted in Ike's eyes?

"I'll have Miss Lamar back before dark tonight, sir." Ike offered Blanche his arm, and together they walked outside, like any man escorting a woman. Blanche would have to order a glass of sweet tea as soon as they arrived at the hotel to calm the heat rushing through her senses.

Touching the tips of her fingers, he lifted them to his lips. "Wait here for a moment, please."

He reappeared at the doorway, yellow rose in hand. "If I may?" After breaking it just below the bloom, his fingers wrapped it around her ear. "Perfect." He made it sound as if he meant *she* was perfect, not the flower, and her skin heated with embarrassment.

Moments later, she returned, and he escorted her down the

street to the hotel. Temperatures had dropped a few degrees with the hint of rain in the air—a pleasant evening for a stroll.

The bellhop opened the door of the hotel for them, and Blanche's skirt swished as she entered. How much more cheerful the hotel lobby was than the parsonage, with comfortable chairs upholstered in bright colors. In this glamour, as much glamour as Roma had to offer, she felt almost dowdy.

Blanche followed Ike's suggestions for the meal. The waiter poured a glass of sweet tea for her, iced water with lemon for Ike, and left them alone. Ike leaned forward. "May I hope that your discussion with Reverend Davenport indicates you have reached a decision? I will confess that I am hoping you will join me on the *Cordelia.*"

She lifted her eyes to meet his. "You said if I came today, you would tell me about my father."

"I can only repeat what I told you earlier: your father gave me instructions to invite you to travel downriver." Ike spread his hands apart on the table. "Your father did not want you to learn about him and about the river at the same time. He wanted you to form your own opinions about life aboard the *Cordelia*, unswayed by either parent's feelings. A lawyer in Brownsville has been authorized to answer all your questions and to inform you of the inheritance your father has left you."

She ran her tongue over her teeth in thought and looked out the window, watching pedestrians strolling the streets. Was she prepared to spend the rest of her life in the community that had nurtured her, without experiencing anything else? She wanted to learn about her father, but she also wanted to experience the world—a small taste, that was all. More than anything she wanted to know her father. "I greatly wish you would tell me what I want to know now." Ire rose with the words.

The waiter reappeared, bearing their food on platters.

Her ineffectual plea seemed to amuse Ike. "I am answering your questions the best way I can. As I have said before, your father felt you would come to know him best on the river. Have you ever been on the Rio Grande?"

She slowly shook her head. "I've never been more than ten miles from Roma." Her eyes peered out the window at the town's dusty street, and she wondered what it would be like to catch the daily stagecoach on a journey to somewhere else. For years she had dreamed of taking a trip, if only to the next stop on the route. She was having her wishes handed to her on a platter. Why not?

Ike laid down his silverware. "Samuel Clemens has romanticized life on the Mississippi. I've been down Old Man River a couple of times, but I prefer the Rio Grande. The 'big river' is a Texas kind of river. It's almost two thousand miles long from its headwaters in the Colorado Mountains to the Gulf of Mexico. I've seen some of that rough country, over in the Big Bend, but the steamboat traffic runs between Roma and Brownsville. It's a country all its own, business on both sides of the river mingling two countries and cultures. A meld of Mississippi Delta and wild river canyons."

"You love it." She couldn't keep surprise out of her voice.

"I guess I do. It's been my home most of my life. I can't imagine living anywhere else."

Like her father. Ike remained silent on the subject. If her father was anything like Ike Gallagher, Blanche could understand how her mother fell for his charm. She couldn't afford to make the same mistake. That was reason enough to stay in Roma: to protect her heart.

But a part of her wanted to discover if the River that her father loved so well ran through her heart as well.

Ike leaned forward, touching her little finger with his own. "Please let me fulfill your father's request."

"I. . .don't know." Stay, and be safe? Or risk everything for the chance of something better?

"I stayed behind on this boat trip. They'll be back a week from now." Reaching into his pocket, he pulled out a small packet of money. "This is to help you with any expenses you might be experiencing. If you decide you wish to join us, you can get word to me at the hotel. You can bring a companion with you, or not. I'll make arrangements for you to have a room and board in case there's a change in the *Cordelia*'s schedule. And now"—he picked up his knife and fork and sliced into a thick steak—"let's enjoy this excellent meal."

Ike kept up a well-informed patter that held Blanche's interest while not making her feel like a naive girl from a small town. The *Cordelia* had taken passengers to the Fitzsimmons-Maher heavy weight title bout held on an island downriver. They both laughed at the burial of a supposed alien in Aurora, and shook their heads at the senseless death of two spectators to a stunt involving a train wreck in Waco.

Neither one of them brought up the question of her joining them aboard the riverboat until Ike walked her back to the parsonage. "Please come. It would have meant a lot to your father—and to me also." He took her hand, kissed it then released it slowly.

He walked away, glancing back a single time. She held her hand where he had kissed it against her cheek.

They both knew she'd sail with them. It was only a matter of time.

Chapter 3

Two weeks passed before Blanche took advantage of Ike's offer. She sorted through her mother's belongings, dismayed that so few items could summarize a life. As she worked, she looked for hints of her father. Surely her mother had kept some memento of the one love of her life. She must have loved him at some point. Mama would not have married a man for anything less. Perhaps she'd thought she could convince him of the error of his river ways, and her bitterness stemmed from her failure to do so.

Tucked at the bottom of the linen drawer, beneath a rose petal sachet, Blanche found a single piece of paper folded into an envelope. "To better times. I will always love you—J.O."

Blanche drew a deep breath. A set of four gems, miniature photographs, lay beneath the envelope. A younger, happier image of her mother than she had grown up with stared at her. Not that people ever smiled in photographs, but her eyes looked brighter than Blanche had ever seen.

But she couldn't take her eyes off the man in the pictures. Even though they were in black and white, the way the light glinted on top of his hair suggested they shared the same auburn tresses. She touched her head; every time her mother had looked at Blanche, she was reminded of her failure to reform her husband. His weatherworn face was open and honest. Blanche searched his features for resemblance to her own but recognized none.

Repeating her father's inscription on the photograph—*I will always love you*—Blanche fought the tears gathering in her eyes. What had happened to the marital vows to love, honor, and protect, that had caused him to leave them alone, unprovided for? This journey was the only opportunity she would have to discover the truth.

A knock drew her attention, and Blanche opened the door to Mrs. Davenport. Steam rose from a napkin-covered plate. The pastor's wife had made sure Blanche enjoyed two hot meals a day as well as breads for breakfast every day since her mother's death. Blanche didn't know if she would have bothered eating otherwise. Her appetite had sunk as deep in the ground as her mother's coffin.

"I brought you some corn pudding and fried chicken." Mrs. Davenport replaced it for the still half-full lunch plate. "You must eat and take care of yourself."

Blanche had managed a few bites of beans and mashed potatoes but not much more. "I've been extra busy."

Mrs. Davenport took a seat. "I will stay with you while you eat tonight. I'll tell you what I used to tell my girls: you can't have dessert until you eat at least three bites of everything on your plate."

That brought a chuckle to Blanche's lips. "Mama used to tell me the same thing, especially when she served me spinach." Her nose wrinkled at the memory. She laid the photograph on the bed and took a seat next to Mrs. Davenport before dipping her fork into the corn pudding. Creamy, slightly sweet, crunchy between her teeth—perfect. Next to it lay a crisped chicken thigh. "Chicken on a weekday. You didn't have to do that."

"I know it's your favorite meal." Mrs. Davenport followed the passage of the piece of chicken to Blanche's mouth with approval. She bit through the skin with a satisfying crunch and pulled the moist meat into her mouth.

Before Blanche knew it, she had stripped the meat from the bone and eaten most of the corn pudding. A smiling Mrs. Davenport handed her a molasses cookie. "You earned it."

Blanche laughed. "Thank you, for everything. I'll miss your home-cooked meals when I leave." A sudden pang of homesickness washed over her. The Davenports were the closest thing she had to family, and Mrs. Davenport had proven herself a true friend. Blanche reminded herself she'd only be gone for a week or a little bit longer.

"Are you sure you must go? You know you have a home with us, for as long as you want one." Mrs. Davenport busied herself packing the dishes back into the picnic basket.

"I know I do. I can never repay your kindness." Mama's friends had repeated variations of the same offer since the funeral. Blanche didn't doubt their genuine concern. But she could no more refuse the opportunity to learn more about her father than she could starve herself to death. "But I've always wondered about my father.

I might have grandparents. . .aunts and uncles. . ." *Brothers or sisters*, but Blanche didn't voice that thought. The implied betrayal of her mother hurt too much. "I've wanted family all my life, and now I have a chance to meet them."

"But." Mrs. Davenport twisted her hands in her lap. "A *riverboat*, Blanche dear. It's not seemly for a young Christian woman of your standing."

Blanche lifted her chin. "I am sure I will be well chaperoned on the boat. I am only making the one trip downriver; no harm will come to me. I'm sure my father. . ." Her voice wobbled at the word. "I'm sure he wouldn't have invited me otherwise." She added a smile, meant to reassure herself as much as her friend. "I will send you a letter when we get to Brownsville. I promise I'll ask for help if I need it."

As if resigned that Blanche wouldn't change her mind, Mrs. Davenport wiped her hands on a napkin and folded it. "How can I help you prepare for the trip?"

By the end of the day, they had sorted things into four piles: clothing and other items to give away, a small pile to throw away, and the valise that held the few items Blanche would take with her. The Davenports would hold the remaining items Blanche wouldn't take with her but wished to keep. Since the Lamars had lived in rented quarters, they had no furniture to worry about. "I hope I'll be able to send for the rest of my things soon."

"There's no hurry, dear."

Blanche had sent a message to Ike at the hotel about her decision to join the *Cordelia,* and he had responded when they returned to port. This last night of her old life, she would spend at the parsonage. Grabbing her valise, she scanned the room that had been her home, her refuge from the world, for most of her life. Reverend Davenport would bring her trunk down to the wharf later. With a final good-bye wish for the life she was leaving behind, she followed Mrs. Davenport out the door.

"Do you see her?"

Ike's sister, Effie, turned sightless eyes in his direction. Her voice stirred his own impatience. "Not yet." The *Cordelia* had made one trip downstream and back since his offer to Blanche.

More than once during the past two weeks, he wondered what decision Miss Blanche Lamar would make. Under the influence of her pastor, she might choose to stay in Prudeville, as he had dubbed the people he met at the funeral. Her unexpected message two days ago had relieved a sadness he didn't know he was experiencing.

He turned as an older man with a pilot's hat clamped on top of salt-and-pepper hair ambled next to him—Old Obie, the boat's pilot. "That's her, I'd bet my life on it." Despite his age, he still had excellent eyesight, a requirement for any riverboat pilot.

Ike spotted her when Old Obie pointed, her bright red hair showing beneath a straw boater.

"Tell me." Effie's hand grasped Ike's arm. "Is it her? What does she look like?"

Ike leaned forward, dangling his arms over the railing. "It's her indeed. Doesn't look like she's changed clothes since the funeral, unless she has identical outfits in her closet." The new hat, the only change in her attire, suggested a woman ready for new experiences.

But as she drew closer, Ike discerned her facial expression. "She doesn't look altogether happy to be here."

"She's scared, Ike. She must be terribly brave, to leave everything familiar behind and try life on the river." Effie nodded her head. "It's up to us to make her feel right at home."

"She looks like she sucked on a lemon for breakfast, that's for sure." Old Obie chuckled. "But she's here. That's the important thing."

"Shall we go down and greet her?" Effie turned a brilliant smile in Ike's direction.

He took her arm. "Obie?"

"I'll wait my turn. You go ahead and welcome her aboard." He headed back to the pilothouse while Ike guided Effie to the street.

If necessary, Effie could maneuver the gangplank without the need of her cane. Even so, he knew she felt safer aboard, where she knew every inch of the boat, than on the less predictable land.

"Maybe you can give her a few pointers on her attire." Ike couldn't wait to see her in something other than her black twill suit.

"What do I know of fashion?"

"More than she does." Effie might not see color, but she had excellent taste in fit, materials, and trims for her clothing. "I have never seen her in anything other than an unrelieved black suit with a white blouse. No flounce to the sleeves or skirt. I'm hoping you can broaden her fashion sense."

"I look forward to it."

He knew the moment Blanche caught sight of them. Her chin lifted and her hesitant steps changed to more of a march. Increasing the pressure on Effie's arm, Ike increased his speed and called out,

"Well met, Miss Lamar! I am pleased you decided to take us up on our offer." Without asking permission, he reached for her valise. "Miss Lamar, this is my sister, Miss Effie Gallagher. Effie, this is Miss Blanche Lamar."

"I have been so eager to meet you, Miss Lamar. My brother has told me so much about you." Effie stuck out her right hand.

Ike studied Blanche's reaction to his sister. Strangers didn't always know how to treat a blind woman. After a moment's hesitation, she met Effie's hand and shook it. "I am pleased to make your acquaintance. You are so kind to share your cabin with me."

"I'm looking forward to it. The *Cordelia* is a beautiful boat." Effie's voice conveyed a measure of pride. "It's been our home ever since our parents died when we were children."

"I don't mind. I am quite used to sharing space." In spite of her brave words, Blanche looked forlorn. Ike had considered offering the use of his cabin instead of having her share Effie's cabin, but that would mean bunking with Old Obie. That situation could create more problems than it solved.

"And it will do me good not to be alone." Blanche spoke the words softly. "Less time to dwell on my sorrow."

Brave words. Blanche was a contradiction, from red hair fiery enough to light a ballroom to black attire appropriate for a mortician's wife. "I am glad you feel that way."

Blanche smiled, and Ike decided he would do whatever he could to make her smile as often as possible. The faint lifting of her lips transformed her from a premature old maid to a lovely young woman. "I'm eager to catch my first glimpse of my father's boat. Lead the way."

Chapter 4

Blanche craned her neck as she walked with the Gallaghers, scanning the docks for her first glimpse of the riverboat that had stolen her father away from her. Long before she had learned about her father's business, she had daydreamed of a day trip downriver, properly chaperoned, of course. It sounded so. . .romantic. But romance and maidenly sighs didn't put food on the table, as her mother was wont to say. For all of her nineteen years she kept her feet pinned to the ground and didn't dare to dream.

For the immediate future, she would live in a fairy-tale world aboard her father's boat. Maybe she would find out she was the long-lost princess, her father the king of the Rio Grande. Her eyes wandered to Ike. If she was the princess, what role did Ike play? Sir Lancelot or court jester? With the ready smile that came to his face, he could be either.

Until she arrived in Brownsville and learned the answers about her father, she could fashion a future out of her dreams. Dreams might lead to future disappointment, but she didn't have much else to cling to for now. Except for the Lord, of course.

Mama had scoffed at Blanche's dreams, saying "God helps those who help themselves." From an early age, Blanche learned to keep her innermost desires to herself, holding them close the way Joseph must have for all those years he spent in Pharaoh's prison.

They turned the corner to the dock, and Effie said, "There she is. Straight ahead." She spoke with so much confidence that Blanche glanced at her face again, wondering if her first impression was wrong. No, the woman's eyes remained focused on some distant sight that no one else could see, and her white cane tapped out a steady rhythm on the street.

"She's something. Whenever I catch a glimpse of her like this, I fall in love with her all over again." Ike had his arms at his waist, his suit jacket pushed behind his back by his fists.

One of Blanche's teachers had used famous steamboat races to teach math: *If a steamboat burns eight cords of wood to travel five miles per hour upstream, how much wood will it take to travel forty miles?* Miss Burton had captured Blanche's attention, as well as many of her classmates, and she had encouraged them to construct scale models of the famous steamboat, the *Robert E. Lee,* while they read *Life on the Mississippi.* All too soon Mama had heard about the project and single-handedly stopped it, much to Blanche's dismay. Now that she knew her father's history, she understood why.

From the pride and affection both the Gallaghers had used to describe the *Cordelia,* Blanche expected to see the same version of the famous floating hotels. Hundreds of passengers could travel aboard boats that had fifty or more staterooms with stained glass ceilings and tessellated floors covered with rich carpets. Perhaps it even rose to four decks.

"There she is." Ike paused and gave Blanche her first clear look at the steamboat that had dominated her thoughts ever since her mother's death. She blinked. Painted green instead of white, a modest two decks instead of three, the gigantic stern wheel silent at the back of the boat. All in all, Blanche swallowed a bit of disappointment. Still, the paint was fresh, including curlicued gold letters announcing *Cordelia*. Crates stacked the decks. Perhaps they hauled more freight than passengers. Why would Mama object to a ship that did nothing more harmful than carry cotton and other products downriver? There was so much she didn't know.

"She may not look like much."

Mr. Gallagher read her mind.

"It's a little smaller than I expected." Blanche wrinkled her nose then held her face still. This boat represented her inheritance. She needed to learn as much as possible about its operations and all aspects of business before she made any judgments.

Effie laughed. "Don't let the *Cordelia* hear you call her an 'it.' She's a lady and expects to be greeted with respect. River and boat, both of them are demanding mistresses."

"I'll try to remember." Were river people superstitious? "Why do you say that? Is traveling downriver dangerous?"

Effie inclined her head in Ike's direction, and he shook his head. "I have lived on the river most of my life, and there's no place I'd rather live. Captain Lamar wouldn't have invited you along if he thought you were in danger."

Blanche felt like she was listening to true statements without hearing the whole truth. Fear fluttered in her stomach, although she knew no place was safe from danger. Her mother had taken sick and died in a matter of days. Fire, thunderstorms, tornados, rainstorms, floods. . .anything could happen even in a small town like Roma. The river was no different, except that she was surrounded by water and she couldn't swim. She swallowed.

"Shall we go?" Ike gestured at the *Cordelia*. "The crew has worked hard to spit and polish every inch of the ship for the captain's daughter. They're eager to meet you."

Blanche smiled. From a poor orphan to an heiress. She lifted her chin with pride and moved forward to meet her destiny.

Old Obie roused himself from his spot high above the *Cordelia,* in the pilothouse. Unable to resist, he raised the binoculars to his eyes for one more look at the young woman accompanying Ike and Effie.

Blanche Marie Lamar. Ike's description hadn't done her justice. But how could one describe such a woman? Even in the wilting summer heat, her clothes looked as stiff as a newly pressed tablecloth, her backbone straight, the tilt of her head determined to look ahead. She wore solid black with a dull gray blouse. Her face had remained somber, with emotions of fear and excitement and hope whispering across her face as she inspected the boat from afar.

But that hair. . .as bright as red light that either delighted or warned a sailor, depending on the time of day. Old Obie would take delight in that hair, an omen that all would go well with her first trip aboard the *Cordelia*. Red sky at night, sailor's delight; red sky at morning, sailor's warning.

Obie watched her confident steps as she strode toward the boat, taking in more details of her delicate facial features, a scattering a freckles on her nose, the rakish angle of the bow under her chin, the sparkle in her brown eyes. When they reached the dock, he put away the binoculars and buzzed around the already gleaming equipment.

Let Ike and Effie introduce Blanche to the crew. He would make her acquaintance later.

As they walked the deck, Ike caught a glimpse of Old Obie's binoculars. If there was any chance Blanche would discover the romance of the river as her father hoped, sooner or later she must make her way to the pilothouse. Old Obie was just the man to teach the young lady the moods of the Rio Grande, from the present summer drought that increased difficulty in navigation to storms that pounded anyone caught in them, from the trees sweeping the riverbanks to the unexpected bridges that appeared with increasing frequency. Adjusting the pilot wheel an inch to the right or left could mean the difference between safe passage or running aground on a sandbar.

Old Obie was master of the pilothouse. Ike had learned a lot from him, but no amount of time had given him the feel for the river that Old Obie had. He was the boat's most valuable employee, the one irreplaceable member of the crew, and well the captain knew it.

The crew had loaded the cotton stored in the warehouse while Ike had absented himself. Splendid pinks, reds, and oranges painted the western sky. If Old Obie agreed, they would set sail tonight. Ike's arm tingled where it touched Blanche's. He looked forward to standing with her on the deck and watching the boat pull away from the dock, feeling the stern wheel come to life, the near deafening turning of the wheels, the water rushing beneath the boat, wind whipping through his hair.

Would the wind tease a lock from Blanche's abundance of red hair, so that it twirled and danced in front of her eyes? Or would an abundance of pins hold each lock in place? He pictured his fingers brushing those curls back against her face, running through the hair hanging loose about her shoulders. He pushed his mind away from the image. Blanche Lamar was a lady, and some images were best left between husband and wife.

The crew lined up to greet them. Everyone had dressed in uniform, as clean and sparkling as the boat. "Are you ready to meet your employees?" He held in the laugh that bubbled in his throat when he heard her suck in her breath at the words.

"Do you have any suggestions on how I should behave?" Pink tinged her cheeks. "This is a new experience for me."

"I will tell you what Ike always tells me," Effie answered for him. "It has helped me get through many difficult situations. Think like an actress and *pretend*. What would you do if you were the captain?"

Color drained from Blanche's cheeks. Effie sensed her faux pas. "That's not good advice for you. You don't know our captain. Well, pretend you're the hostess at a dinner party, or your pastor's wife speaking to the ladies' aid society."

"Just be yourself. You'll do fine." Ike took one step forward but Blanche held back.

"How do I remember all their names? I'm terrible with names," she moaned. "They only have one new name to learn, and it should be familiar—*Lamar*."

"Which is why they will love you. They'll be curious about you. Of course. Who is this mysterious daughter the captain has kept hidden all these years? But they won't ask."

"And if they do, tell one of us," Effie spoke up. "We'll set them straight."

"I'll keep that in mind and try not to be frightened away." Still, Effie's reassurance brought a smile to Blanche's face. "I'll practice with the two of you. What is your position with the crew? Ike, I know your card says 'purser.' I even looked it up in a dictionary. But I still don't quite understand."

"Paperwork and customer service." Ike wasn't ready to explain the full extent of his role on board just yet. His duties regarding passengers involved activities that would make Blanche. . .blanch. He could find some humor in the situation. He put his concerns aside and held out his hand. "Come. We will be beside you all the way. If we wait any longer, they may wonder what is wrong."

Shyly, she accepted his hand and let him lead her forward.

Chapter 5

Blanche put all of Effie and Ike's suggestions into practice as she followed Ike to the boat. Unlike liners that crossed the ocean, the deck lay close to the water, and she could see people lining the main deck before she stepped aboard. The crew was only a little larger than the household where her mother had worked. One white-haired lady had a soft, round face. Blanche instantly felt like she could go down to the kitchen—or was it called a galley?—for a cup of tea and conversation. Blanche relaxed.

In vain she looked for a man dressed in a captain's uniform. Her slight hope that she would find her father alive once she arrived on board, ready to greet and reassure her, was dashed. With his suit and unmistakable air of authority, Ike was clearly in control.

To Blanche's surprise, Effie took the lead in introducing the crew. The round-faced lady who had caught Blanche's attention was indeed the ship's cook, Elaine Harper.

"Tell me your favorite meal, and I'll fix it for you tomorrow night."

Blanche started to protest, but of course the cook wanted to show off for the ship's heiress.

"I should have whatever you want. We carry everything available along the Rio Grande and the Gulf Coast in our pantry."

"I'm looking forward to it." Blanche's smile came naturally. In time, she thought she could get used to this heiress position.

A young woman named Betty was the chef's help. Blanche struggled to commit the names to her memory.

Next came the engineers. Jose and Tomas worked with a brusque Scot. "I'm Harry McDonald. The engine belongs to me. Anything you want to know, come to me. If you want a hot bath, I'm your man."

Blanche almost laughed. "I'm looking forward to it." She wondered if she would remain as immaculate as the engineers did, if she spent time among the coal and steam. Her limited wardrobe had to extend to every situation she'd be facing.

The next staff member Ike introduced addressed that concern. "This is our laundress, Agatha. She also takes care of any tailoring needs that arise. I took the liberty of asking her to design new clothes for your trip downriver."

Blanche gave the woman a second look. Glasses gave her face an unfortunate pinched appearance, but her dress—she thought it was called a tea gown—was as modern, outrageous and comfortable at the same time, as anything Blanche had ever seen in the few glimpses she'd had of the catalogues in the general store. "I don't know what to say."

Agatha looked her up and down. "We'll have fun."

"My mother just died." *I will not cry.* "I want to honor her."

"You don't need to worry. Whatever we do will be tasteful but. . . more suitable for your new life aboard the *Cordelia*."

Blanche appreciated her tact. Too fancy, not fitting well, too worn—she had heard slurs of one kind or another all her life. And she had never had clothes made for her by a professional seamstress. "That does sound like fun. However, I only expect to be here for a single trip."

The laundress bobbed her head. "Just following orders, miss."

After the head server asked her to inspect the evening's dinner service, Blanche wondered how she would fit in everything people wanted of her during a single trip downriver. So far no one had offered to preview the trip's entertainment or show her the pilothouse.

A figure hovered in the darkened room at the top of the boat, the pilothouse. He couldn't leave the wheel unattended, so she would make his acquaintance later. She didn't know whom to ask about the entertainment. Perhaps they didn't provide any, but instead only offered a means to travel downriver; she would learn.

By the time she greeted the last member of the crew, her face felt like it would crack from the constant smile. As the people filed out, Effie spoke, "You must be tired. Dinner isn't for a couple of hours, when you will meet our passengers. If you feel up to it, I have a couple of dresses for you to try."

Blanche wanted to be agreeable, but the implied criticism of her clothes made her uncomfortable. The suit was clean, serviceable, fairly new. The jabot at her neck was a new touch this year.

She swallowed against the fear crowding her throat. Money had always been at a premium in the Lamar household. Mama chose the least expensive, most durable cuts of fabric, from a similar color palette. When Blanche reached her adult stature, they began sharing their wardrobe. The annual changes to her wardrobe dwindled year by year. Mama thought the money could be better spent on other things: feeding the poor and widowed, supporting missionaries, new classrooms for Sunday school. All good, worthy causes that made Blanche feel selfish for wanting a dress with color or frills.

A soft hand touched Blanche's arm. "Let me show you to our room." As Effie led Blanche below deck, the youngest crew member, who looked like she might be a maid, relaxed. How well Blanche understood that feeling—they had passed inspection with the new boss. That gave her a feeling of power, and her back straightened. She would allow Effie to dress her up—but not too much.

"Come around my cabin later this evening then." Ike shook hands with Jason Spurling, a businessman checking out new markets for his products. Part of the problem for the dwindling steamboat business lay in the lack of large population centers on the route. The stops didn't offer good markets for local businesses. The other, bigger problem came with the increased presence of railroads. Not only did trains run to predictable schedules, they also kept their stations at a distance from the boat docks.

As a result, businessmen like Spurling appeared on the boat less and less often, leading to dwindling income. Hopefully, weather and river would cooperate on this trip and he could show Spurling the several opportunities offered by the *Cordelia*.

A peek in the dining room found the head waiter, Smithers, giving the tables a final polish. When Ike was a boy, the dining room was double its present size, with staff to match. According to the old-timers, like Old Obie, even those days paled in comparison to the golden days of the steamboat. He told stories of running out of food because they carried so many passengers. Ike didn't know the line between truth and wishful thinking, but he could imagine.

At the moment, silence reigned in the room, aside from kitchen noises. Where was Effie? She played the piano in the corner before each meal, popular tunes meant to encourage guests to enter and converse with each other.

Blanche must have agreed to a wardrobe makeover. He looked forward to seeing the results.

He went up to the window where Mrs. Harper passed out food. "Do you have Old Obie's tray ready?"

"Right here, sir." She hustled to the window. "Will he be joining us for dinner again soon, Mr. Ike? It's not right for him to eat by himself."

"He'll be taking meals on his own until further notice." Ike gestured for a waiter to take it up to the pilot. Elaine Harper enjoying bending the old man's ear and doing whatever she could to mother the staff. "It's best this way, so if there is something you need to discuss with him, you'll have to catch him in his cabin." He drew up his full height. "And I don't need to remind you not to discuss the situation with Miss Lamar."

She laughed and shooed him away. "I won't be giving away any secrets. You don't have to worry about me. But speaking of Miss

Lamar, she's making her entrance."

Ike glanced over his shoulder and froze for a second. He had gone through Effie's wardrobe, looking for something better than the unrelieved black and white staples of her wardrobe. Even so, the change achieved by a simple dark blue dress amazed him.

The dress was perfectly decorous, somber in color, and, from what Effie had said, a little out of date. But the dark blue instead of the black, with soft mauve touches instead of white, made all the difference. Blanche's hair lay in softly whipped layers on top of her head, and pink sparkled in her cheeks almost as if she wore rouge, something Ike extremely doubted. Her eyes sparkled, too. She lifted a handkerchief to her mouth as if to hide her shy smile.

"You'd better go rescue her before every gentlemen on board approaches her." Mrs. Harper stared at him pointedly.

"I'll do that." He pulled on the cuffs of his shirt, adjusting the studs so they were aligned properly, before walking across the richly carpeted floor. A smile sprang to his lips. "Miss Blanche Lamar." He bowed deeply from the waist. "Your beauty doth bedazzle me."

"You like?" Humor laced Effie's voice.

The color in Blanche's cheeks deepened, and she tugged at the waistline of her skirt, sending it in a slight swirl.

She glanced down, and Ike's eyes followed the direction of her gaze. She was staring at the serviceable, hi-top, lace-up shoes. Even the gleaming oil of a fresh shoeshine couldn't hide the scuffed use marks on the toes. She pulled her foot back, so that the skirts hid it from view.

Ike leaned forward and whispered in her ear. "Don't worry. There are several good cobblers down in Brownsville."

She shook her head. "I never should have come, not if you have to remake me from head to toe."

Effie made a soft sound. "I need to get to the piano. I'll see you at dinner."

"We're not remaking you. Just uncovering the beauty that's always been there. . .and what a few more dollars in the budget can make."

"I never had to go without." Her voice came out strangled.

"I didn't mean to imply otherwise. . ." He drew in a deep breath and didn't speak until Blanche's cheeks returned to a more normal color. "I only wanted to compliment you on how fine you look tonight."

The tinkling sound of piano keys interrupted their conversation, and Ike relaxed. Whatever Mrs. Lamar had taught her daughter, it didn't include how to accept a compliment. He found it refreshing compared to women who had flirtation down to an art form. Unlike those ladies, Blanche made no attempts at pretense.

When Effie shifted to a different song, Ike hummed along. Blanche tilted her head and nodded her chin in time to the music. Underneath the skirt, her feet were probably tapping. "I don't know that song, although it's a catchy tune."

"That's 'The Base Ball Song.' " He belted out a few lines, and Smithers shook his head in mild disapproval. When Ike lowered his head in mock shame, he caught sight of the blank expression on Blanche's face. "You've never been to a baseball game, have you?"

She shook her head. "Roma held a few exhibition games, and some of my friends went. But Mama. . ." She clamped her lips together.

"Mrs. Lamar suggested you had better ways to spend your money?"

Blanche shrugged her shoulders uncomfortably. "I'm afraid that the only music I know, beyond 'America' and the national anthem, are hymns. Music meant to praise God is the best music of all, don't you think?"

How to answer that? "I think God gave us everything to enjoy. As long as there are no scandalous words associated with the melody, surely music reflects praise to God." He grinned. "Even music written for a baseball game." Spotting a familiar face appear at the door, he lowered his voice. "And speaking of baseball. . .do your best to charm the gentleman who is entering the salon. He is the owner of the Brownsville Bats and is considering bringing the entire team downriver to play exhibition games at each town. It would make a big difference in our income."

Chapter 6

Blanche blinked her eyes. The thought of acting as hostess alarmed her. Mrs. Davenport had once shared her secret to making visitors to Christ the King church feel welcome. *People like it when you remember their names.* Blanche had memorized the passenger list and only had to associate the right faces with the names. Be polite, complimentary even. Above all, make the greetings unique to the individual.

The problem was she didn't know a thing about baseball. Maybe that's what she should say—men sometimes liked to show off their superior knowledge. In terms of looks, Mr. Ventura was short where Ike was tall, rotund instead of muscular, with a shock of thick black hair, bushy eyebrows, and a wide smile that invited the world to laugh along with him. *Open my eyes, Lord, to see what You see in this man.*

Before she had time to check her hair or adjust her shirtwaist, Mr. Ventura was in front of her, pumping Ike's hand. "*Buenas noches,*

Señor Gallagher. *Dónde está el capitan?*"

Blanche held her breath. Where was the captain, indeed?

"*No está aquí.*" Ike's answer repeated the obvious: he isn't here. Switching to English, Ike said, "But this is the captain's daughter, Miss Blanche Lamar. Blanche, this is Bart Ventura, baseball owner and one of Brownsville's leading businessmen."

Mr. Ventura shook Blanche's hand, just the right firmness, leaving an impression of strength, before he released it. "*Mucho gusto encontrarle*, Señorita Lamar."

Heat tinged her cheeks. "I'm afraid I don't speak much Spanish, Señor Ventura."

"I was only saying I am very pleased to meet you."

"Likewise. Have you traveled aboard the *Cordelia* before?"

"Once or twice." Ventura slid a sideways glance at Ike. "Mr. Gallagher and I have some interests in common. But you and I, we may have some business to discuss?"

Did everyone in the Rio Grande Valley expect her to conduct business in her father's absence? Before she had even heard the terms of—she dreaded the thought—the will?

But Ike said Ventura's goodwill was important to the continued success of Lamar Industries. So she would do her best.

"That may be so. We can discuss our business as we tour the boat." *Make it personal.* "And I look forward to learning about your Bats. I have never had the privilege of attending a game."

Ventura's chuckle sent a breath across her hand that tingled her fingers. "So I am to sell *you* on the idea of the Bats traveling aboard the *Cordelia*? That is a unique sales tactic, I must say. I look forward to spending more time with you, Miss Lamar."

A reedy man dressed in what she supposed must be a tuxedo—fancier than a Sunday suit, although still in black and white. Smith, Smithson, no—*Smithers*—that was it, the head waiter, came forward. "Glad to have you back aboard, sir. Please follow me to your seat."

After that, a constant stream of passengers promenaded by Blanche. A mother with two children was traveling downriver to visit family. Those two were the only children aboard. A dozen businessmen, a half dozen couples, a few men who looked like Mama called "dandies," and men who lived on family money and dressed in the latest fashions, rounded out the passengers.

Blanche felt her lips curl and forced the sneer into a pleasant smile. Why, Ike himself dressed like a dandy but so far, apart from an unfortunate flare for the dramatic, had acted like a complete gentleman. Mrs. Davenport's second rule came to mind. *Be polite*; maybe they would surprise her.

Thanks to an insatiable appetite for the written word, Blanche was conversant with current news events and books, so she could carry on an intelligent conversation. All the while she smiled and made small talk, she listened to Effie playing the piano. She slipped effortlessly from one song into another. Blanche didn't recognize a single tune, but they ranged from sentimental to lively. All had her wanting to hum along.

Instead of judging, Blanche focused on associating names with faces. In the fleeting seconds between introductions, she reviewed the names of the people already seated. Of all the guests, the young men were the hardest to tell apart. Back in Roma, any one of them would have stood out. Here, they blended together in the similarity of their attire.

The ladies differed in dress and in manner. Roly-poly Mrs. Potter arrived with her thin-faced husband. The pair looked like Jack Sprat and his wife of nursery rhyme fame. They seemed like ordinary, God-fearing folk. At the opposite end of the spectrum, Mrs. Ralston was dressed in a peacock blue gown that looked as if it sported every feather and lacy frill available to the dressmaker's art. The color of her hair rivaled Blanche's, but she suspected that had more to do with a bottle than birth's generosity.

At length, Smithers rang a bell. The piano music stopped. Ike slipped his arm into the crook of Blanche's elbow. "Shall we?"

Blanche wanted to slide into an inconspicuous seat by the kitchen, perhaps, or in a corner. But Ike steered her toward the captain's table, where Mr. Ventura and the Ralstons waited. She lifted her chin and let him lead her to the table. Effie was already at her chair. All the women were seated, but the men stood behind their chairs.

"They're waiting on you to take your seat," Ike offered her whispered instructions.

"Does anyone say grace?" she whispered back, keenly aware of all eyes on her.

"Not ordinarily." Ike seemed taken aback. "Not unless we happen to have a clergyman among the passengers."

Blanche reviewed the names on the list. Not a reverend among them. "Then I will set an example." She called Smithers over. "Please hold off serving the food until I give you the signal."

Ike stood behind her chair and held it as she seated herself, then pushed her closer to the table. She tucked the glistening white napkin into her lap and spoke in her speech-class voice. "Let us take a moment to return silent thanks to the Almighty for the meal we are about to receive." Her bowed head reinforced her meaning. Thankful thoughts warred with worries that she had overstepped her position as Captain's daughter at the first opportunity. She didn't know if anyone had time to return a word of thanks before she raised her head and nodded at Smithers.

Mr. and Mrs. Potter gave her an appreciative smile, Ventura was chuckling, but Ike—Ike stared at her as if he had never encountered anyone quite like her before.

"I never thought to see the like. She kept the whole salon waiting for a good three minutes while she bowed her head in a silent prayer, as pretty as you please." Ike chuckled.

Old Obie glanced at the young man, enjoying his discomfort. Although he kept his eyes fixed on the river, his ears captured every detail of Blanche's first interaction with the passengers. A smile flickered about his mouth. "How did the passengers react?"

"She's a novelty. They were all interested in her."

Old Obie peered through the window at the gathering clouds. "If the sky doesn't clear soon, we may need to shut down for the night. The weather's been dry; we run the risk of going aground when we can't see the water."

"That won't impress Mr. Ventura."

"I know. But an accident would be even worse for business." Old Obie squinted into the fading daylight. If his eyesight ever weakened, his days as a pilot were over. "So far, so good. But tell me, apart from the opening prayer, how did She handle herself?"

The *S* was a capital letter as clearly as if he had held a placard with it written down.

"Well, on the way out, she made a point of greeting everyone by name. That was a pleasant surprise. Smiles and genuine interest in everyone—she's a natural hostess. After the night in her company, Ventura was ready to sign the agreement already." He flipped a coin that rattled on the floor. "Almost."

"So she has some spunk. From what I saw, I was afraid Cordelia had driven it out of her." Old Obie took his pipe from his desk and began puffing. "Did Effie get her out of the widow weeds she arrived in?"

"She was wearing one of Effie's least favorite dresses. Dark blue, with mauve blue gores in the skirt."

"That'd look better on her than on Effie, with her coloring."

"It did." A deep sigh escaped Ike's lips.

Old Obie snapped his head around, pulling the pipe from his mouth. "Oh no. Don't repeat my mistake. If you've heard the story once, you've heard it a hundred times. Test that girl and see if she's river people before you get sweet on her. She might turn out to be a heartbreaker like her mother."

Ike didn't move. "You don't have to worry about that."

"Good." The sky darkened into night but the clouds dissipated— clear sailing ahead. Old Obie rested during the day so he could work the night hours. He didn't trust any of the other pilots to do the job. Below decks, the clock ticked toward nine o'clock at high summer.

Ike headed for the stairs. "I'd better warn you. She's already asking about the pilothouse. She wants to watch and learn. In fact, she seems more excited by that than most of the other functions on board."

Old Obie tamped his pipe and set it back in the bowl. "I'm ready. Let her come."

After a good night's rest, Blanche woke early in the morning. Breakfast would start in an hour. In the bed opposite her, Effie slept peacefully. Blanche stretched her arms and snuggled under the sheet again. If today turned out anything like yesterday, she might not have any more time to herself until she retired to bed tonight, too tired to do anything but fall asleep.

With that in mind, she slipped out of bed with her Bible. With only one day behind her, she already felt the strains and temptations that would come her way on this journey. In her deliberations, she hadn't factored in the absence of a spiritual mentor. She had never traveled more than a few miles away from the advice of Reverend Davenport. Now it would be her and the Lord alone. *Oh, Lord, let me hear Your voice in the middle of the noise of this boat. Let me represent You well.* Blanche read familiar words of admonition from Colossians. "But now ye also put off all these; anger, wrath, malice, blasphemy, filthy communication out of your mouth. . . Put on therefore, as the elect of God, holy and beloved, bowels of mercies, kindness, humbleness of mind, meekness, longsuffering." *Help me to dress myself in the things that matter.*

Effie turned over in her bed. Reluctantly, Blanche put away her Bible and considered her wardrobe. Effie and Ike might insist on different clothing for the evening, but she would wear what made her comfortable in the daytime—her clean and familiar black traveling suit.

She had finished fastening her buttons when Effie yawned. "You're up early."

"Good morning. I thought I would take a turn on deck before breakfast." Blanche turned her boater over in her hands. Should she wear it? Yes, she decided. It provided some protection of her face from the sun. Without it, her skin might burn so red that it wouldn't matter if she blushed.

"Do you want company?" Effie pushed her legs over the side of the bed and reached into her chiffarobe for a dress. "I think I'll wear rose today." She felt the collars of two or three dresses before she pulled out a rose dress.

"How do you do it?"

Effie laughed. "Oh, I have my tricks. For one thing, my buttons have different shapes and textures. The buttons on this dress are round and smooth, like a pearl."

Blanche shook her head in amazement. "I have a hundred questions to ask, but I wanted to take a walk before the day gets started."

"I'll see you at breakfast then."

Should she stay and help? Effie lived on her own and dressed without assistance all the time. Blanche headed out the door.

The room was below decks. Effie had apologized. "Why should I have a room with a view? I can't enjoy it."

Blanche reassured her that she didn't mind. She had free run of the ship. Outside the door, the darkened interior of the hallway left her disoriented. She closed her eyes. Their room was on the left side—the *port* side, she reminded herself. She had to learn shipboard terminology. The stairs should be to her left, past a couple of rooms. Opening her eyes, she headed in that direction.

The plush carpet underneath her feet invited her to remove her shoes. Her toes wiggled, begging to be set free. She tilted her head, imagining it in different colors. Thick tapestries lined the walls. Perhaps they were intended to insulate the hall from the engine noise, but oak paneling or a beige tapestry would be better. Her imagination was running wild; instead of enjoying more luxury than she had ever seen before, she wanted to change it. Was it just the possibility that all this might be hers?

If she didn't stop staring, she wouldn't get in her stroll before breakfast. Spotting the stairs, she climbed to the deck. A cool breeze brushed her cheek. From one end men's voices raised in song, men sounding happy in their work. She looked toward the prow of the boat, where the wheel churned through the water. If she went that way, the spray would tickle her face.

Ahead of her the stairway led to the pilothouse. It was time she made Old Obie's acquaintance.

Chapter 7

Blanche stopped at the bottom of the stairwell, admiring the care taken with this small section of the ship. Here she found the freshly painted walls she expected below, the gleaming brass handrail without a handprint. Years of foot traffic had given the steps a bright sheen.

A sharp, somewhat woodsy scent wafted down the stairs. Blanche's nose wrinkled, striving to identify the smell. Pipe smoke, she decided, a somewhat pleasant odor. Breathing deeply to clear her lungs, she climbed the steps and waited on the top step, suddenly shy.

"Come on in," a raspy voice called. "Ike told me to expect you."

Upon entry to the room, Blanche blinked against the onslaught of sunshine. Pipe smoke thick as fog settled in the air. She coughed and waved her hands in the air.

A chuckle made its way through the haze, and a pipe tapped

against an ashtray. Her eyes still stung, and she didn't dare open her mouth for fear the smoke would trigger another cough. But the chuckle had eased her fears.

"Give 'er a minute, and it will get better. If I'da known when to expect you, I'd have cleaned up ahead of time."

Blanche took a shallow breath and walked in. The air had improved. She turned around, looking at the many instruments, only a sextant one that she recognized. Her gaze fixed on the solitary figure with his back to her, facing the wheel. A weather-worn seamen's cap perched on his head, covering his hair except for a few stray waves at the back of his head the color of a rain cloud. His generous mouth looked equally ready to break into song, smile, or clamp down on the pipe still smoldering in an ashtray made out of driftwood.

Weather lines wrinkled his face. His workmanlike clothes were neat and tidy, but this man was no dandy like Ike. His eyes squinted, studying her as closely as she was studying him. Maybe her imagination was getting away from her again. He probably always looked like that, after a lifetime on the river.

"Miss Lamar." He nodded in her direction.

How should she address him? She had only heard him referred to as Old Obie. "I'm afraid I don't know your name." Heat rushed into her cheeks.

"You can call me Obie. I won't complain if 'Old' slips in there." His lips twitched. "I know my nickname. I don't mind. Figure I earned it, after a lifetime on the river."

A lifetime on the river. . . "Then you must have worked with my father. Captain Lamar."

Again that half smile as he nodded. "Ever since I started on the river. I reckon you could say I knew him about as well as anyone."

Old Obie said it with such an air of finality that the truth hit Blanche. Her father was dead. Tears sprang to her eyes. "I wish I could have known him."

Old Obie's hand reached for his pipe, but he slid it back in his pocket. "You can ask me anything you want to know."

The questions that plagued her, she wouldn't ask a total stranger. *Did he ever mention me? Why did he leave us?* "Did you know my mother?"

"I did indeed. I argued with the cap'n, telling him he had no business straying so far away from the river. I've always blamed myself for what happened. But once he laid eyes on your mother, he was a goner. For a few wild months, he convinced himself he could give up everything he ever knew for her. And he brought stars to her eyes. I was half smitten with her myself."

"So. . .what happened?" She held her breath.

Instead of answering, he grabbed the binoculars and took a step toward the front window. When he swept the river from side to side, his shoulders hitched higher with tension. His generous mouth straightened until it stretched in a thin line. He made a minute adjustment to the wheel. Keeping his hand on the wheel, he reached for a bellpull that dropped through the floor. He tugged it once and received an answering pull. "Steady yourself. They'll be increasing speed by five knots."

Blanche's feet shifted, but she quickly regained her footing. Old Obie stood without speaking, as if he had forgotten her presence.

A bell jingled in the distance, and Blanche waited for the boat to increase speed. When it didn't, she realized that was the breakfast bell. She took a step to the stairwell. "It's time for breakfast."

Old Obie paid her no more attention than if she was a fly buzzing around his face. Repressing her disappointment over the stalled conversation, she headed to the salon.

"You were right." Ike's voice broke into the rhythm of the song Effie was playing.

"What's that?" Effie asked in low tones as her fingers continued to move effortlessly over the piano keys.

"She's wearing her black traveling suit again already waiting at the captain's table."

Effie held back a chuckle. "People don't dress up for breakfast."

Smithers rang a small bell, and Ike helped Effie to the captain's table. Turning in Blanche's direction she asked, "Did you enjoy your stroll?"

"Very much." A story lay behind Blanche's tone; Effie would ask about it later.

"Miss Gallagher, what a pleasure to have you playing for us before our meals."

"Thank you. I enjoy playing." Effie imagined Mrs. Ralston's appearance. People didn't understand when she said she heard colors; but she did. For instance, a song in the key of D, with two sharps, sounded yellow, where as something in D-flat could sound dark purple. Mrs. Ralston's voice felt like a garish green.

"Do you know 'I've Been Working on the Railroad'?" Mrs.

Ralston asked.

Effie tilted her head. Passengers frequently had special requests, and she was happy to accommodate. "Unfortunately not. But if you sing it for me, I can probably pick it up."

Skirts rustled as Blanche stood. "Once again, we will observe a few moments of silence to return thanks for the food."

The simple invitation to return thanks pushed a key in Effie's soul. Even though she didn't make a habit of saying grace, she did turn her thoughts toward God in the silence.

Beside her, Ike shifted in his chair. His presence surprised her this morning. His work entertaining passengers kept him up half the night, and he couldn't work twenty-four hours out of twenty-four.

If she had to guess, she'd attribute his attendance to Blanche. Whether or not he admitted it, she suspected he was half-smitten with the captain's daughter, despite the warnings he had received.

"Amen." Blanche brought the moment of silence to an end.

"What plans do you have for this day?" Ike's coffee cup rattled as he lifted it from the saucer.

"So many people asked for time with me today." Blanche sounded uncertain.

"Agatha has demanded an audience this morning." Effie threw her a lifeline.

"And no one defies Dame Agatha," Ike murmured.

"Why do I need to see the seamstress?"

Ike made a sound half between cough and laugh. Blanche's terrified voice made Effie wonder if she had ever owned a dress not made by her own hands.

"It seems so wasteful to make new dresses for me until I decide whether I'm going to stay with the boat. Truly, I don't need anything new."

Ah, waste not, want not. The captain had mentioned that quality of his wife's character. How did he describe it? *She pinched pennies so tight she wore all the use out of them.*

"I insist." Ike had regained control of his voice. "Agatha is paid a salary, and the material has already been purchased."

"You won't change his mind, and Agatha is an artist with fabric. You might as well enjoy it." Effie determined to help Blanche enjoy this new experience.

"Is her name truly Dame Agatha?" Blanche steered the conversation in a new direction. "What is an English noblewoman doing onboard a riverboat?"

Effie laughed. "That's just her nickname. Because she likes to order everyone around. She probably won't give you a choice about patterns. She doesn't me." Stretching her hand out, she clutched the handle of the orange juice pitcher and poured herself a glass. "The only thing worse than enduring a session with her is missing one. She makes you feel like you've ignored a royal invitation."

Blanche didn't respond until she ate a bite of something—her oatmeal, Effie would guess. "Did she treat the captain that way?"

Good question. Blanche continued to show some spunk.

Nodding, Effie chewed on a strip of bacon. "When you're the queen of it all, everyone has to bow to your wishes. Even a riverboat captain."

"I'll just have to talk some sense into her. That's all. Pass me the biscuits, please."

Effie took the platter in both hands and handed it over. "What else are you hoping to see today?"

"I was hoping to see the engine rooms in the morning, while it is still cool."

"You can go tomorrow. They'll be happy to see you."

"And this afternoon I'm going back to visit with Old Obie."

A spoon clinked against china. Ike was adding sugar to his coffee. "Do you mind if I join you? I can always use another lesson in the ways of the river."

He was smitten, no doubt about it.

Blanche hesitated before answering. "Of course. You don't have to ask my permission." She wouldn't get rid of Ike easily, if only to help the pilot handle the inevitable questions.

Arriving late, the Ralstons took their seats at the table, and Blanche stopped talking. Out of habit, Effie picked up the slack in conversation.

Mrs. Ralston jumped in. "Is your marvelous seamstress available to fashion a dress for me? My *Ladies' Home Journal* caught up with me in Roma, and there is this absolutely marvelous dress I must have."

"I'm sure she'd be happy to—" Blanche offered.

Effie had to cut her off, "—as soon as she finishes with her current project." She was so used to acting as hostess for the *Cordelia,* she'd have to remind herself to give Blanche time to respond. Thoughts of the future troubled her. Of course the captain refused to give away his daughter's birthright, but where did that leave Effie and her brother?

"And what project is that?" The sound of crockery hitting the table pounded Effie's ears, and Mrs. Ralston screeched.

"Apologies, ma'am." Smithers appeared instantly.

Mrs. Ralston huffed. "I'll have to change my dress. *Such* a disappointment. I was hoping to wear this dress for tomorrow night's dinner performance. Will your laundress be able to get it clean before then?"

I bet she knows that our seamstress is also her laundress. Effie plastered a smile on her face, dismissing the suspicion. "Of course, ma'am."

A choking sound came from Blanche's direction, but she didn't say anything. She remained quiet, saying a word here and there, occasionally her spoon striking the plate. Effie offered her the biscuits a second time, and she accepted. "These remind me of my mother's biscuits."

The sadness in her voice reminded her that she had only recently lost her only known family. She must find it difficult to sit with people she had just met, forced into activities she had never done before and trying to be pleasant. No wonder she felt so threatened.

Whether or not she realized it, this trip was designed to test ability to adapt, to survive. Was any of the old Captain in her, or was she an exact duplicate of her mother? "Then she must have been a good cook."

"She was." She pushed back unsteadily in her chair. Ike sprang to his feet to hold it for her. "If you'll excuse me." She moved away from the table at a rapid pace.

"What's wrong with her?" Mrs. Ralston spoke over the clinking of the spoon as if the accident had never happened.

"She just lost her mother." *Why did I speak? We're supposed to accommodate the passengers, not the other way around.*

Nineteen years of living as a servant in someone else's house enabled Blanche to walk out of the dining room with every evidence of self-control. She'd spent a lifetime wearing hand-me-downs, every now and then enjoying a new dress made from leftover scraps of fabric. She glanced down at her serviceable black traveling suit. More than necessity drove her to wear it over and over again. She bought it new, with her own money, and it was both fashionable as well as practical. Her first new dress might be her last new dress, and she wanted it to last.

"Lord, help me to show Your love to Mrs. Ralston. No matter what she thinks about me." How many times had Mama prayed the same words? She had spent her life serving others without complaint, adding extra touches that spelled love. At least every member of the Winthrop family attended church, and Mama had prayed with the two littlest girls. People who didn't know the Lord needed those acts of love even more.

Blanche stumbled into the cabin and sprawled across her berth. Memories of her mother, her countless acts of love even when her words were few, crowded her mind, and her shoulders shook with sobs. She buried her face in her pillow and let the case absorb her tears. She would not appear in front of the seamstress looking like a drowned rat.

Pick yourself up, girl. No time for tears. Ma's words haunted her ears. It was all she needed, for now. She scrubbed her face and prepared to meet the dragon Agatha.

Chapter 8

Is that the one you want to keep our nighttime activities a secret from?" Ralston arched his eyebrows as they watched Blanche leave the dining salon. Effie excused herself and followed behind.

Ike nodded. "She'd demand we search the ship and toss all cards to the bottom of the river—either that, or she might demand to be let out at the next stop."

"Too bad. With that hair of hers, she should know how to have a good time." Ralston's eyes lit with an appreciative gleam. He didn't know what to do with Blanche Lamar.

"You will treat her with the same respect you show my sister. More, since she's the captain's daughter."

"All right." Ralston lifted his hands in surrender. "I promise I won't bother her. That one needs someone to teach her to crack a smile."

"Don't worry. Effie's working on that."

After breakfast, Ike headed to his cabin for a few hours' sleep.

When he passed Agatha's domain, his steps slowed. He had given the seamstress a detailed description of Blanche's attributes, had consulted on which colors he thought would complement her complexion, and had given a masculine impression of current fashions when asked. He appreciated a well-turned-out woman, and Blanche had the potential to put all the society matrons to shame. The captain had teased him about his knowledge of high fashion, but it suited both his personality and his job. No waist overalls or common denim for him.

The door creaked open as he passed, and Effie's cane tapped outside the door. Inhaling her breath sharply, she said, "Ike? Is that you?"

How she recognized him, he had never figured out. "What gave me away this time?"

Laughing, she shut the door behind her. "Your aftershave, of course. Detectable to my sensitive nose beneath the overlay of cinnamon toast and strong coffee. You came at the right time. From Agatha's reaction, Blanche must look amazing."

"She's already sewn a dress?" Agatha was a marvel with the sewing needle, but Blanche had been onboard for less than twenty-four hours.

"Come with me." Effie hustled down the hallway toward the stairs, her cane tapping a steady rhythm. At the stairs, she grabbed for the handrail. "She took your general comments and fashioned a dress, adjusting it according to her observations of Blanche last night, as well as the exact measurements of her traveling outfit."

She dashed into her cabin and returned with a gold haircomb with mother-of-pearl insets in the handle. "I'm going to try my hand at arranging her hair." She tucked the comb into her reticule and left the cabin. Ike followed.

Back in the sewing room, Effie knocked before ducking her head in. "Ike is with me. May he come in?"

Agatha's agreement overrode Blanche's soft protest, and he stepped inside.

Stunning. Breathtaking. Beautiful. Regal. *Warm.* All of those words and yet none of them captured Blanche's transformation.

"Mr. Gallagher. I am so glad that you are here. I think you will agree that this dress suits Miss Lamar's position aboard the *Cordelia.*"

Words failed Ike. He could only nod.

"Miss Gallagher and I are trying to convince Miss Lamar to agree to a few dresses in jewel colors: a gold, perhaps, or sapphire or jade. Any of those would look lovely with her coloring."

Blanche didn't respond. She stood transfixed in front of the mirror, her hand held to a cheek that glowed scarlet between gloved fingers.

"Miss Lamar." Ike took her free hand and raised it to his lips.

The garment Agatha had constructed was simple and modest in design, yet a world removed from Blanche's normal attire. The fitted blouse in warm beige, with vertical stripes of navy blue and ruby red, tucked in nicely at the waist of an eight-gore skirt.

"Sit down, Blanche." Effie knew how to exercise authority as well as her brother. "Let me add the finishing touch."

Blanche sat down in front of a vanity mirror, shaking her head from side to side. Effie's deft fingers pulled every pin from Blanche's head. Luxurious, thick red waves cascaded over Blanche's shoulders and down her back.

Ike settled back to watch Effie work. She had a feel for hair, insisting that each woman's head was different, telling her whether to curl, or brush, or tease.

A few minutes later Effie had sculpted Blanche's hair into a soft bun at the back, the sides held in place with the gold combs. After she tucked a few pins back into the hair, she stepped back. "That should do it."

A pale blush sprang high in Blanche's cheeks and spread down her neck. The smile in her eyes reached her lips, the smile of a woman who knows she looks good.

"You will of course wear that lovely garment when you go up to the pilothouse and let everyone on deck see you," Ike dictated. *No one more so than Old Obie.*

"But what about the dress I was wearing. . .I don't want to create extra work." Blanche offered a feeble protest.

Agatha guffawed. "I do the laundry around here. And I want you to show off my work as soon as possible. You must wear this dress to the evening meal. It is even more important that you look your best when we have additional guests." With a quick nod of her head, she turned to Ike. "Now, Mr. Gallagher. Take your leave so we can continue our work."

"Just a minute." Ike leaned close enough to Blanche to say sotto voce, "You look lovely." The heat rushing into her cheeks tickled the fringes of his mustache, and he hurried out the door before he blushed himself.

Two hours later, Blanche left Agatha's domain, worn out from a hard morning's work. No wonder Ike called her Dame Agatha. She paid no attention to anything Blanche said, as inflexible in her demands as the teacher who had drummed the multiplication tables into her head.

Blanche didn't want to offend Agatha, but she couldn't decide what bothered her more: the colors or the cut of the clothes. "Won't this dress draw attention to me?"

Agatha guffawed. "That's the point."

Effie only smiled before reassuring Blanche that the patterns they had chosen were simple, tasteful, and modest.

For the half hour remaining until the next meal, Blanche decided to retire to her cabin, but she found it hard to relax. If she laid against a pillow or leaned against a chair, she might destroy Effie's delicate handiwork with her hair. The dress wouldn't wrinkle easily, but she couldn't redo the bow by herself. When she removed the gloves, a hangnail on her left hand bothered her. She pulled at it, and a tiny pucker of blood appeared at the root. It dripped onto the perfect white of the gloves. Now what? She couldn't even keep a pair of gloves clean for two hours. Tears formed in her eyes, which made her feel even worse. She couldn't, wouldn't, cry over something as ridiculous as a drop of blood.

Effie entered the room, catching her in mid sob. "You poor dear." She dropped onto the bed beside Blanche. "I had hoped that your dress fitting session would lift your spirits. I always get excited when I'm getting new clothes made."

Ignoring the difference in their perspectives, Blanche pointed to the gloves before remembering Effie couldn't see her gestures. "I got blood on my gloves."

"Is that all? I was afraid Agatha might have forgotten to finish a seam."

Blanche's eyes widened at the thought of walking down the hallway with her chemise showing.

"Give me the offending garment."

When Blanche handed the glove to Effie, she tossed it into the bin with other washables. "I keep several pair at all times. I'm lucky if I can wear a pair for two days."

Blanche sucked in a deep breath. "I don't know how to be fancy." She put a hand to her throat and almost ran her bloodied finger over the top button. She didn't dare. She might smear blood on the dress this time. *I'll never tear a hangnail again.* She hoped she would keep that promise. "Do you have any cures for a hangnail?"

"Don't wear gloves?" Effie smiled. "It will grow out soon enough."

"What did Agatha mean by new guests tonight?" Blanche had wondered about the comment at the time.

"We're stopping at Rio Grande City tonight. Several people usually join us for dinner and the evening's, umm, entertainment. Even more than usual this trip, because we want to impress Señor Ventura. So promise you'll wear the dress tonight. Please."

"Very well." Blanche sighed. She couldn't wait for this trip to be over so that she could go back to where she didn't face new dilemmas every few hours. "Please help me undress. I want to keep this clean until I get to dinner tonight."

After changing into a straight black skirt with dark blue blouse that could hide dirt, she made her way to the deck. She hated being in the bowels of the ship where the air always seemed far too warm.

On deck, she closed her eyes and welcomed the fresh air. The fabrics Ike had chosen for her swam before her eyes. Such. . .color. Before her eyes had landed on the gold brocade, she thought the prettiest thing she had ever seen in her life was a triple rainbow. She had seen one only once, three years ago on her sixteenth birthday. That day, and that rainbow, had changed her life.

The pleasure she felt in the fabrics Agatha spread before her almost exceeded the pleasure of that day. As she reveled in the bold colors, she felt is if she was lusting after another god. She reminded herself that God created color.

And Ike bought it for her, for plain, practical Blanche Lamar. He said they were perfect for her coloring. A part of her wanted to gather the fabric to her bosom and hold it tight in the way she couldn't a rainbow. Another part of her wanted to throw it onto the nearest bonfire as a heathen idol.

Mist sprayed Blanche's face as she leaned over the railing. Unbuttoning the top button of her blouse, she lifted her face to enjoy the cooling drops. It brought a little relief as the sun climbed to its zenith. Raising her hand to her eyebrows to shield her eyes from the sun, she tried to gauge the time until lunch. Could she make it to engineering before the call to the dining room? No. She decided to use the time to walk about the ship instead.

A glimpse into the salon showed Smithers directing the wait staff. Mrs. Ralston came around the corner, and they nodded as they passed in the hallway.

Mrs. Potter appeared at the top of the stairs. When she spotted Blanche, she smiled. "Miss Lamar. How lovely to see you again. And I wanted to tell you how much Mr. Potter and I appreciate your quiet time for prayer at our meals. I confess, I never expected it aboard a steamboat." She chuckled. "Judge not, as the Good Book says."

Heavy footfalls ascended the stairs and Mr. Potter joined them.

"She's speaking the truth. I wondered if you'd mind if I say a word or two to the Almighty out loud, before we eat? Invite some of the others to join in."

"What a wonderful idea. Thank you for suggesting it. I would have done so myself, except it seemed inappropriate somehow." She extended a hand toward the rotund gentleman. "Can I count on you for luncheon in a few minutes?"

"Of course."

Excusing herself, she walked past the deck where the staff cabins were located and stood at the top of the stairway leading into the bowels of the ship. Engines throbbed and heat blasted her in the face. Even if she dressed only in her camisole, she would still feel hot. Tomorrow morning she would leave her room early during the coolest time of day.

The bell rang, calling them to come to the salon. Rarely had a morning provided her so much entertainment. Not much of her time had been put to practical use. None of it had been spiritual, unless she counted her ruminations about rainbows and fabric colors.

But she couldn't remember the last time she had so much fun.

Chapter 9

*E*s *una buena noche, si?*" Face ashen, Bart Ventura leaned against the railing, waiting for the gangplank to extend to the wharf at Smithville. "I know we have only been on the river for twenty-four hours, but I feel better on dry land."

Ike smiled. Any ill effects Ventura felt probably resulted from overindulging in bourbon while playing poker the night before. "Come now, a pleasant day on the river, good food, and now a night in a pleasant community. I can personally recommend Mrs. Hurley's café. The best pork ribs in all of Starr County." He glanced at the lily-white cuffs extending beyond the sleeves of his suit. "Although if we eat barbeque, I need to change clothes."

"My ballplayers like barbeque. We will try the café." Ventura turned the pearl studs of his cuff. After the walkway was extended, the two men strolled into town. "So tell me, are the ladies of the café as lovely as your sister and Miss Lamar?"

Ike's head jerked up at that statement. "So you think Miss Lamar is pretty?"

Bart's laughter rang through the air, loud enough to be heard on board the boat. "So you are thinking that way? That one has spirit underneath all the prim-and-proper manner. And you are just the man to bring it out of her. Bring her along to our game one night. We can teach her how to have a good time."

"I'd rather get honey from a beehive." Ike hoped his suntan hid the heat rushing to his cheeks.

The evening passed pleasantly. The local alcalde, Mayor Fernandez, agreed to an exhibition game by the Brownsville Bats. Later, after they returned to his cabin, Ike won a healthy amount even after he took out the boat's fifty percent cut. Despite the successful evening, he felt unsettled. After an hour of tossing and turning, he arose and cleaned his room, a task he usually left for the maid. After putting everything away, he sprawled in the most comfortable chair in the room and closed his eyes. A few minutes later, his chin nodded forward and he jerked awake.

Face it. He wouldn't get much sleep no matter what he did, so he might as well join the others for breakfast. But if he did that he'd run into Blanche and get stirred up again. No, he'd stop by the salon later to grab a cup of coffee and a bite to eat. The cook usually obliged him even when he showed close to the noon hour.

Ignoring a pounding headache and empty stomach, he stayed in his cabin going over the account books. Totaling up the income received to date, he decided this voyage would be profitable. More and more it looked like Bart Ventura would bring them repeat business. The Roma cotton gin had sent a larger than usual shipment. If they delivered the cotton within a reasonable time, that could turn into increased traffic as well.

What would Blanche think of the gambles businesses took all the time, in the hopes of making money? Expenses had outpaced income for several years. On mornings like this, he sometimes wondered if they could afford to forgo the late nights and uncertainties of gambling. Just as often, his winnings determined whether or not the *Cordelia* stayed afloat.

The grumblings in his stomach increased, and a glance out the window confirmed the late morning hour. As soon as he entered the salon, he headed for the captain's table. Elaine spooned a big portion of eggs onto a plate. Acid rose in Ike's throat. "I think I'll just have coffee this morning. And some dry toast."

"Like that, is it?" Elaine didn't say anything further. She didn't have to. She had nursed him through everything from splinters to his first hangover. Taking a sturdy ceramic mug instead of fancy china, he grabbed a biscuit with the other hand and headed for the one place where he could always find peace. He could depend on Old Obie to listen, and he hurried through the fresh air across the open deck. The worn steps to the pilothouse beckoned.

As soon as his right foot landed on the bottom step, he heard her voice. *Blanche.* His feet raced up the stairs even while a curse rose to his lips.

Dressed once again in her black traveling suit, Blanche stood at the wheel. Her hands grabbed the spokes, her right hand at two o'clock, left at ten. Her fingers curled around the wheel as if the ship would sink if she didn't hold on. Old Obie stood about a foot behind her, his head never moving although Ike knew he saw every nuance of color in the river. He grunted and pointed over Blanche's shoulder. "Do you see anything unusual about that patch of water?"

When Blanche shook her head, Old Obie handed her his binoculars. "Take a closer look." He placed his hands on the wheel while she leaned forward toward the window, adjusting the glasses.

"It looks like there's a shadow under the water. Is that possible?"

Old Obie nodded. "Yup. That's a sandbar. We have to keep the boat away from it or else we could run aground."

"And that's not a good thing."

"Not at all."

Ike hung back, enjoying the interplay between the old sailor and the young lady.

"You turn the boat."

"Oh no. I'll run us straight into it."

"No, you won't. I'll help you." Old Obie shifted position. "Here. Put your right hand next to mine."

Blanche reached out a tentative hand and placed her white hand next to Old Obie's speckled one. Slowly, Old Obie moved the wheel a fraction of an inch at a time, letting Blanche feel the shift of the boat beneath them, until they steered clear of the obstacle.

"I did it!" Blanche sounded as excited as boys at a baseball game. Ike remembered his excitement the first time Old Obie let him take the wheel. Only he didn't have Obie's feeling for the river, the instinct necessary to do a pilot's job. He served the business in other capacities.

But Blanche. . .Blanche might be a natural.

"Well done, Blanche. I'm impressed."

At the sound of Ike's voice, Blanche's right hand escaped the wheel and tucked a strand of hair behind her ear. "Ike. I didn't hear you come up the stairs." She heard the breathiness in her voice and chastised herself.

Old Obie chuckled. "Your mind was all on the river." He turned merry brown eyes on Ike. "The girl is a natural born pilot. I insist she spend time here each day, to better learn the ways of the Big River."

Heat rushed into Blanche's cheeks at the unexpected words of praise. "Don't be ridiculous. I almost ran us aground on that sandbar back there."

"What I saw"—Ike crossed the floor and leaned against the captain's table—"was an apprentice learning from a master. The important thing is that you avoided the sandbar. You're catching on quickly."

If her cheeks weren't already burning, Ike might have blamed the color on his kind words. These two men had spoken more warmly of her abilities in a handful of days than her mother ever did. "There seems to be a lot I don't know." She turned the compliment aside.

"Different areas of expertise. If we had a quiz on Bible facts or recitation, you'd win hands down."

Laughter as big as Santa Claus issued from Old Obie. "He has you there, missy."

A smile crept onto Blanche's face. "You may be right, although others on board might excel, like Mr. and Mrs. Potter. In fact. . ." An idea, so radical, so perfect, jumped into her mind. "We should test that theory out. What would our passengers think about a departure of music for our evening's entertainment?"

"What are you thinking of?"

"A Bible sword drill or possibly a memory contest. I'm sure the Potters would take part, and we could invite the other passengers and crew to join us." Her excitement grew as she talked. "I used to do well at things like this when I was a little girl. I won my very own Bible in my first contest." The pace of her speech increased, the words blending together, so caught up with the possibilities that it took a minute for the disbelief reflected on the two men's faces to register. Her voice trailed off.

"This is a steamboat, not a church." Ike's voice came out high pitched.

Old Obie only shook his head. "That sounds like something Miss Cordelia might suggest. If we were transporting a revival meeting or a church convention, that might work. But people don't pay money to have a bunch of 'thou shalt nots' quoted at them."

Blanche shrank back, her shoulders slumping. Then she squared them and lifted her chin. "You're right, I shouldn't put learning the Bible in the same category as 'entertainment.' But how about a chapel service on Sundays, after breakfast? We must do that much, at least."

Grinning, Ike shook his head. "You won't give up on this, will you?"

Straightening her spine and raising herself to her full height—still nearly a foot shorter than Ike—she nodded. "I at least will spend time on Sunday worshipping Almighty God, and I will welcome anyone who wishes to join me. It would be wonderful if Effie could play some hymns for us to sing."

" 'Amazing Grace.' I always liked that song." Old Obie hummed the first few measures.

"Effie has never studied church music. . ." Ike temporized.

"I already know she plays by ear. I can sing, a little. I can teach her." Blanche relaxed.

Chuckling, Old Obie lifted the binoculars and stared over the river.

"Another sandbar? I didn't know the river was that low." Ike peered through the window.

Blanche joined them, looking in the direction where they focused their attention, scanning for whatever had them concerned. What she saw resembled a submerged tree limb, with a branch sticking above the water. But these men were the experts.

Old Obie lowered his glasses. "It's nothing. Just an old log."

I was right. Pleasure flooded Blanche's spirit. Maybe she was a natural born pilot after all.

Old Obie returned his attention to Blanche. "It sounds like you're going to be busy. Dress fittings, pilot lessons, music lessons. You're fitting into river life just fine." He patted her on the shoulder. "The Rio Grande will grab your heart before you know it."

At that point, the dinner bell rang, and a low growl erupted in the room.

"Skipped breakfast, did you?" Old Obie spoke before he inserted an unlit pipe in his mouth. "You'd better get down to dinner."

"Why don't you join us?" Blanche had never seen Old Obie in the salon.

He waved her concern away. "I'll grab a bite after Pete—he's my relief—shows up."

Ike put his arm through the crook of Blanche's arm and led her to the stairs. She paused and looked over her shoulder. A feather-light touch landed on shoulder.

"Don't worry about Old Obie. Elaine keeps him well fed. As Thoreau said, he hears a different drummer."

After dinner, Blanche convinced Effie to join her at the piano. "I want us to celebrate a time of worship on Sunday."

"And Ike agreed to it?" Effie's cane hesitated a fraction of a second.

Blanche tamped down a desire to remind her that she was the captain's heir and she didn't have to ask anyone's permission. But. . . "I will simply announce that I will retire to the theater for a time of worship after breakfast on Sunday and invite anyone who wishes to join me." She reminded herself she wanted Effie's help—more than that, her friendship. Pasting a smile on her face, she stared again into Effie's sightless eyes. Forced smiles wouldn't win Effie over. Tired of seeking approval in this strange environment, Blanche decided to relax. "From the time I was a little girl, my favorite part of the service was singing hymns. I really want to include a few songs on Sunday. And you are so talented with the piano—will you help me?"

A smile wrinkled those blank-staring eyes. "I'd like that."

"What hymns do you suggest?" Blanche didn't know how much church music Effie had been exposed to.

Effie cupped her hands over the table, her fingers moving as if seeking out piano keys. "I know 'Amazing Grace,' of course. I love Christmas songs, but it's not Christmas. What else? The doxology."

A smile played about her lips. "But if you sing one for me, I can probably pick it up."

Blanche bounced on her feet in time to one of her favorites by Fanny Crosby. "Can we practice right now?"

"The salon is empty now, isn't it?"

"Yes." Blanche answered the question, although Effie probably could name the order in which the passengers had left the room. She went to the piano and pulled out the bench, aligning her body perfectly with middle C. She played a few chords and hummed a few bars of "Amazing Grace," her voice a lovely alto.

"I've never heard you sing before. What a lovely voice you have. Maybe we can sing a duet." As soon as Blanche realized what she had said, heat rushed into her cheeks. "That is, people have told me I have a pleasant voice."

Effie chuckled. "I'm sure you have many talents we know nothing about. We've just met. But you must make me a promise."

"What?" Pleasure at Effie's compliment warmed her.

Effie plunked out a few chords of a melody Blanche had heard her play every night. "You must sing with me one evening."

"Why not?" Why not indeed. Her mind tumbled with possibilities as she guided Effie through a few hymns.

She couldn't remember a time she had felt happier or more at peace than the last two days. She had stayed too busy, and too happy, to spend her days in tears and recriminations.

For the first time, the possibility of living on the river no longer terrified her.

Chapter 10

Should I try to talk her out of this church service she's planning?" Ike lounged against the railing in the pilothouse.

Old Obie didn't object, one of the few people he allowed the liberty of touching anything in his domain. "No need to make an enemy of the girl. She'll be your boss someday, after all." He knew the twinkle in his eyes would take the sting out of his words.

"So you think she'll stay on the river?" More than simple curiosity lay behind Ike's question.

"How do I know? She might be pulling the wool over my eyes the way her mother did to the captain." Old Obie shrugged his shoulders, pretending an indifference he didn't feel. "But I do know this. In less than one week, she's learned more about steamboats than Cordelia did in two years of marriage. Maybe we should test it, let the boat get grounded and see what she thinks about being stuck in one place for a day or two."

Ike groaned. "Don't forget the passengers. We're trying to convince Bart Ventura that we can meet our schedule and that it's safe to bring his team aboard. That's Bart Ventura's biggest concern about bringing his team aboard. Floating them down the river for exhibition games will only work if they can advertise ahead of time. The only reason he's considering the steamboat is that the railroad hasn't made it to Roma yet."

Old Obie looked down the river. Ever changing, yet constant, none of the shifting attitudes of society. "Everybody's in such a rush to get places these days. There was a time when we could relax and take life easy."

Ike pointed to the steam pouring from the smoke stacks. "This from the man who adapted the design of the engine to get the boat to go a few knots faster to win a race?"

"A race is different." Old Obie waved away Ike's reaction, a smile lighting his face. "I won a pretty packet on that race." He sobered. "Of course, that was also the time that Cordelia decided she didn't like noisy engines, running fast, or gambling, and left the river for good." He stuck the unlit pipe in his mouth and chewed on the stem without lighting it.

"If I was making a bet, I'd give at least even odds that Blanche will stick." Ike placed a hand on Obie's shoulder. "She didn't have to come, but she did."

"So did Cordelia. Until she couldn't take it anymore. That just about broke the captain's heart." Old Obie turned his eyes inward to unpleasant memories of dark days.

"We'll know a lot more if. . .when. . .no one shows up at this Sunday service she's planning." Ike straightened away from the railing. "I bet she'd enjoy a time trial. Too bad the river is too low for that."

Old Obie laughed. "She probably would. Maybe we can arrange it."

Ike tossed a coin into the air and caught it with one hand. "At least Effie is having fun. She loves learning new music. She keeps humming this one hymn, 'It Is Well with My Soul.' It was written by someone who lost his family at sea, or so she says."

The sound of a hammer raining blows against wood floated up the stairs. "What's that noise? Did something on deck need repair?"

"No." Ike stared down the stairway. He rounded the corner at the bottom of the staircase in time to find Blanche tacking a sign by the doorway leading below deck. WORSHIP SERVICE headlined the sign in bold letters. The penmanship deserved an award.

Passengers and crew alike drifted by the sign, paused, and read it.

"A church service? Here?" One of Ventura's men questioned.

Ike waited for Blanche's reaction.

"A time for believers in the Lord to gather together to worship. We won't have a sermon, just friends sharing about a Friend."

"I'll probably be sleeping before my shift in the pilothouse." Pete had arrived. "But I wish you well."

He entered the stairwell, pausing when he saw Ike. "That Miss Lamar, she's something else. A church service on any boat. Let alone this boat. Doesn't she know—"

"No." Ike's voice came out more clipped than he meant it to. "And you'd better keep it that way."

"I didn't mean any harm, Mr. Gallagher." The young man's eyes widened. "I won't say a word."

"Good." Ike joined Blanche on deck. A crowd had gathered around her. Their expressions ranged from skeptical to outright humor. Should he rescue her? No. The more he learned about her, the more he discovered surprising strength. Only today he had read in the log book that she spent an hour observing the river in the fading twilight last night.

Today Blanche wore a brown skirt and beige blouse. The brown colors suited her coloring better than black and white, but he looked forward to seeing her in bright colors. Dame Agatha was finishing the gowns as quickly as she could, hopefully before the Sunday service. He grinned at the thought.

"I never thought I'd see the day they would hold a church service on the *Cordelia*. Doesn't the Bible have something to say about God and mammon?" Ralston's comment echoed the sentiments of others reading the sign.

Ike didn't have a clue what "mammon" meant but he didn't like the frown it brought to Blanche's face. The lunch bell rang. "All right, let's break it up. Miss Lamar will welcome anyone who wishes to attend, and I might add that my sister will be playing the piano. And that we are in for some special music. You might find it more enjoyable than you expect."

The crowd broke up, puzzled glances alternating with outright chuckles at Ike's expense.

Ike smiled himself until he saw the hurt in Blanche's eyes. She really cared about the church service. "Don't fret yourself. They mean no harm."

"What do they find so funny? Navy ships have chaplains aboard. Why not a commercial ship?"

Since Ike didn't know how to answer her question without crushing any illusions she might still hold about him, he shrugged. "It's just not the usual thing. May I escort you to dinner, Miss Lamar?"

She nodded and accepted his arm with perfect trust. His heart twisted. How long could he continue hiding the truth from her? Could he? Should he?

The answer was no longer clear.

Blanche slipped into her cabin. Dame Agatha had delivered an emerald green dress with gold piping to her cabin, and she found herself eager to wear it. The new outfits had drawn admiring glances from passengers and crew alike—and from Ike.

If she stayed aboard the *Cordelia* much longer, she'd be as vain as Mrs. Ralston. Sunday, a day dedicated to meditating on the God worthy of all worship, couldn't come soon enough.

The passengers' reaction to the meeting struck her as peculiar. They acted like she was suggesting a preacher go to a house of ill repute. She reminded herself that Jesus said the sick needed a physician, not the healthy. Perhaps their very salvation depended on the service. With a renewed sense of purpose—and a glance in the mirror that confirmed the dress brought out highlights in her eyes and hair—she headed for the dining salon.

The Ralstons arrived a few minutes after she did. Mrs. Ralston greeted her with what appeared to be a genuine smile. Blanche kept reminding herself to *judge not, that ye be not judged.*

Over fresh endive salad, Mrs. Ralston said, "I am glad you are holding the worship service on Sunday. That is sadly lacking in many ships of this kind."

Blanche offered a silent prayer of thanks for the affirmation, and from such an unexpected source. "So can I count on your attendance this Sunday?"

"Of course. And my husband will be happy to join us. Won't you, Mr. Ralston?" She turned her glossed lips on her husband, whose mouth lifted in a half-smile.

He leaned forward and refilled his water glass. "I wouldn't miss it for the world." He winked at Blanche. "I understand that we even have some musical numbers to look forward to."

Blanche opened her mouth to protest, but Effie spoke up first. "You won't have to wait that long. Blanche will sing at tonight's entertainment."

Blanche's head whipped around. Sure, they had practiced together a few times. But she still hadn't decided to go ahead with the performance—singing God's praises was one thing; entertaining the passengers was something else entirely. But she knew better than to voice that argument. "But I'm not ready."

"You'll do fine." Effie patted her hand and wiped her mouth daintily with a napkin. "And I'm sure once people hear you sing, they will be happy to attend the service on Sunday."

Backed into a corner like that, Blanche had to agree.

Ike's face broke out in a wide smile. "What is that saying, that God works in mysterious ways? I look forward to this evening with renewed anticipation. Especially if you will be wearing that fetching dress." He winked, but then his face sobered as his eyes bore into hers. Maybe he didn't believe in her abilities as much he pretended.

Her fears returned, doubled in strength. *Fear not.* The familiar command came to mind, but did it apply to her current situation? God was encouraging Joshua before he crossed the Jordan River to enter the Promised Land.

Come to think of it, Blanche was also on a river, and her own promised land, a possible future with her father, beckoned.

Maybe it applied, after all.

The waves in her stomach refused to go away. She picked at her food, although Elaine had cooked the chicken as tender, as well-flavored, as she had ever tasted. A dish of biscuits and gravy sounded good, but the *Cordelia* stayed away from such simple fare. Eating the biscuit dry brought on a coughing fit. Ike refilled her water glass and handed it to her. In a low voice, he said, "You'll do fine." His tenderness reassured her, and her stomach calmed down enough to finish her meal.

The hour between the end of the meal and the start of the performance dragged like the night before Christmas. She paced the front of the theater, pausing in front of the chair where Effie sat with perfect composure. "I want to go through the song one more time."

"If you sing it again, you'll have the fish singing along." Effie laughed. "You're ready." She wouldn't budge.

Blanche resumed pacing, humming the tune to herself. When she said the words under her breath, she forgot a phrase and panicked. She hadn't felt this nervous since the first time she had taken part in a scripture memory contest. This one performance made her as nervous as she had been when she was eight.

Mr. and Mrs. Potter arrived first, at ten minutes to the hour.

The dear lady crossed the floor to Blanche's side. "I am truly looking forward to this evening. I have been praying for you."

Tears sprang to Blanche's eyes. "Thank you. That means a lot." She turned to the refreshment table. "May I get you some lemonade? Some ginger snaps?"

"Why, thank you, dear. Pour some for yourself first. You look thirsty."

Blanche groped for a glass on the shelf behind her. "I have some water, but thank you."

Bart Ventura came in, studying the newspaper he had purchased the evening before.

Blanche took her mind off her nerves. "What news of your team, Mr. Ventura?"

"The Bats? They're coming along. Coming along. You will have to come to one of their games as my guest. But I ignored another little tidbit that I thought you might find interesting." He handed her the paper, opened to the center page.

Blanche couldn't imagine what news item the businessman thought would interest her, but she accepted the paper. "Female pilot licensed in Mississippi," the headline read. She read on with interest.

A woman named Blanche M. Leathers had taken the test to become a steamboat pilot on the Mississippi River—and passed. The article mentioned her lifetime on the River, and her years of working by her husband's side. "Mrs. Leathers is the first woman to receive a pilot's license." The paper questioned the wisdom of issuing a license to a woman because of the dangerous precedent it set.

Sympathy stirred in Blanche's heart for the woman who

showed so much gumption. The possibilities suggested by her accomplishment stirred something else, something more, something that took her mind off her fear of singing in public.

By the time she finished studying the article, the room had filled. Blanche told herself not to let Ike's absence bother her. She took a seat next to Effie in the front row, folding her hands in her lap, and breathed in and out. The door opened again, and Blanche turned to spot the newcomers. Her heart sped at the sight of Ike, tall, handsome, in his suit.

At his side stood Ole Obie. Dressed in a suit that looked almost as old as Blanche, he joined the traveling company on the *Cordelia* for the first time since her arrival on board.

Chapter 11

The theater had filled with the faces Blanche had come to recognize from their meals together. Murmurs rippled through the crowd, and only a few people took notice of Old Obie and Ike's entrance. Old Obie chose the seat closest to the door. He whispered a few words to Ike, who made his way down the center aisle.

As Ike took his place in front of the audience, Mrs. Ralston brought her hands together. The remainder of the audience took up the applause, with a few men adding catcalls. Heat rushed to Blanche's cheeks, and she rued the fair coloring that went with her bright hair. She took a sip of water from the glass they had brought from the kitchen.

Mrs. Potter reached over and patted her hand. "You'll be fine, dear."

Ike made a dampening motion with his hands, and the noise died down. "Welcome to this evening's entertainment. I know you are looking forward to our program. Mrs. Ralston will entertain us with Helena's monologue from *Much Ado About Nothing.* Our marvelous chef will ply your taste buds with some of her marvelous petit fours. To begin the evening, my sister, Effie, will play a number of Chopin etudes. Then she will accompany Miss Blanche Lamar as she sings a variety of popular songs. And I understand that our two musical ladies have a surprise in store for us."

At the last announcement, the audience once again broke into applause.

"I have promised Miss Lamar that she will retire at a reasonable hour—"

Chuckles, mostly from the men, came at that announcement.

"So let us begin." Ike took a seat and sat back.

Although Blanche didn't recognize the etude that Effie played, her fingers made the piano sing with music that didn't need words. Blanche's heart soared with its beauty, lifting her heart in worship of God. All too soon, the melody ended.

Chef Elaine circled the room. Blanche eyed the delectable miniatures but refused one. She didn't dare chew anything before she sang, or else she might cough in midsong. Mrs. Ralston's recitation could have graced a Broadway stage. Listening to her, Blanche questioned the wisdom of her planned course of action, but she had promised God, if no one else.

As Ike stood to introduce her, Blanche took a long drink and almost spilled it on herself. With a trembling hand, she placed the glass on the tray Elaine passed in front of her.

"And now the moment we've all been waiting for. . .please welcome Miss Blanche Lamar as she serenades us."

Blanche stood to excited applause, and she saw interested smiles on most of the assembled people. At the back, Old Obie looked her in the eye and nodded. Lifting her chin, she straightened her back in perfect posture and walked to the space Ike had vacated.

She bit back the words of apology she wanted to offer. *I've never done this before, please don't expect too much.* Her one word prayer, "Help!" would have to do. Focusing on friendly faces—her eyes swung between Old Obie and Mrs. Potter—she smiled. Effie played the introduction to "America the Beautiful," a patriotic melody as they had decided.

The next song included a more risky choice, juxtaposing "Dixie" to "Mine Eyes Have Seen the Glory." As her voice faded away on the last line, Mrs. Potter openly cried. At the back, Old Obie wiped at his eyes. Blanche relaxed. Her fears that some might complain at her singing the "Yankee" song faded. To her, they were two sides of the same story, the pain and passion felt by both sides. Love for country, love for home, love for God—both armies shared the same feelings. She paused a beat. "God bless America."

"Amen," Mr. Potter said, and others nodded.

After the heaviness of the last song, sentimental songs took over the program. "Miss Gallagher and I agreed that we would like to sing songs by Stephen Foster. Feel free to sing along." Their voices blended as they sang parts of three songs: "Beautiful Dreamer," "Jeanie with the Light Brown Hair," and "Old Folks at Home."

When she heard people singing along, she touched Effie's shoulder to stop. "Let's all sing that last verse again." Everyone joined in singing this time, some clapping, some tapping their feet.

Now or never, Blanche decided. "I also would like to do a

recitation. I'm no actress like Mrs. Ralston. . ." She smiled at the lady and received a smile in return. ". . .but I have repeated this passage to myself many times since my mother's death last month. I offer them as comfort to those of you who may have lost a loved one, in recognition of the God who offers us eternal life." She closed her eyes to focus on God, as she intended, and began reciting the comforting words from the twenty-first chapter of Revelation. "And God shall wipe away all tears from their eyes; and there shall be no more death, neither sorrow, nor crying, neither shall there be any more pain: for the former things are passed away." A single tear slid down her cheek. She opened her eyes. "I miss my mother, but if she hadn't died, I might never have come aboard the *Cordelia*."

Clapping broke out, and Mrs. Ralston stood to her feet. Soon the entire audience joined in the standing ovation. As the applause died down, Ike moved forward and handed her a single, perfect rose. "Let's show our appreciation for Miss Lamar's debut performance tonight."

Applause broke out again, and she wondered if she should bow and sweep out of the theater or how she should respond. Instead she stood there, smiling and nodding. At the height of the applause, Old Obie slipped out of the salon.

As the noise died down, Ike spoke to the group a final time. "Tonight's entertainment is finished. Please finish all the trays our chef has prepared, or else her feelings will be hurt."

After his dismissal, several people came forward to congratulate Blanche individually. Mrs. Ralston made her way to the front of the line. In the same voice she used to recite her monologue, she said, "My dear, you look so lovely tonight. And your voice was even lovelier than your clothes. I, too, lost my mother at a young age." She lowered her voice. "After this evening, I look forward to the Sunday service more than ever."

"I shall look forward to it." Blanche's heart flew to the top of the ceiling.

Bart Ventura came toward the end of the line. "Miss Lamar." Appreciation shone in his dark eyes. "What depths you have. I never suspected. I must bow in appreciation." He suited his action to the words, and she laughed.

Leaning forward, he continued. "I confess, I am confused. I never expected to hear so much about God only an hour before I sit down for a game of poker. It's like your boat can't decide what kind of place it wants to be. . .church or gambling hall." He winked at her before turning to Ike. "I'll see you later."

Blanche mumbled something—she didn't know exactly what—while her mind processed everything she had seen and heard since she arrived aboard the *Cordelia*. As soon as they were alone, she turned on Ike.

"Just where will he be playing poker? In your cabin?"

Ike wanted to curse as he watched Blanche march straight-backed out of the theater. With a few careless words, Ventura had undone all the good, all the humanizing Blanche's short time on the boat had done. Lips thinned, face pale, she lost any resemblance to her larger-than-life father and had transformed back into her mother's image. She might as well have dyed her hair black.

Ike found Ventura waiting for him outside the theater. "I hope I didn't create a problem for you."

Years of experience went into the bonhomie Ike forced into his face. He didn't feel at all charitable toward Ventura at the moment. "It will be fine as soon as I soothe some ruffled feathers." He trotted down the stairs to the girls' cabin.

Effie came out and shut the door behind her. "She really didn't know." As she whispered, she moved Ike down the hall, back toward the stairwell.

"I didn't tell her. . .but I didn't lie about it either. It just never came up."

Effie shook her head. "You knew she wouldn't like it. You could have laid low for this one trip, Ike. Give her a chance to get used to life on the river first."

Ike urged Effie up the stairs and out on deck. A light breeze broke across the prow, teasing his hair. "That's just not possible. I'm good with cards, Effie. I always come out ahead. And. . .we need the money."

"Would one trip bankrupt Lamar Industries?"

"This time, it wasn't just the money. I'm trying to woo Ventura to bring his team aboard. And Ventura's a gambling man. He wouldn't even consider us if he couldn't play a friendly game."

Effie leaned over the railing. "I'm sure you're doing what you think is best. I can't imagine any other way of life. Very little frightens me, but. . ."

"It's like what happened after our parents died and the captain took us in. Only now we are adults, and we're supposed to be able to take care of ourselves." He put an arm around Effie's shoulders. "We'll be okay."

"I'll talk to her." Effie turned sightless eyes on him.

"No." He dragged out the word. "It's time for me to come clean. I probably deserve whatever criticism she offers."

Effie nodded. "Give me a few minutes with her. I'll convince her to meet you on deck."

Unable to stand the waiting, Ike paced the deck. When walking below the shadows of the smokestacks, heat and soot filled the air, the familiar hum of the engines throbbed beneath his feet. Effie loved to come up here. She called it the heart of the ship, and Ike called it his thinking space, but Blanche wouldn't look for him there. He walked on to the pallets of untreated cotton and fruit grown only in the Rio Grande Valley. The scents of summer hung heavy in the air, magnolias and citrus and burning coal. Far different from the cigar-smoke-and-brandy-filled atmosphere of his cabin after a night of poker. Housecleaning tried in vain to remove the smell, so he came on deck every now and then for a breath of fresh air.

Heels tapped on the deck behind him. " 'When I consider thy heavens, the work of thy fingers, the moon and the stars, which thou hast ordained; What is man, that thou art mindful of him? and the son of man, that thou visitest him?' " Blanche's voice floated through the air as she joined him at the rail, keeping about a foot of space between them. Ike drew in a deep breath. She didn't sound angry, but disappointed, rather.

Since he had asked for this meeting, he should initiate the discussion. But where should he start? "I didn't mean for you to find out that way."

"You didn't mean for me to find out at all," Blanche shot back. "You didn't want me to know."

At least she wasn't yelling at him, not quite. "Not right away, no." Gambling aboard a steamboat seemed as natural as a duck paddling down the river. "It's hard to explain. I'm not that good with words."

"Don't treat me like a simpleton." Her voice held a definite hard edge. "You could charm a snake out of his skin if you wanted to. At least do me the courtesy of explaining life on the river, as you will probably say."

"Very well." *I need to see her eyes.* Ike hoisted himself onto the railing so that he was facing Blanche. He tilted back a few inches but righted himself.

"Be careful."

Ike chuckled. "You'd better watch out. Or you'll worry about what happens to me."

"I don't wish you any harm, Mr. Gallagher. My concern is the harm you bring on yourself and this enterprise by playing games of chance."

Ike took a deep breath. "Lamar Industries wouldn't survive without my poker winnings. I understand that steamboats used to earn big profits before the War Between the States. But those days are long over. Things have just gotten worse and worse since I was a child."

Blanche's face looked as pale and stony as the moonlight striking the deck. "Is this steamboat all there is to Lamar Industries? Is the *Cordelia* the totality of my inheritance?"

Chapter 12

Ike tapped his feet against the slats beneath the railings, thinking through his answer. "I'm not at liberty to discuss details about your father's company."

She glared at him. "I have a right to know."

"Of course you do. But, remember, I'm not much older than you are. I grew up on this boat, and I always had clothes on my back and food on the table. That was all I cared about. By the time I was old enough to take part in the business, the captain had grown used to keeping it close to his chest." Ike blinked as memories flooded back. When the captain had taken him and Effie in as children, he had promised they would have a home as long as they needed one.

Those details might soften Blanche's attitude toward her father. "When our parents died, the captain stepped in. I think he missed being a father. When he took care of us, he could pretend he was looking after you." Studying her profile, he couldn't guess what thoughts ran through her mind.

"Maybe so." Face lifted to the heavens, she turned her head to the right and left, surveying the stars. "God knows the stars by name. And He knows when a sparrow falls. He showed His love for you by sending my father to you. But you don't sense His hand on your life. And that's the saddest thing of all."

"You think God used a gambling owner of a steamboat to provide for two orphans?" Ike let his skepticism show. "I should think God would have sent us to a church or something."

"Who can understand the ways of God?" Blanche continued to stare at the sky. "The point is, God knew your need and took care of you. Even if I didn't have a father." Her voice cracked. She turned to face him full-on. "When I am mistress of this vessel—if I am—all your gambling activities will cease. God has provided for me all my life without my resorting to games of chance. He will continue to do so."

You are not the only one depending on the income the Cordelia *provides.* Ike didn't voice the thought as he slipped off the railing. "I will see you in the morning." With a bow of his head, he sauntered across the deck and down the stairs to his cabin.

Blanche's gaze followed Ike until he disappeared down the stairs. Headed to tonight's poker game, no doubt.

How naive she must seem, how innocent. Back home, people held that quality in high esteem. Aboard the *Cordelia,* others laughed at her for not recognizing the obvious.

Tonight should have been a triumph. She had sung, people had laughed and cried, she had even quoted from the Bible to a good response. Even Old Obie had attended.

But all that felt like nothing compared to Bart Ventura's caustic humor. How could a Christian live in a place like this? Bear witness to the saving power of God? She should retreat to her closet and pray the night away. But she hated the thought of descending the stairs and possibly running into someone on their way to the poker game in Ike's cabin.

Lantern light blinked overhead. *Old Obie.* He would listen. As she approached the stairwell, the sign announcing the upcoming church service taunted her with her high hopes.

She climbed the steps as quietly as possible. When she entered the room, Old Obie didn't turn around. She flattened her back against the wall, seeking the words to begin.

"Do you want to take a turn at the wheel?" His voice sliced through the air.

She darted forward, freed from her inertia by the sound of his voice. "Is it safe?" She laid a tentative hand on the wheel. "It is dark out tonight. Not much moonlight."

"I'm right here. If you want to get your pilot's license, you have to know how to run the river at all times of day. So tell me, what do you need to look out for when you're piloting at night?"

Blanche scrambled to remember. "How fast the boat is going. How strong the current is. How close the banks are. What the river bottom is like along here."

Old Obie nodded with each item on the list. "Do you know any of the answers?"

Blanche thought back. "I know we were traveling twelve miles per hour this morning."

Old Obie shook his head. "You must think like a river captain. Not miles. *Knots.*"

"Why did they use the same word for bumps in thread and distance over water?"

Old Obie chuckled. "I don't know. They didn't ask me."

As he led her through the answers to her questions, he occasionally directed her to shift the wheel a fraction to the right or left. The tension that had filled her from earlier in the evening dissipated. "I could stay out here for hours."

That brought another chuckle from Old Obie. "The river is getting ahold of you, girl. Why do you think I spend so many hours up here?"

She voiced the stubborn thought that refused to go away. "I wondered if you were avoiding me."

"Now, why would I do that?"

So you wouldn't have to talk to me about my parents? Wordlessly, she shook her head.

"No, indeed. Truth is, we have a second pilot aboard, but he doesn't have the feel for the river that I do." His hazel eyes slanted sideways at her. "Like you do."

"Do you really think I could be a steamboat pilot?" The idea seemed so audacious, so impossible—so desirable. The possibility challenged her to try something few people had done.

"Absolutely. You just need to get to know the river better." He stepped away from the wheel. "I'll leave you be for a spell. You get any problems, maybe you can sing the river into submission."

She chuckled nervously. Her fingers tightened on the spokes of the wheel.

"Relax. Feel the river."

She breathed deeply, as the music director had taught her to do, in and out, and loosened her grip. Despite the cooler evening air, sweat dotted her forehead. She struggled to see the river water the same way as she could during the day. *Feel the river.*

Looking ahead, she spotted one cypress tree towering higher over the river than the ones around it. She made that her landmark. Once she passed that, she marked an outcropping of the riverbank. She passed three landmarks before Old Obie tapped her on the shoulder. "You done good, but that's long enough for now."

Blanche glanced at the sky, half-expecting the quarter moon to have reached its zenith. It had barely budged.

"You held on for fifteen minutes. That's a good spell for a beginning pilot."

The frank admiration in Old Obie's voice warmed Blanche's heart. As she let go of the wheel, she gathered her courage to mention her reason for coming to the pilothouse. "I learned something tonight."

"That you have an amazing musical gift?" Old Obie shook his head. "I'd think you knew that already."

"No. Mr. Ventura mentioned that Ike runs a poker game in his cabin."

"Yes, he does, most nights."

How could Old Obie sound so matter-of-fact about it? "I wasn't aware the *Cordelia* served as a gambling hall."

"We don't. We don't have a roulette wheel or anyone counting twenty-one."

"But card playing—"

"Is a private game among gentlemen."

"Did—my father—approve?" Was this why her mother had left?

Old Obie's fingers flexed on the wheel. "The captain of a boat does whatever is necessary to keep his customers happy and the boat running. A game of cards every now and then is one of those things."

"So he knew about it. And didn't stop it." Blanche heard the resentment in her voice. The weariness and disappointment that were kept at bay while she piloted the boat rushed back in. "I think I'll go on to bed."

"Wait a minute, girl." One hand on the wheel, Old Obie patted her shoulder with the other. "I know this is all strange for you. And you've been raised to disapprove of gambling in all its forms. And in some ways you're right. But before you think too harshly of Ike, take your time. Get to know him better before you pass judgment on him."

Judge not, that ye be not judged. Blanche didn't expect to hear the echo of God's Word coming from this unexpected source. "I'll try." She took a step in the direction of the stairs, but Old Obie stopped her again.

"I got something for you." Old Obie dug at the back of his desk and pulled out a leather-bound volume. "Here is my logbook for last summer. I thought you might like to study it. Ask me any questions you have." He winked. "Maybe you can learn from my mistakes." He patted her arm awkwardly. "It will all work out. You'll see."

His words left a warm glow, and she felt better for talking to him. "Thanks." She hugged the logbook close to her chest. "And thanks for this as well. I can't wait." Her footsteps down the stairs fell more lightly than they had when she came up.

Given Blanche's reaction to Ventura's revelation about the ongoing poker game, Ike expected her to avoid him. She surprised him by chatting with him the next morning as if they'd had no disagreement. "I haven't made it down to the engine rooms yet. Do you have time to take me this morning?"

Once again she wore her black suit—she seemed to save her new dresses for dinner—but her hair was knotted loosely at the back of her neck rather than pulled into a tight knot on top. She looked quite fetching. He cleared his throat. "Of course."

The noise increased as they descended step by step into the bowels of the ship. He stopped before they reached the bottom, when he would have to shout to be heard. In the flickering lantern light, he looked at Blanche, a smudge of dust already marring her beautiful pale cheeks. "How much do you know about steam engines?"

"It has something to do with heating water to steam and cooling it back to water. But how does it work? How does the energy get to the wheels? I thought steamboats have wheels on both sides. Why is the wheel at the back?" She stopped to take a breath. "I have a lot of questions."

"The wheel is at the stern. It's a stern wheeler."

Her hands were making circles, punctuating each question. The more animated her voice, the brighter her cheeks grew. Her musical talents had gone without any training beyond singing at church.

Old Obie said she was the most natural pilot he had ever met. And now she asked questions like a born engineer. Blanche was a lady of many talents, and the best part was that she didn't even realize it.

"I understand some of the theory, but I can only make minor repairs. McDonald is a magician with the machines. Give him a hammer, rope, and a wrench, and he can fix almost anything." After he explained the layout of the engine room, he led her to the heart of the boat.

"How much coal does it take to heat the tank?" Blanche asked. When McDonald answered, she raised her eyebrows. She probably knew the cost of coal and could calculate the expenses. "Where is the machinery manufactured? How long do they last?" She piled on questions regarding shipping costs, the benefits of steam power compared to other choices, the problems and delays.

Whatever self-righteous habits Blanche mimicked from her mother, she showed a good head for business. If Ike presented the income from the poker games in terms of business profit and loss, she would understand their necessity.

Somehow Blanche's blouse remained pristine as they walked among the engines, even when her fingertips were coated with coal dust. The steam loosened tendrils of red hair that curled over her forehead like tiny flickers of flame. Ike didn't know any other woman, except perhaps Effie, who would be so at ease in the environment. He enjoyed their time together.

As the days passed, Ike waited for Blanche to bring up the subject of gambling, but she seemed as content to avoid it as he was. Although she didn't say another word on the subject, he gathered facts and figures to bolster his argument about the profitability of the enterprise. But she spent the week exploring the boat from stem to stern, asking for his companionship as often as not. Every now and then he caught her reading intently from a leather-bound book that looked suspiciously like one of the ship's logs.

At their last stop, among the stevedores who loaded the ship, Blanche delivered what Ike had come to consider her standard invitation. In each department, she invited the employees to attend the worship service, while making it clear attendance wasn't mandatory. Would that change if she took over running the ship? Would she want to hire a shipboard chaplain?

At Saturday evening's dinner, with Blanche wearing Dame Agatha's latest creation—a brilliant crimson that looked lovely in spite of its clash with Blanche's hair—she grew pensive. "I appreciate all the time you've put into showing me around the *Cordelia* this week. I hope I haven't taken too much time from your duties."

"Not at all." He had lost more sleep for far less pleasant reasons.

"I want to personally invite you to join us for our time of worship tomorrow." She cocked her head to one side, as if uncertain of his response. "Of course you don't have to come, but I think it may surprise you." Color crept into her cheeks. "I would appreciate it."

"I'll think about it." Until that point, Ike had planned on skipping the morning's agenda and catching up on sleep. After her personal invitation, his curiosity overcame his hesitation. What surprise did Blanche have in store?

He decided he wanted to find out.

Chapter 13

Early Sunday morning, Blanche awoke refreshed, one of the few hours of the day when the tight accommodations aboard ship remained quiet. She grabbed her Bible and headed to her favorite chair at the stern of the boat, where mist from the river cooled her face.

After days of planning and preparation and worry, today was the day. None of the nervousness that had assaulted her on the day of the musicale bothered her this morning. She didn't know if there would be three or thirty people present this morning. It didn't matter. God promised to be in the midst when only two or three gathered in His name. She and the Potters made the requisite three. If no one else attended, they could rejoice in the presence of God and renew their commitment to being light and salt to the world of the *Cordelia*.

God knew each person aboard by name. He cared for each one.

She dug out the list she had made, with as many names as she could remember. Digging through her memory for relevant facts, she prayed for each one, adding something beyond "God bless."

At the bottom of the list, she came to the ones she knew the best: Effie. Old Obie. Ike.

How had these three people become so precious to her in such a short time? In some ways she felt closer to them than she did to the people she had known her entire life. With so many items for prayer, she could skip breakfast altogether. But the breakfast bell rang and she decided to join them, to urge them one last time to attend the service. She looked at the sky and whispered aloud, "If there is any one thing they all need, it's Your saving grace. Oh, Lord, use me. The least worthy of all Your servants." *And send them to the service.* She didn't voice that last plea, but God knew her thoughts.

Stomach growling, Blanche slipped into the dining salon behind the Ralstons. When Mr. Potter said grace over breakfast, he reminded the diners about the morning's service. Several heads nodded.

All that prayer had increased her appetite; she piled her plate high with fluffy scrambled eggs, light orange muffins, and a tall glass of fresh-squeezed orange juice. Her old choir master used to advise her to avoid dairy products before singing, so instead of her usual glass of milk, she drank a cup of black coffee.

Conversation flowed around her, with her making appropriate responses from time to time. After breakfast, she would change, but she hadn't decided what she should wear. Her black suit made her the most comfortable, but wearing it seemed ungrateful for all the beautiful clothes God had provided for her. Neither did she want to appear as fancy as a peacock, vying for attention with the God she hoped to glorify.

Ma would wonder why she even had a question. Effie might tell her to wear the dress that made her feel best, but she couldn't advise Blanche about whether a color was too flashy. She considered the question as she buttered a muffin.

Ike leaned in close. "A penny for your thoughts? You're not worried about the service, are you? You'll do fine."

"Not exactly." Ike would have some insight into her question. "I'm trying to decide what to wear. I want to wear one of my new dresses, but I don't want anything too—too. . ."

Chuckling, Ike dabbed at his mouth. "Just like a woman. I didn't know you had it in you."

The muffin lodged in her mouth. Had she become one of those women who thought about nothing more than what she should wear, in one short week?

He straightened his lips, holding his humor in check. "You would look stunning in any of the dresses. I can't advise what is better for church, but I can tell you the difference between day wear and evening wear. I'm fairly sure that day wear would be acceptable for church."

"That sounds reasonable." She swallowed the last crumbs of her muffin with coffee. "So, which is which?" Heat wormed its way onto her cheeks. "They all seem pretty fancy to me."

"Maybe after breakfast? We can ask Effie's opinion as well, about the style if not the color. Unless you want to put the choice up to a vote by the breakfast crowd?"

A hint of a smile blooming, Blanche shook her head. A couple of forkfuls of egg remained on her plate, but she felt full. "I'm ready whenever you are."

The brief explanation of current styles left Blanche befuddled; the differences between the day and evening seemed blurred, but Ike could tell at a glance. Under his guidance, she decided on the beige dress that she had worn on her first day on board. With her hair, she reverted to her old style, pulling it into a tight knot on the top of her head. She didn't want any strands falling into her eyes at an inopportune moment. Effie changed into a dress much like the one Blanche had donned. "Are you ready?"

Effie patted her hair. "Yes." They made their way to the theater where they had held the musicale earlier in the week.

"I can't tell you how much I appreciate your playing for us this morning. I can't imagine worshipping God without music—or singing without a piano. We tried it a few times when our church pianist was ill, but we always sounded like a single bird trying to fill a canyon with sound. Not good at all."

"It's my pleasure." Effie waved aside her thanks. "Besides, I figure it doesn't hurt to add a few good deeds to my account with God."

Effie smiled when she made that statement, but Blanche's heart faltered. Did her friend think a right relationship with God could be earned? She prayed that truth, and so much more, would become clear throughout the course of the morning.

Blanche paused at the entrance to the room and lit the first lantern. Early morning sunlight streamed through windows, throwing the room into dazzle and shadow. Squinting, she decided the sunshine was too bright.

"How does it look?" Tapping with her cane, Effie made her way around the chairs to the piano.

"Too bright." Blanche adjusted blinds over the windows. "That's better. We need to be able to read." Even as she said the words, she realized the cruelty of the comment to someone like Effie. "Do you read Braille?"

Effie nodded. "I learned how, but I haven't had much opportunity to practice. We don't keep many books aboard."

An obvious question shocked Blanche in its simplicity. "Do you have a copy of the Bible in Braille?"

"No, although I read one once, at a school for the blind."

Blanche glanced at the well-worn volume she held in the palm of her hands, with favorite verses marked and notes from Reverend Davenport's sermons written down, smudges on the pages where she had memorized verses and passages. She had prized the Bible ever since she received it at the end of second grade. Once again she felt the rightness of her presence aboard the *Cordelia*. How they hear without a preacher, indeed. As soon as the *Cordelia* arrived at their destination, she would seek a way to obtain a copy of the Bible in Braille for Effie.

"I really liked the verses you read at the musicale. About heaven, and about the wonderful things that happen after death. I like to think of my parents being in a place like that."

Blanche glanced around the room—some setup was still needed—but decided the opportunity to speak to Effie mattered more. "If you died today, do you think you'd go to heaven?"

Effie's shoulders lifted almost imperceptibly. "I hope so. I'm a pretty good person. I figure the good outweighs the bad in the balance scales."

Blanche closed the distance between them and put a single light hand on Effie's shoulder. "The Bible says that not one of us is good enough. God demands perfection, and no one is perfect."

Effie frowned, and her foot tapped the floor. "Then why does the Bible talk about heaven, if none of us is good enough to go there?"

"Because God made another way. Jesus, God's Son, lived the perfect life none of us can. Then He offered Himself to God as a sacrifice for our sins. Remember those scales you talked about? All our sins—yours, mine, everybody else's—all sit on one side. Jesus' death on the other. They balance perfectly. All we have to do is believe it."

Effie tilted her head to one side as if considering what Blanche had said. The Potters came in, and the mood was broken. Blanche prayed that the seed planted in Effie's soul would find fertile soil.

"I'll set the chairs up in rows, shall I?" Mr. Potter suited his action to his words, setting up five rows of chairs. Blanche hoped they would need that many. As he worked, he whistled a few bars of "Blessed Assurance." That reminded Blanche. . .

"Have you ever heard of Fanny Crosby?"

"No. Should I have?" Effie ran her hands lightly over the keyboard, seeking out chords.

"Maybe not. But she writes hymns. And she's blind. She composed the melody Mr. Potter is whistling."

Effie cocked her head and her hands began strumming the keys. "What a lovely melody. What are the words?"

God put that hymn into Mr. Potter's mind. Smiling, Blanche said, " 'Blessed assurance—Jesus is mine.' Just like we were talking about."

"You'll have to teach me the rest of the song."

As Blanche agreed that she would, a figure appeared at the door. Timid Mary, who worked in the kitchen with Elaine and rarely said two words. "Is this where you're holding the church service, Miss Lamar?"

"Why, yes it is." Blanche crossed the room and shook her hand. "Where would you like to sit?"

Mary took a seat in the back row. Blanche suspected she would feel uncomfortable any place close to the front, although in this venue, it didn't matter, at least not to her. As soon as Mary settled in, three stevedores came in. Blanche hoped her face didn't betray her surprise. Somehow she hadn't expected the grizzled, rough-spoken men who made the docks of the Rio Grande their home to attend church. *Thank You, Lord.*

So many people entered over the next five minutes that Blanche couldn't greet each one individually. Out of the corner of her eye she spotted Mrs. Potter helping people find seats. If they had pews, they'd be applying the "SOS" rule—"slide over some."

Ike stood a few paces down the hall, watching people enter the theater. Almost as many people had shown up for the service as had for the musicale. He peeked through the door to see the crowded room while Blanche greeted Mrs. Ralston. Blanche played the part of affable hostess perfectly.

He entered. "You need more chairs."

"You came." Blanche turned a smile on him that he would swear had little to do with church and everything to do with his being a man.

"I wouldn't miss this for the world." He winked at her. "I'll be right back." In the dining room, he grabbed a couple of chairs. Soon they had a sixth row set up against the back wall.

"Thank you." Blanche glanced at the clock. "It's time to start."

"You'll do fine." He repeated his reassurance. He settled back in his chair to watch her go to work. She made her way to the front of the room, stopping to say a few words here and there. At the end of the front row, she paused long enough to square her shoulders then made her way to the podium placed on the stage area.

She moved with a natural grace, one that even her ugly black suits couldn't hide, and which the day dress she had chosen made evident. As soon as her foot reached the top step, silence fell across the room. The tap of her heels on the wooden floor reverberated in the stillness. At first she directed her gaze to the floor—probably praying, Ike realized—then raised her face with a radiant smile.

"Thank you all for joining us here today. We have come together to worship the Lord of lords, the Lord of all. He is the Lord of everything, even the Rio Grande." She took a minute or two describing some things she had observed during her time on board that taught her more about God.

"Miss Effie Gallagher has kindly agreed to accompany us as we sing. I have written down the words to the songs." So saying, she turned around an easel that had a sheet of paper with the words of a poem of some kind written on it. "Please join me in singing a song that praises the God of all creation, 'All Creatures of Our God and King.'"

The song marched along, carrying Ike and the others with it. When the last word finished echoing through the room, Blanche looked straight at Ike and smiled. "I'm not going to be doing all the talking this morning. We don't have a preacher; we're just believers in the Lord Jesus who want to worship. So I'm going to ask for your participation. First of all, I'd like to hear about any of God's 'creatures' you have known and loved. Maybe you had a special pet, or maybe there was a stubborn mule, or maybe a fish you caught in the river. We want to hear about them."

From his seat at the back, Ike saw bent heads and heard whispers circulating among the audience. They needed someone to break the ice. Would she welcome his support? Deciding she would, he raised his hand.

Chapter 14

Y es, Mr. Gallagher?"

A frisson of satisfaction skipped down Ike's spine at the relief in Blanche's voice. Standing, he turned around to face the audience. "We used to have a cat. I wanted a dog, but Mama would only let us have a cat. After our parents died, Effie carried that cat with her everywhere."

At the piano, Effie nodded her head, a smile playing about her lips. "His name was Blackie."

"When Captain Lamar took us in, he said they'd never had a cat on the ship. Blackie sniffed his ankles and rubbed around his legs, the way cats do, and the captain grew stiffer than a piece of cloth soaked in saltwater. I knew how sad Effie would be if she didn't get to keep Blackie, but I didn't know what we were going to do."

Blanche leaned forward to listen, as if eager to hear what her father had done.

"When the captain showed up again the next day, he said they had discovered mice aboard the *Cordelia* and a good mouser would be a welcome addition. If Blackie's owners would join him on board, of course. And so the captain took in two orphans and a cat."

Blanche's smile widened, and Ike thought back to her comments that God was watching over them even back then.

Ike shook his head. "There weren't any mice, of course. Or if there were, Blackie got rid of the evidence."

Blanche cleared her throat. "That's a beautiful story. It sounds like God was taking care of you and your cat. So tell me. What happened to Blackie?"

"He lived to a ripe old age." Effie's fingers tapped out the tune to "Three Blind Mice." She smiled. "He slept on my bed every night."

"Let's keep the *Cordelia* mouse-free." Blanche smiled. "Perhaps we'll get another cat, as a mascot. Thank you for telling us about Blackie, Mr. Gallagher. Does anyone else have a story to share?"

Ahead of Ike, a small hand shot into the air. Before Blanche could call on him, the young child said, "I have a dog. He's almost as big as me."

"Why, then, he must be a big fellow."

The boy straightened in his seat, lifting himself to his full height. "Yes, ma'am, he is. My papa says he eats as much as a horse."

The audience laughed while the child's mother shushed him.

"What is his name?"

Other stories followed. Even Ventura added a humorous anecdote about a stubborn mule he had encountered.

"The Bible says that God gave Adam dominion over animals. I have read about men who go into a cage with lions." Blanche shivered. "I wouldn't dare do that, but I think about that verse when I read the stories. Let's take a moment to thank God for His creatures." She closed her eyes and brought her hands together. "Thank You, heavenly Father, for the gift You have given to us in the animals that share this earth with us. Amen."

The service continued in the same vein. They sang a hymn and Blanche asked an everyday question that she managed to tie back to God or the Bible. After people shared anecdotes, they prayed. Everyone present had told at least one story by the time the hour ended.

Ike never expected the meeting to pass so quickly or so pleasantly. If anyone had come expecting a lecture on the Ten Commandments, he left disappointed. As promised, Blanche steered the conversation in praise of the God she worshiped, one she portrayed as involved in everyday life. The possibility comforted Ike and scared him at the same time.

After the final prayer, he slipped up to the front to wait with Effie at the piano. Blanche joined Mr. and Mrs. Potter at the door in greeting their guests as they left. Over the babble of conversation, Ike heard good comments. He lounged against the wall, a smile playing around his lips. "Who would have thought it."

He had spoken mostly to himself, but Effie responded. "She truly believes in all this, you know. And she reads that Bible of hers every day."

"Whatever else, she's a natural showman. She'll do well at the helm of Lamar Industries, if she's willing to bend some of her principles."

Effie chuckled. "Good luck with that."

The room slowly emptied, and with a start, Ike realized it was almost lunchtime.

"Duty calls," Effie said. "I'd better get down to the salon and begin playing." She caught up with Blanche, murmured a few words, and then departed.

"Where do you want these chairs, Miss Lamar?" Mr. Potter held one in each hand.

"Those came from the dining room." Ike took two more. "The rest of them stay here."

"Mrs. Potter and I will put the other chairs in a circle around the walls, shall we?" Blanche looked at Ike as if seeking his approval.

He nodded. "That will be perfect."

"Thank you for your help."

The way she smiled, with that pretty color in her cheeks, was enough to turn a man's head. "It's my job." Whistling the tune to "Three Blind Mice," he held the door open for Mr. Potter and walked toward the salon.

The aromas of roast chicken and stuffing filled his nostrils before he reached his destination. Was this what people looked forward to on Sundays—church, a good meal, and maybe a nap?

If all church services were like the one this morning, the practice no longer seemed so odd.

"It went well, didn't it?" Blanche looked around the restored theater, empty of their congregation.

"God was with you, dear." Mrs. Potter sank into a chair with a grateful *oomph.* "People enjoyed themselves."

Blanche frowned at that comment. "It wasn't meant as entertainment."

"Of course not." Mrs. Potter patted the seat next to her, and Blanche accepted the implied invitation. "You worshipped the Lord with your whole heart. People were touched and maybe thought about God in a new way. I think it was just right."

The luncheon bell rang. "I believe Elaine has roast chicken on the menu today." Blanche's mouth watered at the thought. "Let's not keep the company waiting."

Over the food-laden tables, Blanche glanced around the room, making a mental checklist of who had attended the service and who hadn't. Several passengers had stayed away, perhaps taking advantage of the extra time to sleep. Mr. Ventura's presence had provided the biggest surprise.

Ike had come.

Old Obie hadn't.

The handful of crew members absent from the service were involved with keeping the ship running. Everyone should have an opportunity to attend. She would speak with Ike about rotating shifts to make that possible. She nodded, pleased with the decision. Would Old Obie come in that case? She didn't have a clue.

"What's going on in that pretty little head of yours?" Ike dabbed his mustache with his napkin.

He just called me pretty. "I was thinking about ways to make it possible for everyone to attend the worship service, at least on alternate weeks."

"I should have known." He shook his head. "I would venture

a guess that not everyone will come, but after the turnout this morning, I'm not so sure."

"Yes." Unable to help herself, she asked, "What did you think of the service?"

His blue eyes darkened, as if calculating the answer to her question. "It wasn't what I expected. I guess I was expecting more hellfire and brimstone."

"While hell is as real as heaven, I prefer to remember that God loved us enough to send His Son to die for us."

He nodded but didn't comment. She was probably hoping for too much to expect him to do a complete about-face after one service that didn't even include a clear presentation of the Gospel.

"What changes do you have in mind for the schedule?" His fingers drummed the table.

"Nothing major. I realize that some men must work on Sundays, to keep the boat running." What would Ike say to docking on Sundays? She thought she knew and suppressed a smile. "But can they alternate weekends so that everyone has an opportunity to attend a Sunday service, if they want to?"

A smile curled Ike's lips. "For someone who has only committed to one trip downriver, you want to make a lot of changes. Or have you decided to make the *Cordelia* your home?"

Blanche jerked back at that. "I—no, not yet." She dredged out a smile. "How about a one-time change? For next Sunday?"

Ike's smile grew wider. "We can do that, sure." He winked. "And hope it becomes a permanent change."

Does Ike want me to stay? Blanche wished she had a fan to cool her face. *I shouldn't care what he thinks of me.* Mama had warned her often enough to beware of men with sweet words and wicked ways.

Then again, Mama didn't approve of anyone—including Blanche. Nothing she ever did was good enough for her mother. Mama would be shocked and disappointed at Blanche's decisions since her death. Her shoulders drooped. "Please make the arrangements for next Sunday, then."

Her appetite disappeared. The lemon squeezed into the sweet tea turned sour in her mouth. She forced down the last couple of bites of mashed potatoes and excused herself from the table.

At the top of the stairs, she hesitated. Did she want to walk the deck, or should she head to her cabin? The light breeze rippling across the water called to her, but she decided against open air. After the morning's excitement, she felt the need for solitude and quiet, time to consider her life, like self-reflection in preparation for the Lord's Supper. A pang of homesickness for Christ the King Church struck her. She missed the sonorous organ that accompanied the hymns, Reverend Davenport's sometimes dry but always challenging sermons, the loving fellowship that surrounded her at all times. In her cabin, she disrobed and stretched out on her berth. One by one she pulled up events from the past week for review.

"Poor dear." Effie put a finger to her lips and gently closed the door behind her. "She must be tuckered out. Out like a light on her bed."

"That sounds like a good idea." Ike didn't bother hiding his yawn. "I think I'll do the same."

Effie laughed. "You've had a time of it. I've seen more of you this week than I usually do in a month. Before you rest, though, come with me on deck." She felt her way to a deck chair and settled down, arranging her skirt so that it flounced prettily. An umbrella protected her from the heat of the midday sun.

Ike took the seat next to her and spread his legs in front of him. With the umbrella shading his face and his stomach full, hymns from the morning lulled him to an almost doze. Closing his eyes, he said, "Go ahead and tell me what's on your mind before I fall asleep."

"That's not necessary." Effie's light chuckle tickled his ears as she pulled a light blanket over his form. "Rest while you can. Maybe hidden away up here people will leave you alone." Soft footfalls receded in the distance, and he relaxed into a light doze. *Just a few minutes.*

The next thing Ike knew, the aromas of the evening meal awakened him from the best sleep he'd had in a week. For a brief moment, he kept his eyes closed. An elusive image had imprinted itself on his mind during a dream, of a lovely maiden with fiery hair and a spirit to match, dressed in the improbable colors of a peacock. But the memory proved elusive, disappearing as soon as he opened his eyes.

He swung his legs over the side of the chair and rotated his shoulders and neck, working out the kinks from sleeping upright. He glanced at his suit, glad it wasn't much creased from his unexpected outdoor nap.

He glanced up at the pilothouse. If he went right up, he had enough time before supper to tell Old Obie about the morning's service as promised. Tugging at the lapels of his jacket and whistling through his teeth, he bounded up the steps with renewed enthusiasm.

"You're a cheerful soul today." As usual, Old Obie didn't turn, but kept his eyes fixed on the river ahead.

"I had a most refreshing nap, thanks to Effie." Ike joined Old Obie at the window. The pilot made a minute adjustment to the wheel. Ike strained forward, scanning the water for a hint that had caused Old Obie's reaction. Giving up, he shrugged. "I don't know how you do it. I never see whatever you see."

"That Blanche girl. She sees a lot of them." In spite of the matter-of-fact voice, pride showed through Old Obie's words. "She's a natural."

Ike turned his back on the river so that he faced his friend and mentor. "Do you think it will make a difference? That she'll stay? She'll never be a pilot."

"Don't see why not. Not since they made that woman a pilot over on the Mississippi."

Ike had his doubts, but he didn't argue them. "She's got a lot of tricks up her sleeve. You should have seen her this morning." As he described the service, he realized how much he had come to admire her. "Sometimes she seems like a nervous cat, ready to run away at the first sign of trouble. Then she gets up in front of everybody like she's been doing it all her life."

Old Obie looked at Ike out of the corner of his eyes for a second before he turned his attention to the river. "She's got courage. And backbone. The backbone comes straight from her mother, but the courage. . .maybe her father had something to do with that. At least I like to think so."

The longer Blanche spent on the river, the more of her father's qualities she displayed. Ike grinned, and Old Obie looked at him, teeth bared in a matching smile.

Chapter 15

Blanche woke up, stretched out on top of the covers of her bed. She stared at the ceiling of the cramped cabin. "What am I doing here?"

"You're awake. Good. I was beginning to think I would need to wake you up so you wouldn't miss dinner."

Blanche glanced at the only chair in the room, where Effie sat working a pair of knitting needles. She raised up on her elbows. "Is it that late?" Rubbing her eyes, she stood and went to the wardrobe. She'd wear her black traveling suit, a penance for the insights she had during her earlier time of reflection.

Reaching the end of the row, Effie paused in her knitting. "I don't mean to pry, but I've been told I'm a good listener." She turned the row and started moving the needles again.

Blanche watched her flying fingers. "Do you ever drop a stitch?"

"Of course." Effie's laughter tickled Blanche's ears. "But that's true for everyone who knits. And then I go back to find my mistake and fix it. Once I had to start over again from the beginning."

Give me words. "That's like what happens when a person becomes a Christian."

Effie's face scrunched while she recounted the stitches on her needle. "I don't understand."

"Everyone makes mistakes and breaks God's laws. Jesus died for those sins. When we ask God to forgive us, He takes away all of those mistakes. He makes us into new people."

"I've never thought of it that way." Effie continued down the row then tucked the knitting into her bag. "When we were little, before our parents died, Ike and I used to go to Sunday school. One day our teacher asked us if we wanted to ask Jesus into our hearts. I didn't know what she meant, but I knew I loved Jesus and so I prayed with her." A smile played on her lips. "I haven't thought of that for a long time."

Blanche's heart sped and she threw her arms around Effie's shoulders. "That means we are sisters in the Lord." And what about Ike? The question dangled in Blanche's mind but she didn't voice it.

Blanche felt Effie's smile without seeing it. "I always wanted a sister." Effie returned the hug before stepping away. "I'd better get down to the salon. It's almost time for dinner." With a whisper of fabric, she left the cabin.

Blanche wanted to call her back, but God would give her another opening. As children, Effie and Ike had heard the Gospel. But when their parents died, they no longer received regular religious instruction.

Blanche would double her prayers for the captain—her father.

When he took the children in, they stopped attending church. Righteous anger sang along her nerves. How could he? Charging out of the room, she headed for the pilothouse.

Her route took her past shining brass fixtures, and Blanche caught sight of her reflection. Lines marred her forehead and lips, her slitted eyes looked stormy dark. Even the hair that escaped her bun looked like flames of fire ready to devour anything that got in her path.

She stared at her image, the resemblance to her mother obvious. Nothing about that angry face spoke of God's love. No wonder her father had run away. Flushed and sickened, Blanche bolted to the railing and leaned over the side. Her stomach heaved, and she opened her mouth. Nothing came up, but acid burned the back of her throat.

Oh, Lord, forgive me. A fresh breeze blew across the bow, and she breathed deeply of the clean, cool, scent. Closing her eyes, she recalled the morning's service, voices raised in songs of praise to the Lord. Overhead a bird called. She followed its flight to a tree branch on the opposite bank, and she thought whimsically of the two languages spoken on either side of this great river, but how the birds only spoke one language and God understood all of them. "All creatures of our God and king." The hymn from the morning bubbled up in her throat and burst out. Starting as barely more than a whisper, it grew until she sang with full voice, unmindful of anyone else who might be on deck.

When her voice trailed away, a solitary clap of hands welcomed the end. Heat rising in her cheeks, she checked her reflection in the brass again. The angry lines that bothered her earlier were gone, replaced with color and life and, yes, joy. God extended His grace to her even when she was her most ungracious. She turned to greet her audience.

Renewing his applause, Obie stepped out of the shadow of the stairwell. "You sing with all your heart." He could also have said she sang well, with the voice of an angel. But the color in her cheeks told him he had chosen the right words.

"Thank you." She regained her composure. "I don't believe I've ever seen you anywhere except the pilothouse." Putting her hand over her mouth, she gasped. "Except for the musicale the other night."

His lips widened in a broad grin. "I'll let the assistant pilot hold the wheel for a few hours, until full-dark. Walk with me?"

When she agreed, he took her arm and walked to the bow of the boat, used mostly by the crew. "Ike tells me the service went well this morning."

"It wasn't much. We shared testimonies and songs. No preaching."

"Sometimes the only Bible people read is your life. And a lot of people are watching you, weighing your actions." He patted her arm.

Blanche stiffened. Silence accompanied them as they walked a few more feet.

"They did the same thing to your mother, of course." When they reached the stairwell, he leaned against the side rail, remaining in the open air instead of the confined space on the steps.

Obie couldn't read her expression. Did she think he was comparing her to her mother? He hadn't thought much of Cordelia's "Bible."

"Am I. . .very much like her?"

He took off his pilot's hat and twisted it back and forth in his hand while he considered his answer. "Yes. And no. You could probably say the same of most children and their parents, I suppose." He pointed his finger at Blanche. "The captain would be pleased that she didn't manage to snuff all the life out of you. You love your God, that's clear enough, but there seems to be more to your faith than a list of dos and don'ts."

A joyful smile followed Blanche's flinch. "That means a lot to me. Jesus lives in me. He's a part of everything I do and say."

"I know." Obie winked. "You might even convince an old reprobate like me to listen one of these days."

A smile spread across her face. "I would like that, very much."

"I'm sure you would." He took her right hand in his and patted it. "I don't want to give you the wrong idea about your mother. The captain adored her. He just couldn't live with her." An old longing swept over Obie.

"You were sweet on my mother, weren't you?"

The pilot needed to do a better job of masking the longing. "Some might say so. But she only ever had eyes for Captain Jedidiah Lamar, his high-falutin' manners and snake-oil charm, not an old river rat like me." He shook his head. "You see things more clearly than Cordelia ever did. You keep that quality, girl."

Impulsively, she hugged him. Heat slammed into his cheeks and he plopped his hat back on his head. "Thank you kindly." He let go of her hand and walked into the darkness of the stairwell.

It had been quite a day.

After sunset, Ike waited in his cabin for his poker cronies to show up. Bart Ventura arrived first, followed by Ralston. Ike poured drinks for the three of them while they waited to see if anyone else would join them. No one did.

"It looks like it's just us tonight." Ike gestured for his guests to sit down and slit open a new pack of cards, a weekly ritual. The cards Bart provided featured the logo of the Brownsville Bats—a black bat wrapping its wings around a Louisville slugger. Mr. and Mrs. Ventura provided the inspiration for the king and queen, and the manager served as the jack. "Ventura Market" was blazoned beneath the logo. "I like these." He gestured with the pack in his hand before shuffling them.

"We'll give a deck to everyone who attends the games we're setting up. Might draw business for both of us." Ventura winked. "Unless Miss Lamar shakes things up more than she already has."

Ike fanned the cards on the table and continued shuffling. "The captain made sure that won't happen."

Ralston slanted his eyes in Ike's direction. "Does she know we've continued our friendly game?"

He shrugged. "Not as far as I know. And I intend to keep it that way as long as possible." After shuffling the cards twice more, he tossed them to the other men, one at a time around the table. "This may be her only trip downriver."

Ventura and Ralston exchanged a look. "She'll be back." Ventura spoke with Latin assurance. "We can see it, even if you can't."

His words disturbed Ike, and he stroked his ear in an unexpected tell when he turned his cards over. Ralston arched an eyebrow and grinned. *I might as well toss my cards on the table.* As expected, he played a mediocre hand.

Ralston bent his head in Ventura's direction. "That's our secret to winning. Keep talking about Miss Lamar."

Chuckling, Ventura nodded. "Maybe he'll be convicted, and he'll stop taking our money."

Taking a sip of whiskey, Ike swished it around his mouth, bringing calm back to his spirit. "That's not going to happen." He leaned back in his chair, a complete picture of peace. "We *welcome* your contributions to our coffers."

From there on, the game turned serious. Perhaps Ike could blame his lack of luck on one glass of whiskey too many, but he suspected it had more to do with the thoughts swirling through his mind about Blanche.

Ventura lost more than Ike did. Over the course of the trip, he had easily lost a thousand dollars. More money disappeared into his baseball team. He ran a profitable business, but how much of his apparent prosperity was smoke and mirrors? A flicker of guilt washed over Ike, but he shook it off. Ventura's financial well-being wasn't his responsibility. The *Cordelia*'s future was.

Ike's guests left a little early, which suited him fine. Not yet sleepy, he sat by the porthole, studying the reflection of the moon on the water. He fancied Blanche staring at the same view, except the girls' cabin lacked portholes. The only people definitely awake this hour were the engineer on the evening shift and Old Obie. As a child, Ike used to explore the decks till all hours of the night. He knew every inch of the ship; he could probably rebuild it from memory.

Until Blanche, the only other person he had ever seen with the same passion for the *Cordelia* was the captain.

He closed his eyes. Why did Blanche keep cropping up in his every thought? Shrugging out of his suit coat and removing his bow tie, he slipped out of his room. This late at night, he risked comfort, hoping the night air would cool his troubled emotions.

He made his way through the bowels of the ship, nodding at the engineer from a distance, allowing the sweat to build up and roll down his back. He skipped the deck with the passenger rooms. As disheveled as he was, he had no desire to run into anyone. A stop at the salon netted him a sugar cookie with a cup of cool water. After two more glasses slaked his thirst, he returned to the hall, opening the door to the theater. Flicking on a gas lamp, he walked the perimeter, his mind placing the passengers in their appropriate seats. Almost everyone on board had attended the worship service. More than attended, they actively participated and enjoyed the experience. The support surprised him. Blanche Lamar's simple trip down the Rio Grande was going to change life aboard the *Cordelia* in ways no one had imagined when the captain first proposed his plan.

One long stride brought him to the stage, and he walked to the spot where Blanche had presided over the gathering with such skill. She didn't use any fancy tricks or powerful oratory, only sweet sincerity and genuine kindness shining from her eyes. No one could resist. Him least of all, even if he didn't understand all this talk about a Savior. He didn't understand, but he wanted to believe, at least as far as Blanche was concerned.

Blanche. He couldn't afford to like her. Lamar Industries might not survive with her running the business. Tired of worrying about her, he jumped off the stage and scurried up the steps to the deck.

His long legs ate up the deck as he paced back and forth. Long ago, Effie memorized the number of steps from one spot to another until she could walk about without the aid of a cane. Ike did the same thing, adjusting the number of steps as his legs grew longer.

If only the *Cordelia* was a bigger boat, he wouldn't pass over the same spots time and again, listening to the same creaks. His shoe might miss the nail he had hammered down more times than he could count, although it always came loose again.

The moon sank low, and the sky lightened a smidgeon. Below the railing, the river rippled invisibly around the prow of the ship, and the wheel churned slowly. When the visibility decreased, Old Obie kept the speed down. He had every inch of the river memorized, the same way Ike knew the decks of the ship, but the river constantly changed. Even in the darkest reaches of the night, Old Obie could tell something was wrong within half a foot.

The light in the pilothouse testified to Old Obie's presence, and he would welcome Ike's company. As tempting as the idea sounded, Ike needed to puzzle out this problem on his own. When the captain turned everyday affairs over to Ike, he vowed to lessen his worries. That meant Ike kept some things to himself. Railroads began to make their presence felt even down here in the Rio Grande valley, and business profits had dropped every year under his management.

Ike didn't know how long the *Cordelia* could stay in business. If he really cared for Blanche, he would make sure she had a miserable trip and never want to come back.

That shouldn't be a problem. All he had to do was tell her he ran a nightly gambling hall that kept them in business.

She'd run back to Roma in a second and retreat into the shell of the woman she could become.

He didn't know which loss would bring more grief—the loss of the *Cordelia* or the departure of Blanche Lamar.

Whichever way things turned out, he'd let down his captain.

Chapter 16

Blanche straightened in her chair and stretched her arms, rolling up the map of the river Old Obie had given to her and slipping it into a case. As she read the logs, she marked down every spot where he mentioned obstructions and other warning signs to study. When not studying the maps, she stared at the river as it sped by, so that she could identify the potential problems she knew were there.

Now that she had finished reading the logs, she would indulge in one of her favorite activities: heading to the pilothouse and steering the boat under Old Obie's watchful eye. Even though she hadn't reached a decision about whether she would stay on the river or return to Roma for good, she had developed a passion for earning her pilot's license. The study was not only fun, it also made dull subjects like math and science important in a way that her teacher never managed.

Five new dresses hung in her closet. Colors and stylish cuts, which seemed inappropriate and prideful in her mother's domain, were perfectly acceptable in this setting. God's flowers of every shade and shape filled the earth all year long. Why would He prefer His people to dress in uniform black and white? She enjoyed the dresses Madame Agatha had made for her, even if she only brought them out for special occasions when she returned to Roma.

Today she donned her persimmon-colored dress, a shade of red her mother would have insisted clashed with her hair. But the color made her feel alive, like the first rays of daylight awakening the earth. She thought Old Obie would approve.

Realizing she had dawdled a little too long over her attire, she hurried to the pilothouse. She dabbed at the unladylike sheen of sweat on her forehead with a handkerchief and headed in.

The soft scent of rose water alerted Obie to Blanche's presence. "I was wondering when you would come."

"I apologize." Her voice was hushed, less confident than usual. "I spent so much time studying the maps that I rushed to get here."

Satin whispered against the wall, and Obie turned around, a smile spreading across his face. "Dame Agatha has done well. You look lovely, my dear."

Red a shade between her hair and dress flooded Blanche's cheeks. "Thank you, kind sir." She dipped in a curtsy and giggled.

"You are most welcome." He waved his hand, inviting her to turn around. She pirouetted for his approval, shaking a little as she completed the turn. In that moment, she looked so much like her mother that Obie's heart constricted. "Your mother would have looked lovely in that dress. I saw her in a red dress one time. Then she hung it at the back of the closet."

Blanche dropped to the soles of her feet. "I never saw her in red, not even at Christmas."

"I'm not surprised, but that's unfortunate. Bold colors brought out her coloring, made her beautiful, but she was more comfortable in the background." He glanced at Blanche's feet. "Perhaps Ike can do something in the matter of new shoes."

Blanche sneaked the toes of her boots under her skirts. "These are perfectly serviceable."

Obie laughed out loud. "You sounded just like Cordelia."

Blanche kept her gaze on the floor.

"That's not a bad thing." He gentled his voice. "But you are not her. To use words that Cordelia herself might use, God created you, a separate and beautiful young woman. He welcomes your laughter. In heaven, Cordelia would want you to be happy." In a low voice almost more to himself than to her, he said, "The captain wanted her to be happy, but he couldn't do it. They loved each other but made each other miserable." He lifted Blanche's chin with one gnarly finger. "Never doubt that your parents loved each other, and their child."

Tears welled up in her eyes. "My mother loved me?" Her voice broke as she said the words.

"Never doubt it."

It felt like the most natural thing in the world to take her in his arms and rest her head on his shoulder, comforting her as she cried.

Ike searched the boat to inform Blanche of his dinner plans in the town of La Joya with Bart Ventura. As expected, he found her in the pilothouse.

He wanted to pinch himself at the transformation. Could the woman wearing the persimmon-colored dress in mid-afternoon be the same woman he first saw at the funeral a few short weeks ago? She, who always wore black and white, until that first cream-colored dress Dame Agatha had made for her sight unseen?

Neither one of them paid attention to his arrival.

"What's coming up in the next mile of the river?" Old Obie lounged at the side, ready to step in if she made an error. Given the fact he still hovered behind Ike on the rare occasions he took the wheel, the pilot was offering Blanche a tremendous compliment. Did she know?

She laughed, a lighthearted sound that Ike would love to hear every day. Her happiness mattered more than a compliment. He leaned against the wall, watching them chat.

"There should be a sandbar right up there, to the left of the poplar tree." She leaned forward, as Ike had seen Old Obie do time and time again. "I see the shadow. Over there." She raised a draped arm, her delicate hand pointing a single finger.

The pilot nodded. "So how do you correct?"

"If it was spring, runoff would raise the river level and I wouldn't have to worry." She drew in her features as if running through options in her head. "The water goes down in summer, but we've had several afternoon showers. I'm not sure."

"Look at the shadow again. Use your eyes."

Blanche tilted her head. "I think the boat can pass over it."

Old Obie didn't speak.

"But—I'll ask them to slow the engines?"

Old Obie remained silent, and Ike laughed. The two of them turned and stared at him.

"That's a favorite trick of Obie's. He's testing your confidence." Ike came forward. "Which means you are correct."

Shaking his head, Old Obie smiled. "Don't go telling her all my secrets."

Blanche laid her hand on the bell she used for alerting the engine room to slow down. Both men nodded, and she pulled it. She tilted her head, her ears peeking out beneath her halo of hair, as if seeking the telltale sounds of the bottom of the boat scraping the riverbed. The prow glided forward, past the danger zone, and Blanche's grip on the wheel relaxed.

"Well done." Ike brought his hands together in a single clap. "Not only will you be one of the few women with a pilot's license, but you will also earn it the fastest if you keep things up at this rate."

The grin on Blanche's face was more little boy than young woman.

"She still needs hours on the river." Old Obie was a little stingier with his praise. "She's had just enough experience to be cocky and think she knows it all."

"I could never do that." Blanche shook her head.

"Not on purpose, no. But you might look for what you expect to be there and not see what is different."

"That takes a lifetime." She acknowledged his experience. "My father was lucky to have you."

Old Obie cast an amused glance at Ike, and he stifled a laugh. "We put in a lot of years together." The pilot nodded.

"Don't let him fool you. You're his prize pupil, and he knows it." Ike changed his plans for the night. "I know how we can celebrate. We are stopping in La Joya tonight. Why don't you come with me? Meet the customers who use the boat for shipping, and then go out to dinner? There's a wonderful restaurant that serves the best steaks on the Rio Grande."

Blanche kept her eyes trained on the river, avoiding his gaze. In a flat voice, she asked, "Will Mr. Ventura join us? I thought you introduced him to town officials at each stop."

Ike arched an eyebrow. "So you were paying attention."

"Of course. Every place we have stopped has agreed to exhibition games. You've done a good bit of business for Lamar Industries." She glanced over her shoulder, the expression in her brown eyes an enigma. "I will come with you, if Effie will consent to host dinner for the evening."

"She will." Ike grinned. "She has before. I will suggest that Mr. Ventura visit the town council on his own this time. We'll be in Brownsville before we know it. I'd like to do something special before we reach the end of the line." He came forward and leaned against the window, so that he could see Blanche from the front. "You look like a vision in that dress. You will light up the restaurant."

Blanche's hand went to her throat, and she looked at the ruffled cuffs at the end of her sleeves. "I. . .will think about it."

"I will meet you at your cabin then, about fifteen minutes after we dock. Until then." He nodded his head and withdrew.

Whistling, Ike debated whether or not to return to his cabin. During this time of day, he often rested for a few hours. But today thoughts of his upcoming dinner with Blanche filled his mind, and he knew he wouldn't sleep. Effie would say he should lie down, rest his body if not his mind. He'd rather sweat out his uncertainty than lie in bed and dwell on it.

While Ike dawdled at the top of the stairs, Ventura climbed from below deck. "What's on your mind?"

Ike rolled his shoulders and balled his fingers into a fist. "This is one of those rare occasions that I wish I lived on land. A long ride on horseback sounds perfect, or perhaps an hour toiling the soil."

Ventura threw back his head and laughed. "I can see you on the back of a horse, but turning the sod like a farmer? That would make the headline on towns all up and down the river."

"You may be right." Ike unclenched his fists and turned sideways, imitating the swing of a bat. "Perhaps a friendly game of baseball with your Bats."

"It's physical exercise you're wanting. . ." Ventura rubbed his chin, considering. "I might be able to accommodate you. Perhaps a sparring bout, between you and me? With a friendly wager on the outcome? My man could keep the score."

"Where?" The idea held appeal. Channel his energy into quick jabs. Punch his feelings into line. "We don't have a gymnasium on board."

"The theater is large enough. And we are unlikely to be disturbed there at this time of day." Ventura pulled out a pocket watch. "What say you? I'll go get my man."

"Easy money, Ventura. Easy money. I have ten years on you,

man. Shall I spot you a point or two?"

"Not necessary." Ventura grinned. "You don't know everything about me. Fifteen minutes?"

"I'll see you there."

"And you can bring a second, if you wish."

"Duel at dawn?" Ike trotted down the stairs. In his cabin, he rustled through his clothing. His stylish wardrobe filled him with pride, but he had precious little suitable for a boxing match. He settled for the clothes he wore when helping the stevedores loading and unloading—worn slacks, a shirt with loose buttonholes and a few paint splashes on the sleeves. What else? A pair of leather gloves might protect his hands. Slipping them into his pocket, he went to the theater.

Ventura danced around the floor, his feet shifting and arms darting with an invisible partner. As the door shut behind Ike, he looked up. "Where's your second?"

"I didn't bring one." Ike said. "You won't last more than five minutes."

"How much do you want to bet?" Ventura grinned.

"Oh, I don't know. One dollar a point? Five?"

"Five. Let's keep it interesting." Ventura handed his pocket watch to his man. "Terms. One point for every hit landed. Punches only allowed above the waist. Two five-minute bouts, a third if we are tied. Agreed?"

"Agreed. Are you sure you don't want me to spot you a point or two?"

"No chance."

After Ventura's second moved the chairs to the perimeter walls, he met Ike in the middle, where they knocked their knuckles together.

"Shall we separate six paces before we come out swinging?" Ike couldn't get over how much this felt like a duel.

"A yard should be plenty." Ventura backed up a few feet. Both of them waited for a signal from his second. At his nod, Ventura darted forward, swinging his right fist. Ike shifted, but the blow glanced off his chin.

"One point!" Ventura danced back. Ike threw right, left, right, but Ventura dodged all of them.

Ike's estimation of his opponent rose a notch or two. Ventura was tougher than he looked.

"We grow them strong in Old Mexico. Like a bantam rooster. Small and tough." Ventura grinned as he darted forward and swung his left hand toward Ike's chest. Ike avoided the blow.

As they continued to dance around each other, feinting, avoiding, darting forward, Ike worked up a sweat. This room would smell like the engine room. He'd have to give special instructions to the cleaning crew tomorrow.

"Five minutes." The second called. "Halt."

The first period ended with Ventura ahead two points to one. Ventura tossed a towel to Ike. In the absence of a bucket of cold water, he accepted it and wiped at the sweat pouring from his face and neck and down his arms.

"Take your places."

Ike copied Ventura's stance, holding his elbows in close, protecting his vulnerable chest. This time he landed the first blow on Ventura. "Even."

Ventura circled Ike, moving him to the left, his weak side. "Not for long." He darted in and landed his right fist beneath Ike's protective block with his left arm.

Ike resisted the urge to jump back and protect the injured area. He would smart tomorrow. Instead, he channeled his aggravation into vigilance and landed a second punch before time was called again. Ike took his seat, swiped at his face with the now-damp towel, and wished he had a cold drink.

"What is going on in here?"

Ike's head snapped up and his gaze collided with the astonished glare of Blanche Lamar. "We're. . .letting off steam."

"You're fighting! I heard you all the way at the end of the hall." She took a step into the room, glanced at Ventura, but crossed to Ike. "You're hurt." Her finger pointed to his chin. "I'll get some cold water."

"In Mr. Gallagher's defense, I'm the one who suggested this." Ventura stood up. "Nurse him later. We're not done yet. The next man who lands a hit wins."

"This is a game?" Blanche looked as mystified as women always had since they watched boys fight in the schoolyard.

"It's not so much a game as a way—"

Ike hastened to interrupt. "I felt the need of exercise, and my choices on board are limited. Ventura came up with this suggestion. Now, if you will excuse me. . ." He stood and crossed the distance to Ventura in one long stride. His hands lashed out, left, right, left, and all three landed.

Chapter 17

Ike raised his arms in the universal signal of victory. Gasping, Blanche stepped in Ventura's direction to make sure he was uninjured.

"Well done! We'll settle things later." Ventura accepted his man's towel and buried his face in its folds. Swinging the towel around his neck, he smiled as if he hadn't lost the bout. "Good day, Gallagher. Miss Lamar. I will see you later." A tune whistling between his teeth, he walked out the door, happy with the world.

Blanche counted to ten once, then twice. "Was that really necessary?"

"Of course not." The corner of Ike's mouth lifted in a half smile. "But it was fun."

"Grown men, fighting like two boys in the schoolyard." She shook her head. "I thought the two of you were friends."

"Have you ever heard of boxing?"

Blanche shook her head.

"It's a kind of organized fight. With rules."

"You still were hurt. Your chin is already turning color." She peered at it, questioning whether what she saw was a bruise or his whiskers. Her fingers stretched out to check before she pulled back, embarrassed by her close examination of the man.

He touched his side and winced. "I didn't expect you to leave the pilothouse so early."

Old Obie had sent her out early with strict instructions to rest and fix her hair for the evening, but she wouldn't give Ike the satisfaction of telling him so. "I was just taking a break before we come to La Joya. I was on my way to my cabin when I heard all the commotion in here." She drew a deep breath. "Since it appears you will live, I will go on ahead."

"I'll see you this evening then." Ike grabbed a towel and walked her to the door. "Looking like a gentleman, I promise you."

Blanche watched his back as he walked away. Damp patches darkened his shirt where it stuck to his skin. Dressed in these clothes, he looked more like farmers she had seen working around Roma, and less like the suave man of the world. They transformed him into a real man with muscles, one who sweated when he worked—strong enough to defend his family. She turned away, heat spreading into her cheeks and down her arms. So, he was a man, like any other man. A man who had invited her to dinner at a restaurant.

Confused by her feelings, she slowed her steps, seeking direction. She should go to her cabin, grab her Bible, and ask God to clear her momentary muddle. What she did instead was return to the pilothouse.

"Back so soon?" Old Obie gestured her forward. "It's just as well. We are almost at La Joya."

"I thought so. I want to watch you pull up to the dock."

"Maybe you want to do it yourself?" The corners of Old Obie's hazel eyes crinkled as he patted the wheel.

"I would like that." Learning something new would take her mind off Ike. Old Obie did an amazing job of explaining how to pilot the sternwheeler. As long as he stayed by her side, she'd be willing to risk it. She stared into the depths of the water, as dark and murky as Ike's brown eyes.

". . .but the river is deep enough here to get close to the wharf. No ferry needed."

"A ferry?" she said stupidly.

"To move the cargo to the town." He tilted his head toward his shoulder. "You haven't been listening. Something is on your mind. What is it? You can tell me."

Blanche shifted from one foot to another. His listening ear had drawn her to the pilothouse in the first place, but she found it difficult to put her feelings into words. "I ran into Ike." Her voice sounded strangled.

"It is a small ship." His measured tones invited her to explain further.

She wouldn't mention the fight she had seen between Ike and Ventura. "He had changed clothes. I have never seen him dressed in anything except his suit before."

"I think I understand. It was like you were seeing him for the first time."

"Yes." The word came out as a whisper. "He was injured."

"There was an accident?" Old Obie stiffened at the wheel, knees flexed as if he were prepared to spring into action.

"It was no accident. He and Mr. Ventura engaged in fisticuffs—on purpose." Her voice grew stronger as her indignation asserted itself.

The older man laughed. "I would guess that you haven't spent much time around men."

Blanche shook her head.

"When you were at school, did you ever see two boys get into a fight?"

She nodded.

"And afterward they were best friends?"

Her face tightened in concentration. "That was so strange."

"Boys—men—are like that. They take pleasure in physical challenges." His eyes crinkled, waves lapping in the hazel of his eyes.

"I believe you." She shook her head. "Although it still seems strange." Ike's image floated in her memory again. What she had seen bothered her far more than memories of childish playground tussles.

The mirth in Old Obie's eyes altered, transformed into concern. "If you want the opinion of an old river rat like me, I'll give it to you."

You're like the father I never knew. The thought sent more uncertainty swirling through her. In this arena, she trusted Old Obie more than she would Reverend Davenport. Her pastor was a good Christian man, but she couldn't imagine him raising his hands in a fight between friends. "I'm listening."

"Life in Roma hasn't prepared you for life aboard a steamboat, and you haven't met many men like Ike. But people are people, and

Ike Gallagher is like a son to me. He's a good man. The captain trusted him. He earned his position in the crew." Coughing, Old Obie wiped his sleeve against his mouth, closed his eyes, and sagged against the wheel. He opened his eyes, drew a deep breath, and clasped the wheel with both hands.

"I've kept you from your rest time today." Blanche backed away.

He pulled in his lips, pain creasing his face. "I get to rest all night, as soon as we arrive at La Joya. You go on and get ready. I'll be fine." The lines on his face argued against the strength he projected in his voice.

Blanche promised herself she would check on him when she returned. On impulse, she threw her arms around his shoulders, stooped from carrying the weight of the world. "I like to think my father was a lot like you."

"That's right kind of you, Blanche." He wiped at moist eyes. "Now, go on, before tears blind me and I can't see to pilot the boat." He wiped his hands on his shirt and clasped the wheel with both hands.

Blanche paused at the head of the stairs, glancing at him over her shoulder. Her own eyes filled, and she hurried down to the main deck. Today, emotions she had rarely felt scraped against each other. She'd have to ask God to protect her heart tonight, or else she might break down and do something foolish.

Ike stared at his wardrobe, full of the latest in men's fashions in a variety of fabrics and colors, with tasteful accessories. Fewer choices would make his decision easier. He hadn't missed the gleam of appreciation in Blanche's eyes when she saw him after the match with Ventura. But dressing in workday clothes felt like an insult. In fact, the restaurant where he planned to go required a suit jacket. Without a jacket and tie, he would not be admitted.

He settled on wearing a suit coat without a vest, neither black nor white, but pale gray. He rejected the dark blue shirt, hesitated over pale blue, and reluctantly picked out the white with his usual bow tie. His hand hovered over his pocket watch. *Take it,* he decided, and tucked it into the front pocket of his black slacks.

Did Blanche spend half as much time as he did worrying what to wear? He shook his head. It didn't matter. Even a potato sack couldn't hide her figure or her beautiful face, the sparkle in her eyes when she was excited.

Face it. You're smitten. He shook his head. The feelings would pass. They had to. Blanche Lamar would no more settle for a gambler like him than he would become a Sunday pew sitter, although that possibility no longer seemed as impossible as it once had.

"I'm ready."

At Blanche's soft voice, Ike turned around. Her hair was swept up in a style that spoke of Effie's flawless hands, held in place by a white comb. Black leather toes peeked from beneath the hem of her dress. A few simple changes made her even more beautiful than she was before, if that were possible.

A slow, warm smile spread across his face. If she was a different sort of woman, he might have whistled. Instead, he let his admiration linger for a moment. Then he swept his hat from his head and bowed before extending his hand to take her arm. "I will be the envy of every man in La Joya tonight."

She ducked her head, sending the feather attached to the comb aflutter, shining against the vivid color of her hair. "I doubt that." She raised her head. A brief glimmer in her eyes suggested she appreciated the trouble he had taken with his appearance. One gloved hand reached toward his chin but stopped short of touching him. "Is it sore?"

"I'll live." Ike led Blanche down the wharf, the heels of her shoes clicking on the wood of the wharf. He had held many women's arms before, but never had one felt so fragile, never had the desire to protect one surged so strong in him. "I have hired a carriage to meet us at the wharf."

Her head swiveled, her nose twitching as she breathed, eyes widening as she took in the appearance of the town ahead. She could have been someone just released from prison, seeing home with new eyes.

She caught the expression on his face and laughed. "I've never been so far from home before."

Home. Roma was her home, not the *Cordelia.* Ike pushed the thought out of his mind. "How does it compare?"

They reached the end of the wharf where their carriage awaited them. The livery had outdone themselves, sending a sparkling white carriage with matching horses to pull it.

He offered his hand to help her step up for a ride designed to impress Blanche, but she looked down the street instead. "How far is the restaurant? I would like to walk if possible. It's such a lovely evening."

"And you haven't been able to walk far in any direction for over a week. I understand the feeling. Yes, we can walk." Stifling his disappointment, Ike explained the situation to the driver.

"She is the señorita?" The driver's mustache quivered beneath his smile.

Ike nodded. "She has a yen to take a walk."

He nodded. "Keep her happy, that one. You are a fortunate man to have such a lovely lady on your arm."

Ike's grin widened. "I intend to do everything I can to keep her happy." He gave the driver some money for his trouble. The smile stayed on his face as he walked back to Blanche.

"The restaurant is this way." Ike felt like he was ten feet tall as he walked with Blanche at his side. Block by block, they turned heads. Men followed their progress with envy, women with interest.

Blanche remained oblivious of the attention, instead sweeping her head from side to side, as if memorizing the route.

"Is it so very different from Roma?" Ike asked.

She stopped their progress, studying a church on the opposite corner. A statue of the Virgin Mary out front dominated the buildings around it. Squinting, Ike read the sign: LA IGLESIA DE LA VIRGEN DE GUADALUPE.

"In some ways it resembles Roma," Blanche said. "I wonder if that's the largest church in town."

Ike looked at the adobe structure, gleaming white. He shrugged. "I honestly don't know."

"Of course not." She said the words half under her breath, but he could hear the disappointment.

They resumed walking. Every few feet she'd stop and stare in the front window of a building. After each stop, her pace increased, until she was nearly skipping down the street.

"You're having fun."

"Of course." Blanche spread her arms, taking in the street. "If I close my eyes and just breathe in the air, it would seem like I'm back home in Roma." She inhaled deeply. "Sawdust and horses. Honeysuckle and pine. Baked bread and chilies." Opening her eyes, she scuffed the dirt underfoot with the toe of her shoe. "I even like having the ground under my feet."

Some of Ike's good humor seeped away with her outburst. Was she so homesick for Roma so soon? "I feel the same way when I have to be away from the *Cordelia* for more than an overnight stay. The mist of the water on my face, the smoothness of the floorboards and railing, Elaine's good cooking."

Something across the street caught her attention. Instead of responding to his comments, she pointed across the street. "Look! There's a mercantile. Do we have time to stop?"

Ike fingered the watch in his pocket but didn't pull it out. He wanted to keep this evening carefree, not worried about the clock. "Let's." His sister had taught him how much women enjoyed shopping.

"Oh, thank you." Blanche stepped down from the boardwalk in the direction of the store.

"Of course." Ike trailed behind, curious about which section of the store would attract her first. Her choices would reveal a lot about her.

Once through the door, again she breathed deeply. Ike followed her example, his mind sorting through the odors—licorice, pickles, tobacco.

Blanche's swift run through the store surprised him. She bypassed the baubles that had caught the attention of a pair of young girls who were chattering over the counter. She also strode past the sewing supplies, Effie's favorite section.

A bookshelf distracted her for a moment. Her fingers ran along the spines of the books. Shaking her head, she turned to him. "Do you know if there is a bookstore in Brownsville?"

"Ventura will know."

"They probably won't have what I'm looking for in stock." She backtracked to the sewing area and picked up a pincushion. "If I order something, can it be delivered directly to the boat?"

"Of course." Did that mean she was committed to stay long enough to receive a package? Ike's hopes resurrected.

Blanche lifted a box of stationery to her nose. "Rose-scented. Very nice." She paid for it and they left the store.

"You're going to write some letters." He almost made it a question.

"I have special plans for this stationery." She didn't elaborate. "I'll get started as soon as we get back to the boat tonight."

Her hint of a promise of future plans concerning the boat lifted his spirits. So did getting back on board the *Cordelia*.

Land was fun to visit, but he wouldn't want to live there.

Chapter 18

"Did Ike buy you roses?" Effie asked when Blanche entered the cabin. She had stayed up to chat with Blanche after her dinner with Ike. What fun these days had been, sharing her cabin as if Blanche were her sister.

"You're still awake!" A sigh accompanied the whoosh of the chair cushion. "Is he in the habit of giving girls flowers?"

"Only a special few." A smile played around Effie's lips. "He did give you flowers, I can tell."

"No flowers, just a lovely dinner and conversation."

Effie sniffed the air, detecting a light floral scent. "I thought I smelled them."

"If you're smelling roses, it's from a box of stationery that I bought."

"Oh, I almost wish I could write a letter, if it meant I could enjoy that scent every time I opened the box."

Blanche handed Effie a sheet of the paper. "Here. Keep this. Perhaps you would like to place it in your bureau drawer, like a sachet."

Effie brought the sheet to her nose and sighed as she breathed it in. "I'll put it under my pillow, so that I can enjoy it as I fall asleep." She tucked the stationery into her bed and pulled out her knitting. "Will you be coming to bed soon?"

"Not for a few minutes. I have some notes I want to write." The tip of a pen scratched against paper while Effie worked on an intricate shawl. An hour passed before they called it quits for the night. Blanche continued her project for all the following day. After breakfast the second morning, she set down her pen at last. "Done."

"I won't ask what has kept you so busy these last two days." Effie changed yarn colors for her shawl. "You have given me pleasure, filling our room with the scent of your stationery while you've been writing so busily."

"You make the perfect roommate. I could wrap all your Christmas presents right in front of you, and you wouldn't know what they were."

"Don't be so sure about that. I've fooled a lot of people that way." Effie laughed. "I can tell a lot by the sounds something makes, or the scent. And the feel, of course. I used to drive Ike crazy, when I could guess and he couldn't."

"So what do you think I've been doing?"

"Writing something, of course. But what you've been writing, or to whom, I don't know. I would guess you have written letters, and to more than one person. You've opened several envelopes."

"You are good at this guessing game." Blanche didn't explain any more, and Effie didn't press.

"Are you looking forward to arriving in Brownsville? We should be there tomorrow or the day after at the latest."

A small silence formed around the word *Brownsville*. "I am hoping to have my questions answered."

Effie switched back to the original yarn color. "What if you don't like the answers?"

"God promises a good future, plans to prosper me and not to harm me. Not necessarily wealth, but whatever answers I find are ones that will help me."

"I wish I had your faith."

"My pastor used to say it wasn't the amount of faith that a person has—the Bible talks about faith as small as a mustard seed—but the object of our faith. God is big, even if my faith is small."

Effie shook her head. Such thinking went against everything she understood about religion. "God seemed big to me when I was a little girl. Then my parents died, and I realized even He couldn't make everything right."

"But He brought Old Obie into your lives about that time, didn't He? I know losing your parents when you were so little must have been terrible. But God still took care of you." The pleading tone in Blanche's voice got Effie's attention.

Effie stuck her tongue between her lips, a habit she had when she was concentrating on something, and counted the number of stitches in the row. "Didn't drop a one. I always check after I have to change yarn." She turned her sightless eyes in Blanche's direction. "I only know that sometimes the answers God gives aren't the ones I want. And I hope you're not disappointed with what you learn."

Blanche caught her breath. "I can't say I won't be disappointed. But if I am, know this. The problem is with me. God is good, all the time."

Effie's half-smile returned. "I know that's what you believe." She tucked the yarn away. "Are you ready to leave?"

Blanche dropped several envelopes into a bag. "Now I am."

Rising early the next morning, Blanche donned her black suit to better blend into the lingering nighttime shadows, and made her way around the ship she had come to know as well as the hallways and rooms of her childhood home. First she headed for the salon, where she went to each table and left envelopes addressed to their guests.

Finding the right words to thank each passenger for their business had come fairly easily. She tucked a couple of envelopes into the waiting muffin baskets, trusting that the kitchen staff would discover them in the process of serving breakfast. Elaine was already at work, but aside from nodding good morning, she stayed at the back of the kitchen, preparing bread and other baked goods for the day.

Next Blanche headed to the crew's quarters. A special envelope went to Dame Agatha, who would shake her double chins in severe disappointment if she spotted her prize customer in her "dowdy country clothes," as she had described Blanche's suit. The transformation the lady's needle had wrought in Blanche still confounded her, changing her in ways she still didn't understand. About half the crew remained abed, and Blanche slipped notes for everyone under their cabin doors. She added Effie's letter to Ike's, trusting he would read it to her. She brought that envelope to her nose, hoping the stationery would hold the scent a long time.

Last of all, Blanche headed for the pilothouse, where Old Obie stood on watch. She couldn't leave it at his cabin, since she didn't know which cabin was his. As for letting Ike deliver the note, she decided to keep it between the two of them.

The bow of the boat parted liquid gold as they slid into sunrise. If she could capture it, she would make a fortune that no amount of money could buy. She waited on deck, watching the water turn from black to gold to blood red. *Red,* the color of blood. The color of joy. She'd felt such joy on the excursion to La Joya with Ike. Then she reminded herself that he was an unbeliever. Someone she could never marry. She placed her hand over her heart as if she could protect herself from the unwanted emotions flooding through her. She feared it was already too late.

She touched the remaining letter in her pocket. Effie had laughed when she asked for Old Obie's full name. "That's a closely guarded secret. You'll have to ask him yourself." Humming a few bars of "When Morning Gilds the Skies," Blanche mounted the stairs.

Sunshine outlined Old Obie's form in fiery reds. "My songbird is up early this morning." He turned, and Blanche saw he was holding a cup in his hand.

"Coffee."

He laughed. "Do you want some?" He dug out a coffee mug and poured from a pot that would look right at a campfire.

She sipped it and sighed. "Perfect." She enjoyed coffee first thing in the morning, before the day became too warm. Drinking deeply, she studied the river. To the left she spotted a submerged log. Maps indicated a sandbar on the right, but the water level would carry them over it without a problem. "How do you adjust for the sun on the water?"

"I slow down and look out the side windows instead. Fog is worse. More than one morning, I've had to stop the engines until visibility improved." He tapped the wheel. "A good pilot is never afraid to stop if necessary. Don't let an anxious owner push you to do something that is unsafe."

"You sound like I will actually get to pilot the boat one day."

"Of course you will. I have no doubt."

She finished her coffee and set the mug down. Taking care that her fingers were clean, she pulled out the envelope. "This is for you. I would have addressed it, but I don't know your full name."

"A letter." He didn't offer his name. "I haven't had one of these in a long time. Should I open it now?"

Suddenly shy, she shook her head. "It's not much. Just something to remember me by."

He turned his complete attention on her, piercing her with his gaze. "I won't ever forget you. It's not possible. And I still hope you will choose to make your home on the river, so I won't need something to remind me. But, I will treasure this." He gestured with the letter. "As I would treasure anything that you give to me."

Ike dressed slowly, as if delay on his part could prevent the coming revelations from the captain's lawyer. He read the few lines of

Blanche's letter to him again. The balanced message, poised between a polite letter of appreciation and a personal note to a friend, betrayed more than she intended to, he suspected. He lifted the paper to his nose and breathed in. Every time he passed a rosebush, he would remember this letter.

Oh, Blanche. Would she feel the same way after she talked to the lawyer, only a few hours from now?

Bringing the letter to his lips and placing Effie's letter in his suit pocket, he headed for breakfast. He treasured these hours of uncluttered friendship, hoping against hope that she wouldn't reject him once she knew the truth. When he glanced up at the pilothouse, Old Obie waved for him to come.

The click of heels behind him announced Blanche's arrival. "Do we have a scheduled time with the lawyer?"

Ike noted, with amusement, that Blanche had returned to the security of her black traveling suit for this business appointment. "Not exactly. We didn't know when we would arrive. But they are expecting us sometime this week."

They rode in the carriage to the offices of Cox, Carver, and Chavez in relative silence. Ike knew the answers to most of the questions Blanche had held at bay since they left Roma. Neither one of them indulged in idle speculation as the carriage drove them to the office on East Washington Street, adjacent to Washington Park.

"That must be their office." Blanche pointed to the modest storefront office. "Mr. Carver was my father's lawyer?"

Ike nodded. He circled the carriage and helped her down. Her smattering of freckles stood out darker than usual on her skin, color having fled her face. He didn't have any words to reassure her. He offered her his arm and led her inside.

A young man Ike had never met before sat at the front desk. He half rose from his chair. "May I help you?"

Something resembling panic filled Blanche's eyes. Ike took a step forward. "Blanche Lamar and Ike Gallagher, here to see Mr. Carver."

The man's nose quivered. "Do you have an appointment?"

"No." Blanche backed up a step.

"He is expecting us this week." Ike moved forward. "Why don't you let him know we're here? We can wait." He escorted Blanche to a chair.

The young clerk frowned. "That's not possible."

Before Ike could retort, Blanche spoke. "Pardon me, what is your name?"

Her request erased the unpleasant young man's frown. "I am Walter Brown, ma'am."

Blanche glanced at Ike. "Mr. Brown, we'd like to make an appointment. Is there an opening with Mr. Carver this afternoon?"

"That is what I was attempting to explain." Brown glared at Ike. "Mr. Carver has business out of town today. He will return next week. May I schedule an appointment for you?" Leaning forward, he unbent a little. "Can Mr. Cox assist you? He is available today."

Blanche looked at Ike, her eyes sending a silent plea, but Ike didn't care to discuss the situation with someone reading the file for the first time. Struggling to make his voice pleasant, he said, "We don't expect to be in Brownsville that long. Is there any possibility that Mr. Carver will return earlier than next week?"

Brown scanned the calendar in front of him. "His court case is scheduled to last through this week. There is always the possibility it will end early, but we do not expect it." He offered an apologetic smile. "And it could also, unfortunately, last longer."

Ike nodded. "Then let us make an appointment for Friday afternoon, and hope he returns earlier than expected."

Brown held the pen in his hand for a moment before making a note on the appointment book. "Two o'clock on Friday afternoon, Mr. Gallagher and Miss Lamar to meet with Mr. Carver." He copied the information onto a calling card and handed it to Blanche. "I cannot guarantee that Mr. Carver will have returned."

"We understand." Blanche glanced at the card before tucking it into her reticule. "Thank you, Mr. Brown. You have been most kind."

"It's my pleasure, Miss Lamar."

The sun beat down on their heads as they exited the building. As instructed, the carriage had left to return in an hour. Blanche clasped her reticule. The courage she had demonstrated only minutes earlier had disappeared, and she looked anxious for their ride.

"Mr. Brown would not object if we want to wait inside until the carriage returns. Or we could walk a couple of blocks in that direction." Ike pointed to the right, toward the center of town they had passed a short time earlier. "We could find a bakery or a mercantile."

"A walk sounds pleasant." Blanche accepted his arm at her elbow and shifted her reticule to her other hand. "I would love to go shopping again, but I shouldn't spend any more money. God promised to provide for my needs, but knickknacks don't fall into that category."

The look of longing that filled her face told him all he needed to know about the absence of nonessential items from her childhood. He wished he could buy her an entire cabinet full of curios from every town in the river and more beside.

"The letters were a wonderful idea." The words she had written to him had seared themselves in his brain. *Dear Ike. . .friendship. . . support. . .you have made me feel special.* She had even copied a Bible verse, something about God loving him. "Creative. Personal. Everyone is talking about them." He smiled.

"You didn't mention the low cost." Blanche's smile let him know she meant no offense. "Thank you. I learned a lot about giving from my mother. We never had much money, but we always had enough to give away."

"I felt the same way, growing up on the *Cordelia.* We always had what we needed, and we knew the captain loved us. Those are things money can't buy."

"Just like God's love." She nodded. "He was there for you, even back then."

Chapter 19

T his isn't the quality of cotton we have come to expect from Roma." The owner of the textile factory, a Mr. Draper, shook his head over the pallets that had been delivered from the decks of the *Cordelia*.

Blanche stood uncertainly by the carriage. She didn't know how to respond. In the past, her only business consisted of dealing with school supplies and food from the local mercantile in Roma. But from the time she had spent reviewing the accounts for Lamar Industries, she knew delivery of cotton played a big role in continued profitability. Was this kind of complaint common?

The chief stevedore shrugged. "I just load it and unload it, boss."

"And I'm telling you, this isn't what I ordered." Draper's voice grew agitated.

This disagreement was going around in circles, and she took a step forward. "Do you have a copy of the order you placed?"

"What's that?" Mr. Draper switched his gaze to her. "Who are you?"

"I am Blanche Lamar. Captain Lamar was my father. I'm sure there's been some misunderstanding. The order might clear it up."

Mr. Draper looked at Ike out of the corner of his eye, who nodded. Blanche stepped on her irritation. How long had Ike been handling business for her father?

"I have a copy in my office." Mr. Draper headed for the small adobe building at the back of the property. "This way."

Ike held a chair for her while Mr. Draper rustled through his file drawer. He laid a sheet of paper in front of her. "This is what I ordered."

The handwriting was legible, but that didn't make the meaning any clearer. She'd guess it referred to the weight and quality of the raw cotton. Did she have to understand the cotton business to operate a profitable steamboat operation?

Ike zeroed in on the heart of the problem. "You requested six bundles. We delivered the requested half dozen. Any problems you have with the product, you need to take up with the farmer."

"And if I refuse delivery?"

Were all business owners this belligerent?

"That is acceptable, as long as you pay for the return shipment."

Panic rose in her throat. She thanked God for Ike's presence and calm demeanor. She didn't know if she could speak.

The two men continued arranging the details while she tried to relax. She clasped her hands in her lap, tapping her fingers against her palm, settled her back against the chair, and let a smile play on her face. A lemon drop might renew the moisture inside her mouth.

They could stop at the mercantile for some penny candy. She could afford that much. Visions of hard candy ran through her mind while she ran her tongue around the inside of her cheek. From the posture of both Ike and Mr. Draper, she guessed they had engaged in this duel of words many times before.

I still have so much to learn.

Including the information the lawyer would convey. As his associate had predicted, Mr. Carver didn't return early. With the completion of today's business, the *Cordelia* was ready to return to Roma. They couldn't justify spending an additional three days in Brownsville so she could talk with the lawyer.

Ike shook Mr. Draper's hand, and he turned to her. "Is that acceptable to you, Blanche?"

She hadn't followed all the steps of the negotiation. "Th–that's fine."

"Good. Then we'll be on our way." They left the office by one of the many side streets in Brownsville. All roads led to the river eventually, at least they did in Roma. Follow the flow of traffic, follow the smells, follow the birds, and she would find the wharves.

"How do you want to spend your last night on land?" Ike had relaxed, perhaps glad that the business had finished.

The words sounded a gong in her heart. Was this her last time in Brownsville? She didn't dare risk another trip down the river. One time had already turned her whole world upside down.

She also didn't know if she wanted to settle in Roma; she had changed from the person she was. The meeting with the lawyer should have provided some direction, but for some reason God hadn't allowed that to happen.

"What are you thinking?" Ike nudged her shoulder. "You went somewhere far away."

Blanche brought her thoughts back to the presence of Ike at her side, the community of Brownsville out before them. "You don't have to keep me company. Did you already have plans?"

"Nothing, except this." He reached into his pocket and flashed three tickets before her. "Ventura has invited us to join the Brownsville Bats for a baseball game."

The carriage returned for them, and Effie sat next to the driver. "Have you told Blanche yet?" Her smile was as warm as the white cotton dress with gay red stripes she wore.

"Just now." Blanche realized Ike's clothes matched Effie's, thin red pinstripes in his shirt and a red bow tie. "Someone should have told me to wear red."

"You noticed." Ike's lips lifted in a lopsided smile. "The team's colors are red and white."

Blanche glanced at her black suit and decided that it would cover a multitude of sins, with all the dust and spills possible at a baseball diamond.

"You have been to games before." Blanche made it a statement, not a question.

"As often as possible." Effie's light laughter rippled through the air. "You're wondering why a blind woman wants to go to a baseball game."

"The thought did cross my mind." Blanche accepted Ike's arm as he assisted her into the carriage.

"The ballpark, please," Ike said to the driver. The horse moved at a slow trot.

"There must be more to baseball than watching men running around the bases."

"Oh my, yes. A bag of peanuts and a box of Cracker Jack."

"Cracker Jack? What is that?"

"A delicious snack that Elaine would never allow in her kitchen." Ike rubbed his stomach in anticipation. "Caramel corn with peanuts. There is something to be said for the pleasures of childhood."

"I can't wait to taste it."

"And hot dogs and pretzels and—"

"Stop! You're giving me a stomachache."

"Do you mind if we walk the rest of the way?" Effie glanced over her shoulder. "I enjoy a chance to stretch my legs. We'll take a carriage back after the game."

Blanche nodded. Soon the three of them were walking down the street, Ike's hand tucked through the crook of Blanche's elbow. He made her feel protected, special. Tonight he was offering her another new experience. "Effie, what do you think of baseball?"

"I love it. I hope you enjoy it. Have you ever played?"

Blanche paused in her steps. "What, me, play baseball? No." Shock showed in her voice. "Girls don't play baseball. Do they?"

"Maybe in the schoolyard. Even I have played catch." Effie kicked a pinecone and caught it with her hand. "They tell me I caught nearly as many balls as the girls who can see." Pushing her hands out, she said, "Here, catch."

The pinecone brushed the ends of Blanche's fingers before dropping to the ground. She giggled.

"I guess you won't be catching any fly balls today." Ike smacked his fist into his palm. "I'll have to catch one for you."

"Fly ball?" The image of a ball with tiny white wings brought a smile to Blanche's face.

"Let's get to our seats. I'll explain it all to you."

Their "seats" turned out to be bleachers. Blanche tucked her skirt beneath her, hoping to avoid soiling the fabric.

Peanut shells crunched beneath their feet. "Ah. The sound of peanuts." Effie lifted the hem of her skirt and settled down next to Blanche.

"What do you want to eat? Hot dogs, Cracker Jack, peanuts? Candy?" Leaning in close, he whispered, "Beer?"

"Ike!" A giggle accompanied Effie's reprimand.

"I take that as a no."

Blanche considered. "I don't know. They all sound good. Except beer, of course."

"I'll get one for each of us, together with Dr. Pepper." Ike left a handkerchief to mark his place, on Blanche's right. "I'll be right back."

"Is he always like this before a game?" Blanche watched him half run down to a vendor carrying a box full of snacks supported by a shoulder harness.

"Turns back into a little boy all over again? Yes. I think it does him good."

Blanche leaned forward to see Ike's retreating back. He encountered the vendor, the pitch of his head suggesting laughter, filling his arms with food. "He's buying enough to feed everyone here."

Effie laughed. "He does that on purpose. He sneaks it back on ship and then skips breakfast for a day or two. I think Elaine knows his secret, but she lets him get away with it."

Blanche had brought sweets home from a friend's house once or twice, but Mother had never caught on.

Impossible. In the short time Blanche had shared Effie's cabin, she knew one or two of the places she kept special treats, and could guess at others. Mother must have known most of Blanche's secrets, but she had pretended otherwise. The thought warmed her down to her toes. Mother had allowed her the small piece of childhood.

Ike returned with his arms laden with food. "Here's a bag of peanuts for you, and one for Effie, and one for me."

Removing a peanut, Blanche squeezed the shell. It crushed beneath her fingers, popping the nut onto the floor. The shattered shell clung to her skirt. She tried to pick it off.

"Just brush it underfoot." Ike handed her another nut. "We get to make all the mess we want to here at the game." He snapped a shell in half and dropped two peanuts into his hand before he dropped his shells onto the floor. Lifting his foot, he ground them into powder.

Blanche gingerly brushed off her skirt. She succeeded in getting the second nut. "It's salty."

"They roast and salt them before bagging them." Ike popped another one in his mouth. "The game is starting." Ike pointed to the field, where nine men had taken positions. The men tossed balls—at least Blanche assumed they were balls. It was hard to tell, as quickly as they sailed through the air. One man stood on a mound in the middle of the diamond, throwing to a man crouched behind a bag. They all wore matching outfits, white with the words "Brownsville Bats" emblazoned in red over a cartoon bat holding a baseball bat.

Ike's hat sported the same ridiculous picture.

Munching on their snacks, they talked and laughed while the team continued throwing balls. Everyone ignored what was happening on the field. Eventually they cleared the field and a brass band marched out.

"Ah, now we're about to start."

Mr. Ventura walked in front of the band. Spreading his arms like Blanche imagined a circus ringmaster might, he said, "Ladies and gentlemen, please rise for the national anthem." Seconds later they were singing "The Star-Spangled Banner."

As soon as they finished singing, the Bats returned to the field, joined by a man swinging a bat. On the first pitch, his bat connected with the ball.

"Leadoff homerun. Not looking good." Ike popped a piece of caramel corn in his mouth.

Effie patted Blanche's hand. "Do you understand any of this?"

"Honestly?" Blanche shook her head. "No."

"I'll explain it to you." Ike's chest seemed to expand as he began explaining the system of hits, balls, strikes, and runs that made the difference between winning and losing.

"So they can make a run two ways. They either hit the ball over the fence into the crowd, where anyone can get hurt." She pretended offense. A couple of balls had felt like they whizzed by her ears. "Or they can hit the ball and run to the base and try to make it around all four bases."

Ike opened his mouth, as if ready to explain more. Shaking his head, he said, "There are foul balls and strikes and steals and. . .but that's it in a nutshell."

"And the Bats are winning. They have seven runs, and the Hurricanes only have six."

"It's a good thing that the Bats have the last at bat." Effie popped a peppermint candy into her mouth. "The game is too close to pick a winner yet."

The game ended with the Bats winning by a final score of nine to six. Smiles wreathed Ike and Effie's faces, and Blanche felt sure she looked the same. "Come, let's congratulate Ventura on the win." Ike offered his arm, and Blanche accepted it.

"Are all the games this exciting?" Blanche heard the breathless sound of her voice, as if she had been the one running the bases instead of the teams.

"Some more, some less. Sometimes the pitchers keep the batters off base. That's exciting, in a different sort of way."

The three of them wormed their way through the crowd that was going in the opposite direction, surging toward the gates. Blanche was glad for Ike's presence. Without him, the noise and the bustle might have paralyzed her.

"Ventura was successful in arranging games in all the towns between here and Roma?"

"They're looking forward to it."

"So am I." *If I'm here.* Depending on what the absent lawyer had to tell her, she had to find work, soon. The trip on the *Cordelia* had been enough adventure to satisfy her for two lifetimes.

"There he is." Ike pointed to the spot where Ventura stood in front of the Bats' bench. Instead of the smile Blanche expected, a frown creased his face as he spoke with a young lad. He looked vaguely familiar; about the time they reached Ventura, Blanche placed him as one of the young stevedores who had helped unload the boat upon their arrival.

Ventura caught sight of them and gestured for them to draw close. "Jim-boy thought he might catch you here at the game. There's been an accident."

Chapter 20

W hat happened?" Ike asked sharply.

"Has someone been injured?" Blanche asked at the same time.

Ventura nodded to young Jim-boy. "We was loading the cotton back on board, sir. Mr. Draper sent it back. I wondered about that, but he had all the proper paperwork so I thought it was all right."

"He didn't waste any time." Ike grimaced. "But yes, that's fine. What happened?"

"Since you wasn't there, I went to ask the Cap'n, sir. He came down on deck, and the crane slipped and knocked into him. Knocked him clean out."

"The *captain*?" A glance at Blanche reminded Ike of another reality. Her skin paled beneath the light sunburn, and her breath came out in short gasps.

Ike couldn't afford that distraction now. He had to find out the extent of the injuries. "Have you sent for a doctor?"

"He's onboard already. And I came to find you, straightaway."

"The *captain?*" Blanche's eyes went wide. "Captain Lamar—*my father*—has been on the ship the whole time?" She turned agonizing eyes in his direction.

Worry warred with guilt. "I'll explain it to you later. Right now, we have to get back to the boat."

Blanche whirled, turning her anger on Effie. "You must have known."

Effie's mouth worked, but she couldn't seem to find words to respond either. "Let's get back to the ship. I'll explain while Ike sees to things."

"Don't bother." Blanche's voice was cold. "I want to meet my father." She headed toward the exit, Ike hurrying after her. When he caught up with her, she stopped, tears streaming down her cheeks. "I don't know the quickest way back."

"We'll walk. The crowd would only delay a carriage, even if we could find one. Come with us. We all want to get back as quickly as possible."

After Effie offered a few more details that Jim-boy had supplied, they walked in silence. Ike was torn between worry about the captain, injured and unconscious, and what it could mean to Blanche.

The plan for father and daughter to get to know each other before making Blanche aware of their connection didn't allow for illness. What if something interfered, denying them the opportunity? All the preaching against gambling didn't stir Ike's soul, but that single deceit weighed on his conscience.

Ike weaved his way through the streets without thought, trusting his instincts to lead his feet aright. When the *Cordelia* came into view, Blanche sped up. He matched her step for step, wanting to get there first, to ease the discovery for her.

She pressed forward, leaving him a little breathless when he swept past her on the gangway. "Where is the captain? How is he?"

"Mr. Gallagher, I presume?" A small man, with a bushy salt-and-pepper mustache and no-nonsense cut of a suit coat, greeted him. "John Foster. I'm the doctor they called in."

Blanche placed herself between Ike and the doctor. With a glare at Ike, she said, "How is Captain Lamar?" Only a slight waver in her voice betrayed her overwhelming emotions.

Dr. Foster glanced at Ike, which only fueled Blanche's anger.

"Doctor, this is the captain's daughter, Blanche Lamar."

"I see." The man turned to Blanche apologetically. "I was given to understand there was no family to notify."

Notify. The word hung between them with horrifying import.

"Is he—" Ike left the question unfinished.

Dr. Foster flinched, as if he realized what his words had implied. "Oh no. Nothing like that. He's had a nasty bump to his head, but he regained consciousness while I was with him, and was alert to his surroundings. That's a good sign." He smiled reassuringly at Blanche while explaining the signs they should watch for: disorientation, problems with eyesight, fever—the usual. "The most important thing is to keep him quiet for a few days, give his body a chance to heal. I hear he can be stubborn. Can you keep him to his bed?"

"I'll make sure he doesn't move," Ike said.

"Will you be back, to check on him?" Blanche asked.

"Of course. I'll come by morning and evening. If problems arise, feel free to call for me in between times." Shifting his black bag to his other hand and nodding at Blanche, Dr. Foster walked down the wharf.

Tapping her right foot, Blanche turned the full force of her glare on Ike and Effie. "Are you ready to introduce me to my father?"

So close. Blanche had been on the boat with her father for more than a week, and no one told her. Every time the facts repeated themselves in her mind, her anger increased. They had no right, no right at all, to keep the truth from her.

She wanted to scream in frustration, but their discussion with the doctor had already brought curious glances from the crew. Lowering her voice, she said, "Where is he? *Who* is he?"

Effie looked resigned, but Ike looked almost—sheepish. An air of uncertainty clung to the usually cocky purser.

"Come this way." Effie walked toward the bow of the ship, past the pilothouse. Blanche glanced up. Old Obie's replacement was there. The pilot must have known about the deception as well. No wonder her mother had warned her against steamboats. People she had trusted had turned out to be nothing more than thieves and liars.

"This way." Effie headed toward the cramped stairs at the end of the boat. "His quarters are nothing special. He said Ike needed the captain's cabin more; all he wanted was a place to lie his head. That's just the kind of person he is."

Effie's voice trailed away as they circled down the stairs, ending up in the bowels of the ship, hot and steamy and dark except for a few lamps down the hall. She stopped in front of a dingy black door, no different in appearance from the three before, and hesitated. "This isn't how he wanted you to find out. Please. . .think kindly on him. Listen to what he has to say."

The door swung open, and Elaine the cook came out, carrying an empty tray. "Mr. Gallagher. I'm so glad you're back. I was just bringing some of tonight's supper, like always."

"Thank you, Elaine." Ike placed a hand on the doorknob. "Let me go in first, explain what happened."

"That I found out my father has been hiding from me? Go ahead, warn him. That's more than anyone did for me." Reeling from the shock, Blanche knew she sounded bitter.

Ike offered an apologetic smile before slipping around the door. The wait felt like an eternity, but it couldn't have been more than five minutes before he reappeared. "He's expecting you."

"Do you want me—"

Blanche forestalled Effie's question. "No, I want to be alone with him." When neither one moved, she added, "I can find my way back." Turning her back on them, she opened the door and paused. What would she discover inside? Her heart welled up in a single-word prayer. *Help.*

For a room awash in lantern light, Blanche had a hard time making out the figure on the bed. Ginger-and-gray hair she had only ever seen in tufts beneath a hat. . . .

"Cordelia. You've come back."

Old Obie's voice welcomed her into his cabin.

Chapter 21

Blanche's heart skipped beats. *It can't be.* Thump, thump. *Of course.* Thump, thump. *I always knew.*

"You." She reached his side in three quick steps, took a seat on a plain, straight-backed chair, and took his hands in hers.

"Can you forgive me, girl?" Old Obie's eyes searched hers.

"*You're* my father." Wonder filled Blanche's voice. She couldn't answer him. Not yet. "But my father's name is J.O. Lamar."

"Jedidiah Obadiah Lamar. My mama and pa were good, God-fearing folk." Old Obie chuckled. "But I've been Old Obie for more years than I can count."

Blanche noticed the envelope she had written to Old Obie tucked under the edge of his lamp. No wonder Effie wouldn't tell her his real name. Doing so would have revealed their closely guarded precious secret.

Old Obie followed the direction of her gaze. "I've memorized your letter, word for word. In it, you said I'd become like a father to you." He looked away, down the length of the bed, to where he kicked at his covers. "I hope learning I'm your father for real isn't too big of a disappointment."

Blanche stared at her feet. "I meant what I said." She forced herself to meet his eyes. "But I can't connect the man who was teaching me all about life on the river with a father who would lie to me. Deny our relationship."

"My dear girl."

Blanche gritted her teeth. She wasn't his girl, dear or otherwise.

"I have never denied you. I had no way of knowing what Cordelia had told you about me. I hoped, you see, that if you liked Old Obie the pilot, you might be able to like Captain J.O. Lamar, your father." He locked his fingers together and stretched his arms in front of him. "I guess I got what I deserved, not telling you up front."

Blanche studied the light and shadows on his face. She had dreamed of meeting her father all of her life, and now that she had, she didn't know what to think. The man before her was complex, contradictory, charming, and irresponsible, all at the same time. "I don't know how I feel about things. Not yet." She leaned forward and took his right hand. "But I do know I care about you, whether I call you Old Obie or. . .Father." With her other hand, she brushed his hair away from his eyes. "I think a part of me knew as soon as I saw your hair. I just didn't want to admit it."

"A halo of fire around your head." Old Obie reached up and pulled down a tendril from her hair. "I was ridiculously pleased that a part of you took after me, and worried that you would make the connection." His eyes drifted shut.

"I've tired you too much." Worry thundered through Blanche.

Old Obie opened his eyes a slit. "I like having you here. I have a lot to tell you. . ." His eyelids fluttered shut again. ". . .as soon as I sleep a little while."

"Don't worry. I won't go anywhere, as long as you want me here." She had spoken to herself more than to him, but he squeezed her fingers. They sat there, hand in hand, while he drifted back to sleep.

Should I let him sleep? Blanche had some idea that people knocked unconscious should stay awake. But the doctor hadn't said anything, and her—father—was clearly alive. His head thrashing back and forth, he muttered unintelligible words.

At last she had learned the truth about her father. Part of her oscillated between fear and disbelief. But the biggest part of her rejoiced, head over heels happy to learn Old Obie was her father.

The way he was thrashing about couldn't be good for him. Blanche thought of fractious infants she had cared for on occasion. Singing while she rocked them helped. She couldn't rock her father but she could sing. She began with Christmas carols.

At the end of "Away in a Manger" mumbled words continued to stream from his lips. After "Joy to the World," his words had changed to an occasional groan. They died away to soft snores when she finished the final verse of "Silent Night."

Advent onboard ship might not resemble the Christmas traditions she had grown up with, but how would they celebrate the birth of the Lord Jesus? And what brought her to thinking so far ahead? She wouldn't be on the *Cordelia* in December. Would she?

The answer depended on the man lying beside her. She tapped her fingers against his palm, sending up a confused prayer. Thanksgiving and prayers for his salvation warred with anger and questions about why God let things work out this way.

"They're both sound asleep." Effie closed the door quietly behind her. "I would take over so she could go to our cabin, but she is sleeping so peacefully I hate to disturb her."

"She'll wake up with a crick in her neck." Ike spoke from experience, from the times he had fallen asleep in his chair after a particularly long night.

"And joy in her heart. We should have told her a long time ago." Effie sighed. "I'll bring something down from the dining room in case she gets hungry later."

"Good idea. I'll be here, waiting." Keeping watch by the door for the night seemed like the least he could do. The two of them had tangled his heart and soul. He had no illusions. If Old Obie died, Blanche would leave the *Cordelia* at the next town.

He banged his head against the hallway wall just as Effie reappeared. Her steps sped up. "Is everything all right?"

"As far as I know."

She whisked open the door, and Ike followed behind. Blanche's halo of red hair was splayed across the coverlet on the bed, her hand still entwined with Old Obie's. He was going to check for a pulse, but he saw the coverlet rise and fall. "They look peaceful."

Effie lifted her fingers to her lips and opened the door. "I'll be out in a moment," he whispered. Bending over, he listened for Old Obie's breathing. It was even, relaxed—none of the signs the doctor had warned him about. His eyes strayed to Blanche. Faint blue lines showed in her neck and on the back of her hands. From this new angle, she was even more beautiful.

He pushed himself up and left the room before he got any more notions about Blanche.

He left the room, to find Effie waiting in the hall, a plate in her hand. She handed him a thick roast beef sandwich with a slab of apple pie. "You didn't eat much supper."

"This would be even better with a glass of milk." Ike's smile showed in his voice.

"Like this?" Effie brought her right hand out from behind her back. "As long as we can share it. I brought a couple of cookies for myself."

Ike leaned against the wall and took a bite. Thick, juicy. He devoured the rest in short order.

"I wish we had told her a long time ago." Effie nibbled on her cookie. "I wanted to. Her faith in God is so real. I wonder what this will do to her. I've been thinking about the decision I made myself, so many years ago."

The juice in the sandwich turned to dust in Ike's mouth. "Are you a Christian now?"

"I guess. . .I always have been, according to Blanche. I hope she can forgive me for not telling her." Shaking her head, she yawned.

"Go get some sleep. There is no reason for us all to lose a good night's rest."

Effie's face crumbled and she set down the glass. "He's been a father to me, too."

Ike gathered her next to him and let his tears join hers. After the sobs stopped, he held her in a loose embrace. "Old Obie will be okay. He has to be." He flashed back to the day their parents had been injured, when they were waiting for news. He had said the same thing back then, but their parents still had died.

"No one lives forever, Ike." Pushing her hands against his chest, Effie put distance between them. "I will go to my cabin, although I doubt if I'll sleep. You will let me know if anything changes?"

"Of course. Let me walk you back." After Effie turned in, Ike continued to the dining salon and grabbed a chair. Furniture was preferable to sitting on the floor. He unbuttoned the top few buttons on his shirt, removed his jacket, tossed it on his bed on the way past, and headed back to Old Obie's cabin.

When he arrived back at the door to Old Obie's cabin, he heard soft murmurs from inside. Part of him wanted to open the door, to sit with the man who had been like a father to him for most of his life, to offer and receive strength. But that would be selfish. Father and daughter needed time alone together, time that might be limited.

Leaning his head against the hallway wall, Ike could hear the tone of the conversation, every now and then a word discernible. Several times he thought he heard "Cordelia," although he didn't know if they were discussing the boat or Blanche's mother. Laughter followed tears.

Their conversation was none of his business, but he couldn't shut his ears so he wouldn't hear. When the chair proved no more comfortable than the floor would have been, Ike gave up his vigil and went up to the deck. He rolled up the arms of his shirt and let the evening breeze cool his arms and neck.

With Old Obie ill, responsibility for the *Cordelia* fell on Ike. They couldn't afford to stay in Brownsville for too long. Every day the boat remained in port, they lost money. Old Obie would tell him to go, to take care of business, not to let sentimentality overrule business sense. But even if he was willing to leave Old Obie in Brownsville, the loss of their primary pilot would hamper their progress. Once they left Brownsville, they might not return for three weeks.

A lot could happen in three weeks. Staring at the waterline reminded him that life streamed by like the boat rippling down the river. The moon's reflection drew Ike's gaze to the sky. He opened his mouth to howl, but instead he said, "Oh, God. Help us."

God. If God controlled man's life from birth to death, then Ike was talking to the right person. He had never doubted God's existence; God just never seemed relevant to his everyday life.

"From what Blanche says, You're not too pleased with the way I've lived my life. But I'm not asking for me. I'm asking for Old Obie. He gave us a home when we needed one. And I'm asking for Blanche. And I know You must care about her. She certainly brags on You all the time. So please make our stubborn old captain better."

He remained on deck a while longer, staring up at the sky, unsure what he was expecting. For God to thunder back an answer? For Old Obie to jump out of bed and run upstairs?

Nothing happened. Wind ruffled through his shirt, bringing some comfort. After an hour, he returned to his station by the door. The pillow he used as a headrest muffled the murmurings still emanating from the cabin. With a calmer spirit than an hour earlier, he fell into a light sleep.

"It was love at first sight." Obie drew out precious memories that he should have shared with Blanche as soon as they met. "On both sides." He dipped his spoon into the soup they had found when they awakened.

"What made you fall in love with Mother?" It was obvious that Blanche hungered for every detail he could provide.

"She was so beautiful, with that halo of dark hair and long, slender fingers that I wanted to kiss one at a time. Her brown eyes revealed the warmth she hid behind her severe exterior." He sighed. "She was as beautiful on the inside as on the outside. I learned that as we spent our days together. One long, amazing week in Roma."

Blanche chewed her sandwich, eyes wide.

"You are probably wondering why she fell in love with me." Obie shrugged, and the blanket slid down his chest. "I don't know. I had never met anyone like her before, but I like to think it was more than that."

Blanche's eyes misted over. "I can think of some qualities she might have loved."

"And what might those be?" With each spoonful of soup, he felt stronger. "She didn't tell you much about me, did she?"

Blanche shook her head. "But I know what I've seen for myself. You are kind and generous, and you know how to bring out the best in people." She took a deep breath. "I never thought I could pilot a boat, but you made it easy for me to learn." She averted her gaze, picking at her food.

"You have a knack for it."

The conversation continued between them, flowing gently. Obie told her about his family, all of them dead. "I'm sorry. I know you were hoping to find family."

She told him about some of her best childhood memories. So far they had avoided the topic that had driven a loving couple apart. He knew she would bring it up eventually.

After she chased the last crumb of the piecrust from her plate, Blanche cleared her throat, and he knew what was coming.

"You say your parents were church people. They gave you two biblical names."

"They made sure I knew about it. Jedidiah was another name for King Solomon. And Obadiah was a book in the Bible. It was so short they made me memorize it once upon a time."

"Can you still remember it?"

"Bits and pieces. I remember something about fire. . ." Obie closed his eyes, searching old memories. Then he looked at her. " 'And the house of Jacob shall be a fire, and the house of Joseph a flame, and the house of Esau for stubble, and they shall kindle in them, and devour them.' I dreamed about all that fire." He chuckled.

"Do you believe in God? In the Bible?"

Obie didn't have a problem answering that question. "Of course. Only a fool doesn't believe in God."

"But have you asked Jesus to be your Savior?"

There. She'd asked the question. It hung between them.

Now Obie hesitated. "I always intended to. But I figured I had plenty of time. I wanted to enjoy my life first. Then I drove your mother away, the best woman to walk God's green earth." He closed his eyes to block the pain. "It's too late for an old sinner like me."

Chapter 22

Blanche couldn't speak for a moment. Tears clogged her throat. She sipped her tea to moisten her mouth, all the while shaking her head. "It's never too late. Not as long as you are alive and breathing."

"Figured you'd say that." He set aside his pie, only half-eaten. "But I know what I know. I've spent a lifetime saying no to God, I'm not going to be a hypocrite and ask Him to save me now."

A tear rolled down Blanche's cheek, and she turned her head so he wouldn't see.

"Ah, sweetheart, don't feel bad for me. Having you in my life is more of a blessing than I had any right to expect. I've had a good life, and meeting you, why, that's the frosting on the cake."

Blanche couldn't stop her tears. "I'll pray that you see the truth."

He patted her hand. "And now, if you don't mind, it's late at night for this old man. I want to rest." He closed his eyes. Blanche waited, praying, while her father slipped into sleep. When he began gently snoring, she planted a kiss on his forehead. At peace, she decided to set the half-eaten tray of food outside the cabin and try to sleep. When she opened the door, she found Ike in a chair, his head slammed back against a pillow, arms crossed. Whiskers darkened his cheeks. With his shirt unbuttoned at the neck, no suit jacket, and sleeves rolled up, he looked almost. . .heroic.

She wanted to hold on to her anger for not telling her the truth about her father, but how could she when he guarded the door like a knight of old? Laying the tray on the floor, she found an extra blanket and tucked it around Ike's shoulders. Back inside her father's room, she fell asleep as soon as she closed her eyes.

When Ike woke up in the morning, someone had covered him with a blanket. Blanche? What a homey, motherly touch. He shrugged off the good feeling that gave him. He didn't need a mother.

The breakfast bell sounded as he pulled out his pocket watch. Everyone would want an update on Old Obie's condition. He knocked on the door, and when no one answered, he turned the doorknob and entered. Blanche's hair was splayed across the white coverlet. He forced his gaze away from the display and watched Old Obie's chest rise and fall. His mouth hung open, and his breath rasped a little. His color concerned Ike; he'd check on him again after breakfast and see if anything had changed.

He allowed himself to look at Blanche again. With the blanket she had given to him, he returned the favor, easing it across her back. His fingers tingled where they skimmed her neck.

The bell sounded again, and he jerked his hand away. He had dallied long enough. Smithers arched an eyebrow when Ike strolled into the dining room, but no one else commented on his late arrival. The headwaiter brought him a plate piled high with all kinds of good food; Elaine must have poured her worries into her cooking.

"How is he?" Effie's drawn face showed the aftereffects of a sleepless night.

"I'm not sure." Ike grimaced. He brought a cup of coffee to his lips, swallowing the scalding liquid down without a qualm. "Give me a few minutes to eat, and I'll tell the crew. Then I want you to come with me, to check on him."

"Why? What's wrong?"

People turned in their direction at the sound of her raised voice, and she lowered her head. "What happened?"

"I didn't like the way he looked." Ike forced himself to take a few bites and then stood.

The room fell silent.

"Captain Lamar survived the night. As far as I can tell, he spent the night comfortably. He was still asleep when I came downstairs," Ike announced.

Question marks formed on the faces circled around him. He held up a hand. "That's all I know. At this point, I am uncertain when we will leave Brownsville. Until then, continue your regular work schedule."

As the workers filed out, Ike sought out Smithers. "Go ahead about your duties. I'll take care of my dishes."

Smithers nodded and withdrew.

Ike stopped by the serving window. "If you prepare a tray for the captain and Miss Lamar, I'll bring the food to them."

"The poor dears." Elaine whisked around, creating a masterpiece of appearance and taste.

Effie waited with Ike while Elaine put the platter together. As she finished, the door burst open.

Blanche stopped as soon as she spotted them. "Come quick. He's taken a turn for the worse."

Chapter 23

Ike leapt to his feet, Effie at his elbow. "Is he—" He stopped shy of the dreaded word.

"No." The word exploded from Blanche's mouth. "But he sounds like he's having trouble breathing." Tears pooled in her eyes. "He sounds like Mother did before she died."

Effie let out a strangled cry.

"I'll send for the doctor." With the call to action, Ike felt an icy calm descend on him. "You stay here and grab a bite to eat while Effie stays with the captain."

"But—"

"Five minutes one way or the other isn't going to matter. And if anything at all happens, I'll send someone right away."

When Blanche repeated her protest, Effie stood her ground. "This would be a good time for that prayer you're so fond of."

"Prayer isn't a genie's bottle that you can demand whatever you want." Blanche looked sick to her stomach as she stared at the pile of fluffy eggs in front of her. She dug her fork in and brought it to her mouth. "Go on," Ike urged.

Effie headed in the direction of Old Obie's cabin, her white cane tapping the way down the familiar route of the corridor. Ike ran down the gangway to find a porter on the wharves.

"I need to get a message to Dr. Foster. Do you know where his office is?"

The man nodded, and Ike gave him enough money to take a cab. "Ask him to come as quickly as possible. Captain Lamar has taken a turn for the worse."

With that business taken care of, he raced back to the *Cordelia*. He headed for the stairs. He met with Blanche as she was leaving the dining room. "I've sent someone to fetch the doctor and bring him right back."

"Good." She had bitten her lips until red beaded on her flesh. She moved so quickly that he had to hustle to catch up. If she had the freedom of movement of men's trousers, she would have traipsed down the stairs two at a time. As it was, her feet sped down the stairs with the lightness of ballet slippers. His feet hammered the steps loud enough to wake anyone still attempting to sleep.

A handful of the crew had gathered outside the door, keeping a silent vigil. "Mr. Gallagher. Miss Lamar," the head engineer addressed them. "I thought we would stay here, in case you needed help."

Blanche cleared her throat. "That's a kindly thought, Mr. MacDonald. One of you should remain on deck and bring the doctor down when he arrives."

"I'll go up." One of the waiters disappeared in the direction of the stairwell.

Ike opened the door and motioned for Blanche to enter first.

"I bet that's them now." Effie looked up as she heard them enter the room.

Old Obie lay on a pile of pillows that failed in its purpose of easing his breathing. He burst into a fit of coughing.

"Papa." Blanche dashed forward. "You should be sleeping."

"Don't have time to sleep. There are things that need saying." Old Obie speared Ike with his gaze. "I'll have a minute with you then I want to be alone with my daughter." Renewed coughing made Ike wonder how he could speak. "Sorry, Blanche, but I need you to go out for just a few minutes."

Effie took Blanche by the elbow and led her out. As the door closed behind them, the color drained from Old Obie's face, and he collapsed against the pillow in a coughing fit. Ike darted to his side.

Old Obie waved him back. "I'm not long for this world."

"Don't be foolish. Dr. Foster will be here in a few minutes. He'll fix you up with a snap of his fingers."

The captain frowned at him. "Don't lie to me, young man. You can fool a lot of other people, but not me. Now listen up."

He coughed again, and helplessness burned through Ike. Wordlessly, he handed him a clean handkerchief. When the captain used it to swipe his mouth, it came away filled with phlegm.

"There are two things I've done right in my life. Maybe three. One was taking you and Effie in when you were children. You think it was an act of kindness, but I'm the one who was blessed with two children who brought me so much joy."

Ike swallowed past the lump in his throat and coughed. "Let's call us even then. You've given us far more than we could ever repay."

Old Obie patted his hand, his fingers barely tapping his skin. "You're a good man. The son I never had." He dropped his hand. "Then there's the *Cordelia*. She's a good ship, and I'm proud of her time on the river." A slight tinge of color came back into his cheeks. "And now there's Blanche. I'm a proud old cuss, and I'm prouder of her than anything else." A sigh brought on another fit of coughing. "But now that's another burden on my conscience. I hoped for more time with her, but such is not to be. I need you to promise me something."

"Anything. You just need to ask." Ike dredged a smile from the depths of his grief. "And if it's for Blanche, you don't have to ask."

This time, Old Obie's cough came out as a watery laugh. "Like that, is it? I figured as much. And you have my blessing, you know that, don't you?"

Relieved, Ike nodded.

"She won't want your help, you know. She'll fight you. But I figure that with her moral backbone and your business sense, you stand a good chance of keeping the *Cordelia* in business for a while longer. That's the only legacy I have to leave her, and I want it to last as long as possible."

"Your legacy is much more than that."

"I'm counting on you to tell her my story." Old Obie struggled back to a sitting position, cleared his mouth another time with the handkerchief, and smoothed the coverlet across his legs. "Now, go out there and send my girl in."

"Yes, sir." Ike laid a hand on Old Obie's shoulder. "I'll do everything in my power."

"I'm counting on it."

Blanche jumped to her feet as soon as Ike opened the door. She placed her hand on the doorknob, but Ike stood in her way.

"He loves you, you know. Don't be too hard on him for not telling you the truth earlier."

Blanche's mind blanked, and she blinked her eyes. "I know that." She paused at the entrance. "Send in the doctor as soon as he gets here."

"Of course."

She brushed past Ike in the tight confines of the entrance and closed the door.

"My girl." Old Obie had combed his hair, and a smile wreathed his face. "You don't know what joy you have brought to my life. I wish we could have had more time together."

"And we will." He looked so much better that she could almost believe it. Until he coughed again, a cough that drew from the soles of his feet.

"Maybe we will. But just in case. . ." Coughs racked his chest.

Blanche couldn't hide her dismay. "The doctor should be here any time."

"Then let me talk before he gets here. First thing is, I know you have your doubts about Ike. But you need to give him a chance. He's a good man." His failing strength punctuated his words.

"I wouldn't speak so plain, if I had more time. But I'd like to see you settled, and I don't know a better man than Ike Gallagher."

Ike. "He may be as good as you say, but he's not a Christian." The words brought tears to her eyes. *And neither are you.* "And I can't be interested in anyone who isn't a Christian."

"And that's the other thing." He glanced away, revealing deep lines at the corners of his eyes. "I've been thinking about what you said. You told me it's never too late. Do you have any reason for thinking that way, besides wishing it was so?"

The heaviness in Blanche's heart lifted. "Oh, Papa." A smile, bright enough to light the dark cabin, burst on his face. "You don't know how long I've wanted to hear you say that." She realized she had betrayed herself, in the best possible way, of course. "Yes, Papa. I've always known God is my heavenly Father, but now He has given me back my earthly father. If nothing else told me God loves both of us—that does." Even if she could stem the tears flooding her eyes, she wouldn't. They were happy tears, tears of rejoicing and love.

"Ah, darlin'." Tears glistened in his eyes. "Of course God loves you. It's me I'm wondering about."

"But our meeting again was God's gift to you, as well as me. But your question. All kinds of people came to our church and gave testimonies of the lives they lived before the Lord saved them. They did some awful things. But they claimed the promise that God will save everyone who calls upon His name."

Papa shook his head. "I don't want to disillusion you, but I've heard some of those stories, too. The same men went straight from church to the nearest saloon and bellied up to the bar and ordered a round of whiskey."

Lord, give me the right words. "I'm so sorry to hear that. Not entirely surprised. Some of the men said they slid back into their old ways, two, three, even half a dozen times, before they stayed on the straight and narrow."

A glance at her father's face told her that he didn't entirely believe it, but she went on. "Then there's the stories in the Bible. The man who was crucified next to Jesus was a thief and a murderer, sentenced to death—and Jesus promised, 'Today shalt thou be with me in paradise.' He's the only one I know of who became a Christian right at the end, but there are others who did all kinds of bad things. Both Moses and King David killed a man, Paul hunted down Christians, Peter denied the Lord." She paused long enough to draw a deep breath.

"Add another talent to the list of things I'm discovering about you. You're a preacher."

A woman preacher? She laughed at the thought. "I guess Jesus said it best. 'They that be whole need not a physician, but they that are sick.' "

"That makes sense. I haven't gone near a doctor in years. Why pay out good money when you're feeling okay and listen to him tell you how you ought to change your ways if you want to stay well?" He coughed again. "I guess that's how I've treated God."

"Think about how quick the doctor came when Ike called him yesterday. God doesn't even have to run. He's standing at the door to your heart, knocking. Waiting for you to let Him in."

"Is it really as simple as that?"

"It is." Blanche suspected her eyes were shining, between excitement and tears. " 'For whosoever shall call upon the name of the Lord shall be saved.' "

Blanche's heart leapt, certain her mother rejoiced with her as Jedidiah Obadiah Lamar at last returned to the God he had spurned for so long.

Ike paced up and down the hallway. What was taking the doctor so long? Every turn or two he paused by the door, listening to the soft murmurs of conversation. However short their time together was, Ike was glad to the soles of his feet that Old Obie and Blanche had found each other.

As still as Ike was nervous, Effie sat in the chair Ike had slept in, plying her knitting needles. Only an occasional tremor in her shoulders hinted at her distress. Her needles stopped clicking, and Ike stopped his pacing. "He's here."

Running to the bottom of the steps, Ike saw the doctor taking the stairs at a good clip. "You made it."

"I was setting a broken leg when the messenger came in. What has happened?"

Effie turned those uncomfortable, sightless eyes in his direction. "It's his breathing. He's coughing. It sounds like his lungs."

A frown creased the doctor's face. "I'm sorry to hear that." Pausing at the door, he inclined his ear to listen. "Who's in there with him?"

"Blanche. His daughter."

"Why don't you wait with her while I examine the captain." After knocking, he opened the door, Ike following behind.

Blanche held Old Obie's hand, softly singing "Amazing Grace." The old man's eyes were closed, a smile on his face, a harsh rattling sound emanating from his chest chasing it away every now and then.

She stopped abruptly in mid-verse. "Dr. Foster, I'm so glad you're here."

Old Obie's eyes flew open. "Back here to disturb a sick man, doctor?"

"Come with me." Ike put an arm around Blanche's shoulders as if it was the most natural thing in the world and led her out of the cabin. She collapsed against his chest, so that he supported her weight. Every instinct in him wanted to shield her from this pain. She felt as fragile as a butterfly's wing in his arms.

Effie stood outside the door, her knitting returned to its bag. "I could use a cup of tea about now."

"Coffee for me." Blanche took the seat that Effie had abandoned. "I need all my wits about me."

"Come with us."

People usually obeyed when Effie used that no-nonsense voice, but Blanche remained seated. "I want to be here when the doctor comes out."

"You heard what the lady said. Do you mind asking Elaine to send down coffee and muffins?" He wasn't hungry, but he hoped he could get Blanche to eat something.

Effie gathered her skirts and straightened her back. "We'll fix up a tray. I'll be back in a few minutes. I hope to see Old Obie after the doctor leaves." Her voice came close to breaking. Neither Blanche nor Ike spoke as her soft footfalls headed up the steps.

"I've been selfish, keeping him all to myself." Blanche spoke in a low voice. "He's like a father to both of you."

"No, I understand. And so does Effie. We're already provided for. I'm sure he wants to do the same for you."

"Yes." She took a shaky breath. "God will provide for me, but I've stopped guessing what form that will take."

Chapter 24

Ike leaned against the wall opposite Blanche, his eyes trained on the floor, his ears straining for every sound coming through the door. Within a few minutes, Effie returned. She set a food-laden tray on the floor and joined Ike at the wall. The next time the door cracked, Blanche jumped to her feet and Ike and Effie took a step forward.

The somber expression on the doctor's face told Ike everything he needed to know even before he shook his head. "There is nothing I can do. Keep him comfortable. I've left some laudanum, but I doubt he'll take it. Says he can't afford to waste whatever time he has left."

Effie shuffled forward. "Can I go in to see him?"

"Of course."

Blanche trailed behind the doctor while Effie went into the cabin. Ike looked at Effie, then at Blanche. Which one?

"Stay with Effie. I'll be all right." Blanche called over her shoulder. "She needs you now more than ever." Accepting the doctor's arm, she disappeared from view.

When Ike opened the door, Effie sat next to Old Obie on the bed, holding him in a sitting position, her head leaning on his shoulder. ". . .made her happy." A small laugh escaped through her tears.

"Mind if I join you?"

Effie's head tilted in the direction of his voice. "Come in."

He took the seat beside the bed, the same one Blanche had occupied through the night.

"You know where the papers are?" Old Obie's voice held a small bit of his old strength.

Ike knew what papers he meant. "Yes."

Old Obie nodded. "I've made some changes, though. You'll have to see Carver to learn what's up."

"Don't talk like that." Effie raised her head from his shoulder. "You and Blanche have years ahead of you."

"We don't know, do we?"

Something had changed. Old Obie's voice didn't sound so much stronger as more resolved. "Now that I've made things right with God, I'm ready to go, if it's my time. I don't want you feeling bad on my account."

Made things right with God? The words tripped in Ike's mind.

"Don't look so shocked, son." A ghost of Old Obie's smile returned. "I never doubted the truth of the Gospel. And this little accident has shown me that I need God after all. If you're as smart as I think you are, you won't wait as long as I did to recognize the fact." A fit of coughing interrupted any further talk.

"Take the laudanum. It will ease your cough." Ike picked up the bottle from the nightstand.

Old Obie shook his head. "It'll put me to sleep." He winked. "I want to enjoy every minute I have left."

Refusing Elaine's insistence that she take a short rest in her cabin, Blanche balanced a tray with a bowl of chicken and dumplings on her arms. "It's his favorite comfort food. Maybe I can convince him to take a few bites."

The savory smell teased Blanche's nostrils, and her stomach grumbled. Maybe if she ate a bite, she would encourage her father to eat as well. When she entered the cabin, he was chatting with Ike and Effie as if it was an ordinary day.

"Come in. We were just talking about the day Ike jumped into the river from the deck. Scared us all half to death, he did."

"I got wet, that was all." Ike shrugged. "At least I knew how to swim."

"It was the middle of the winter. And you caught a cold." Her father's voice held a teasing note.

"And here I thought you were proud of my little escapade."

Ike's laughter sounded more forced than her father's.

"Elaine sent food for all of us." Propping the door open, Blanche set down a tray filled with chicken and dumplings, chicken salad sandwiches, tea, and cookies, and then took the seat Ike offered. "Now eat up. Your cook scares me. I don't want to report that you refused her food." She lifted half the sandwich to her mouth and took a bite. While she chewed, she dipped the soup spoon into the bowl and extracted a single dumpling. Eyes twinkling, Old Obie opened his mouth. He seemed to have trouble chewing, so for the next spoon, she offered broth only. That went down more easily. By the time they finished, she had eaten half a sandwich and most of the broth in the bowl was gone.

"That's enough." Old Obie settled back against the pillow. A little bit of color had returned to his face, and Blanche allowed a small beacon of hope to arise in her heart. Then she reminded herself what the doctor had said: a day, two at the most, more likely less.

Ike disappeared through the door and returned with an extra chair. Effie shifted from the bed to the chair, smoothing the spot where she had sat. Blanche's fingers itched to smooth the hair back from her father's brow, to offer the comfort Effie did, but Old Obie was as much Effie's father as he was hers. Ike took a seat on a weathered sea chest, his long legs folded in front of him.

Effie and Ike kept up the reminiscences. . .escapades that Effie shared in equal measure with her brother. . .while her father added an occasional grunt or comment. The longer they talked, the less he contributed, his eyes closing for brief spells in between coughs. A westerly sun burned through the porthole when his eyes sought out Blanche. She knelt on the floor beside his bed. "What do you want, Papa?"

Across the bed from her, Ike's eyebrows lifted and he smiled at the word.

"I want to hear you sing. Some of those hymns you're so fond of." The words that only a day ago might have sounded like a reproach now rang with bell-like clarity in her ears. "Sing Christmas carols. Those are my favorites."

"Mine, too." Blanche cleared her throat then in a low voice began "Silent Night, Holy Night." Effie's hands moved across her lap as if she was playing along on the piano. Blanche jumbled some of the verses together, but no one seemed to care. Her father's breathing eased.

As the last note faded, he opened his eyes. Struggling to a seated position so that he could see all three of them, he speared each of them with his gaze in turn. "I don't want you to feel bad for me. I am ready to go. God, in His mercy, reunited me with my daughter and restored me to Himself. You are my family. Take care of each other."

The speech sapped his energy, and he collapsed back on the pillow. "Stay with me. Please." The words came out as a whisper.

"You don't have to ask." Blanche pressed his hand. "Do you want me to sing some more?"

At her father's nod, she held his hand and sang as the songs occurred to her, from Christmas carols to Stephen Foster ballads to Gospel songs. His breathing rasped, and slowed down. While she sang "Lead Kindly Light," his fingers relaxed in her grip.

Silence descended, no one moving. Blanche locked eyes with Ike, and he pushed himself up from his sitting position. He leaned over the bed, placed his hand over her father's nose and mouth, and then felt at the side of his neck for a pulse. Shaking his head, he said, "He's gone."

Effie sobbed, tears falling from eyes that peered not into their faces but into their souls. Tears clustered in Blanche's eyes, but she didn't cry. Her mouth dried. She couldn't speak or cry. How could

God take both parents from her in such a short time? Wordlessly, she stood to her feet.

Ike pulled her close to his side, his chest heaving with grief. "It's time you rested."

Blanche found her voice. "Join me, Effie."

"But someone needs to. . .I need to—"

"I'll take care of it." Ike helped his sister to her feet. With his arms supporting both women, they left the cabin.

Blanche had to handle all the details of her mother's death by herself. She tried to dredge up gratitude for Ike's strong presence, but all she felt was grief.

"Ashes to ashes, dust to dust." The pastor of the local community church spoke the familiar words.

Ike knew the pastor from other funerals. Old Obie wasn't the first person to die aboard the *Cordelia*, and his funeral wasn't the first one he had arranged. Because of his parents' deaths, Ike had experienced death from a young age. But aside from his mother and father, whom he had loved with a child's simplicity and intensity, he had never lost someone he loved until now.

He opened his mind, etching every detail of the funeral on his memory. A good-sized congregation, including all the *Cordelia*'s crew and many local businessmen, attended. Others may have come in after Ike took his seat at the front with Effie and Blanche. She had insisted that they join her as members of Old Obie's immediate family.

The pastor adjusted his glasses on his nose and glanced at the notes he had made. Blanche stared straight ahead, while Effie held a handkerchief to her eyes. The preacher cleared his throat. "In addition to being a well-respected businessman of the river trade, Captain Lamar was blessed to find his long-lost daughter in the last few weeks of his life."

At those words, Blanche's reserve broke, and a single tear rolled down her cheek. Ike ached to place his arm around her shoulders, but this wasn't the time nor the place for such familiarity.

The pastor continued. "He is survived by his daughter, Blanche Lamar, and by his two adopted children, Isaac and Effie Gallagher."

Blanche had also insisted on their inclusion in the obituary.

"In recent days, Captain Lamar made peace with God. Even as we gather here to mourn his passing, he is in the place where God has wiped all tears from his eyes. If he were here, he would urge you not to mourn as those without hope. He would challenge you to find that same hope, of eternal life, that he at last embraced."

The words fell like a snake's venom and sank teeth into Ike's soul. The preacher's comments might bring comfort to others, but not to him. The Old Obie he had known and loved wasn't a religious man. And Ike resented the implication that he must become a Christian himself to honor the man who had been like a father to him. He closed his mind to the remainder of the sermon, only cuing back in when music emanated from the piano. Standing, he helped both women to their feet and walked behind them to the front where the casket lay.

Blanche trembled, and he tightened his hold on her, to make sure she didn't buckle at the knees. Effie's hand formed a fist.

Blanche noticed the movement as well. "He looks good. He's dressed in a navy blue suit, a pocket handkerchief tucked in the pocket. They slicked his hair away from his face. I wish he had his cap on." Her voice cracked.

Feet shuffled behind them. "I'm sure he looks fine." Effie relaxed her hand. "Let's go."

In the basement, people streamed by. Everyone shared a memory of Old Obie's laughter, his sense of humor, a trip down the river, his solid business sense. After the first few, Ike gritted his teeth, wishing the well-wishers would leave them alone. How Blanche kept her composure, he didn't know. This scene must remind her of the loss of her mother, only a few weeks ago.

One man lingered at the end of the line, waiting to speak with them—Carver, the lawyer. At length he approached and acknowledged Ike with a nod. After expressing his condolences, he mentioned that he was handling the captain's final affairs. "Shall I join you aboard the *Cordelia* to go over the terms of the will, or do you want to come to my office?"

"The *Cordelia*—" Blanche began.

"Let's meet at your office." Ike interposed. He didn't want the crew speculating about the future until he heard from the lawyer. "The sooner, the better. We have already delayed our departure."

The lawyer shot him a sharp glance, and Ike wondered again how the future would change. What would he do, and where would he go, if he could no longer call the *Cordelia* home? More importantly, what would Effie do?

The lawyer turned his attention to Blanche. "Would tomorrow afternoon suit you?"

Blanche blinked. "But tomorrow is Sunday." She looked from Ike to the lawyer. "Do you normally do business on the Lord's day, Mr. Carver?"

His eyebrows rose. "I thought you would prefer to take care of things before Monday."

Blanche glanced at Ike, and he nodded. "That would be best. Perhaps we can meet later this afternoon?"

They arranged to meet at half past two.

Ike didn't have much of an appetite, which was well as guests continued interrupting them to speak another kind word. Blanche ate even less than he did, mostly sipping sweet tea. Effie stared straight ahead without saying a word. Within half an hour, Blanche was yawning. Perhaps the last few days had caught up with her. Ike sought out the pastor. "This has been a difficult day for my sister and Miss Lamar. Is there a room where they can withdraw for a short time?"

The pastor led them next door to the parsonage. His wife invited the ladies to retire to one of the guestrooms before offering Ike a comfortable seat in the front parlor. The next thing he knew, the pastor was gently shaking his shoulder. "I hate to bother you, but you mentioned an appointment this afternoon?"

The grandfather clock rang two bells. Blanche came down the hall, looking somewhat refreshed from her brief rest. A smile had returned to Effie's face. "Thank you for giving us refuge. It has been a difficult few days."

"Churches have always offered sanctuary." The pastor's smile offered understanding. "We could do no less. I have hitched up my carriage, and I will take you to your appointment."

A couple of minutes before the half hour, they pulled up in front of a single-story building that housed three of the city's law offices. Ike assisted first Effie, then Blanche, out of the carriage.

"I'll wait out here," their host said. "It's a long walk back to the wharves."

"Thank you." Blanche managed to get the word out. She took short breaths between biting on her lower lip to keep panic from setting in full force. She had lived a lifetime since Ike had walked into Christ the King Church at her mother's funeral and turned her life upside down. In reality, only a month had passed.

God, give me strength and wisdom. She had already completed her first quest, finding her father. She had also found an unexpected family in Ike and Effie. However, her desire for a relationship with her father had been cut short. Soon she would know what provisions he had made for her in his will, if anything.

What if he left her penniless? Fighting the urge to pant, she accepted Ike's arm and walked up the steps to the office to learn her future.

Chapter 25

Blanche was surprised when Mr. Carver met them at the door himself. "Please pardon the informality. My clerk doesn't work on Saturdays. Would you care for a cup of coffee? A glass of cool water?" He gestured to a sideboard that held glasses and cups, together with a pitcher of cream and a sugar bowl. Blanche would have preferred tea, but she accepted a glass of water to keep her mouth moistened. As much coffee as she had drunk in the past few days, she was afraid she'd turn into a coffee bean if she drank more.

Only Ike was brave enough to take more coffee. Effie declined anything to drink. A few minutes later, they had taken their seats in Mr. Carver's office.

The lawyer turned his gaze on each of them in turn, a trick Blanche recognized from singing in public—make a connection with the members of the audience. The simple gesture helped her relax, prepared to hear what he had to say.

"I have had dealings with Mr. Gallagher in the past, and I have had the pleasure of meeting Miss Gallagher before. I looked forward to making your acquaintance, Miss Lamar, but I am sorry it is under these circumstances." He paused, took off his glasses, and wiped at his eyes.

Putting his glasses back on, he assumed a serious expression and opened a file in front of him. "Captain Lamar has always kept his affairs in good order. He came to me on Thursday instructing me to draw up a new will."

Effie let out a soft moan.

"So he came here on the day he had the accident." Ike spoke the words that were on all their minds.

"Yes."

Ike frowned. "So which will is in effect? The one he had previously drawn up or the one with changes?"

That's right, Ike knew the terms of the old will. The lawyer's announcement must be as unsettling for the brother and sister as for her.

"The new will is in effect. The captain always waited while we drew up whatever document he needed and had it witnessed. He didn't like to wait on the fortunes of the river for his legal matters."

Ike sat back straight in the chair, eyes intent on the lawyer, but he didn't speak.

"He said he had recently had a change in family circumstances. He was delighted to have you in his life again, Miss Lamar, and wanted to be sure you were provided for."

The tears Blanche had held at bay for the morning welled up and tumbled out. *This isn't the time or place. What must this lawyer think of me?* But no amount of self-criticism stopped her tears. She pressed the handkerchief she had tucked into her pocket to her eyes. No one spoke. Effie placed a hand on Blanche's arm while Ike rested his hand on her shoulder.

She drew in a shaky breath. Wordlessly, Ike handed her a fresh handkerchief. Nodding, she gave the others a smile. "I believe I'm ready to go on."

"Are you sure you don't want to come back another time?" Mr. Carver leaned back in his chair, not rushing her, open to whatever happened.

"No. I'm ready to listen. We can't make any plans until we know where we stand." She wiped the last of the traces of tears from her face and crumpled the handkerchief in her lap. She focused on the diploma behind the lawyer's head, testifying to the successful completion of his college studies at the University of Texas.

"I assume that the captain added his daughter to the will. How significant were the other changes?" Ike asked about the heart of the matter.

At Ike's query, the lawyer spread his hands. "Captain Lamar brought in the most recent financial information from Lamar Industries. The *Cordelia*, while still showing a profit, no longer brings in the money that it did when he first set sail. He wanted to be fair to everyone concerned."

Blanche's blood pounded in her ears. She didn't want any provision her father made for her to put others in jeopardy.

Ike nodded, but his face gave away none of his emotions.

"He left token amounts to all the employees who had worked for him for a minimum of a year. He also requested that every effort be made to retain any employees who choose to stay with the boat."

"Of course."

"He regretted that he didn't have more cash for the three of you. Most of his capital was tied up in the business. Of his cash, he left half to his daughter and the other fifty percent to be split between Isaac and Effie Gallagher." He named the amount. "It's not much, but the captain hoped it would help ease the transition."

Blanche sat back. Not much, perhaps. She wouldn't be rich. But it would provide a living, more than she had from her mother. "And the boat?" Her father's pride and joy.

A smile played around the lawyer's lips. "Here, Captain Lamar's wishes were a trifle unusual." He looked straight at Blanche. "The boat belongs to you, Miss Lamar. It was your father's wish that you study for a pilot's license. I questioned that direction, but he informed me that a lady pilot on the Mississippi recently accomplished the feat." His smile widened a fraction. "But the ownership comes with one important stipulation." He turned his attention to include Ike. "Miss Lamar owns the *Cordelia* provided she leaves the running of day-to-day operations in Mr. Gallagher's hands, with a salary commensurate with his position. If this is a problem for either one of you, the *Cordelia* will be sold and the profit divided among the three of you."

Ike threw his head back and laughed. "The old salt."

Tilting her head, Blanche glanced at Ike. "Is this arrangement acceptable to you? It sounds like you will be doing the majority of the work while I control the money."

Ike shifted in the chair. "What about my sister?"

"Yes, what about me?" Effie spoke for the first time.

"She should have a salary for her work. She acts as hostess and she arranges entertainment." Blanche sounded like an owner already.

Ike opened his mouth about the entertainment then closed it. Blanche wouldn't welcome his comments.

"Oh, that's not necessary. The *Cordelia* has always been my home."

"It still will be your home, but that doesn't mean you should work for free." Blanche smiled. "No argument."

"You're sounding like the captain already." Ike put encouragement in his tone.

"Captain Blanche Lamar." Blanche's face lit up more than at any point all week. "I like the sound of that." Then she grew serious again, worry darkening her eyes to walnut brown. "But I do have one concern. I know you host games of chance for passengers in your room. I am willing to enter into this partnership only if you agree to end all gambling activity."

Ike ground his fists together, keeping a smile on his face. If he hesitated too long, she wouldn't believe anything he said. "I promise not to do anything that will bring trouble to the *Cordelia* or bring disgrace on the Lamar name."

Tiny wrinkles tented between her eyebrows. Ike held his breath. His promise didn't quite match her request. He admired Blanche with all his heart, but he couldn't work under the conditions she wanted to lay down. He extended his hand. "Are we partners?"

"Yes." A thin smile took away some of the wariness in her eyes.

"We will work out the details as we go." She stared at his hand for a moment before accepting it. Her handshake was surprisingly firm, but nothing about Blanche shocked him anymore.

No one spoke much after that. Blanche spoke in monosyllables at the evening meal. The crew remained quiet, so still that Ike could hear the teapot whistling in the kitchen.

Blanche struggled to her feet to address the group. "I'm sure you have questions about the future. I don't have any answers for you tonight. I appreciate your patience while we figure things out." She placed a trembling hand on Ike's shoulder. "I am going to bed and hopefully sleep. Take things slow tomorrow. But first thing Monday morning, we'll get together and make plans for the trip back to Roma."

Old Obie's death had accomplished one important thing: Blanche would remain aboard the *Cordelia* for the foreseeable future. Whether the business would survive, he wouldn't risk a bet. His desire to take action, to get away from this city of death and mourning, to return to the business of riding the river and making money, chafed against Blanche's desire to spend an extra day in Brownsville—a Sunday, at that.

After a quiet evening—Ike couldn't name the last Saturday night he hadn't spent playing cards—he slept soundly, awakening shortly before breakfast. After a good night's rest, he had a better perspective on Blanche's day of forced inactivity. After all, she hadn't demanded everyone attend a worship service, and she hadn't said *he* couldn't work. His initiative should please her. He shook his head. No. She'd be happier if he sought out a church for Sunday morning worship.

Blanche didn't come to breakfast. Ike considered bringing a tray to her cabin but decided against it. The earlier he left, the sooner he could finish his business in town. After sending a message to Ventura to meet him for lunch, he took the list of items that customers upriver needed and headed to the warehouse district. The greater the margin between what the cost of the purchase and the amount he was authorized to spend, the more profit Lamar Industries would make. He enjoyed the challenge of the hunt.

First up: fabrics. A seamstress in Roma had a specific request for silk taffeta. He knew the best sources.

Greg Palmer, a portly man, greeted him at the door. "Mr. Gallagher, I didn't know if we would see you on this trip. We were saddened to learn of Captain Lamar's passing."

After accepting the condolences, Ike waited while Palmer disappeared into the bowels of the warehouse to bring out the requested materials. Ike took advantage of the break to walk up and down the aisles, studying the variety of colors and textures and shine. He found himself measuring each bolt against how they would appear on Blanche. Materials that were practical, yet beautiful. Vibrant colors, but not ones that would shout out loud. She would look good even if she only had dark calicos in her wardrobe. Classy and classic, in other words.

He forced himself to walk the aisles a second time, thinking in terms of the shop owners along the river route. This warehouse carried everything needed for a well-dressed lady's wardrobe, from fabrics from around the world to sewing notions. To purchase other items requested by merchants in Roma, he would have to make several more stops.

The warehouse manager wheeled the bolts of materials to

the center table. Ike examined them, looking for those minute imperfections that could bring about a reduced price. A water stain appeared on a tiny section of mustard-colored silk. *Perfect.* He haggled with the manager until they arrived at a price that was more than Ike wanted to pay, but less than he expected to.

"Thank you for doing business with Lamar Industries." Ike made arrangements for delivery of the materials. After he doffed his hat in a salute, he headed to the next warehouse.

Several hours later, Ike left the final warehouse, dust dirtying the light gray of his suit and grinding into the creases on his hands. Sweat had welded his hat to his head. Levi's would make more sense, but then he'd reduce himself to the level of the working man. Dressing as a man of means served to keep prices at a profitable level. He would enter the day's purchases in the account books this afternoon.

As he walked back in the direction of the *Cordelia,* a thought struck him. Perhaps Blanche would have preferred to shop with them. But Old Obie had left daily operations up to him, and shopping fell into that category, didn't it?

When he turned onto the wharf leading to the steamboat, the deck lacked its usual bustle. The Lady *Cordelia* looked sad, almost dead, lacking signs of life. Part of him hoped Blanche would be waiting for him at the railing, and he felt strangely empty at her absence.

Ike resisted the urge to wipe his grimy palms on his already dirtied suit. He would change, leave his clothes for Agatha, and head to the captain's quarters to update the books. Sunday's slower pace usually brought him pleasure, but today loneliness and grief weighed him down. The prospect of Sunday afternoons gathered around the kitchen table, replete with food his wife had prepared, their children gamboling around the table legs—that held appeal. Children with curly, flame-red hair and the captain's hazel eyes.

The *Cordelia's* accounts should distract him from thoughts of marriage and family. He wished he could hand Blanche a fortune, not a business on the brink of failure.

Tomorrow Blanche was expecting a full accounting of the state of affairs with Lamar Industries. While entering the days' purchases, he realized no one had noted the goods delivered from upriver. He pawed through the papers on the desk and found everything except the receipt for the cotton. Chewing the end of his pencil, he studied the room, searching for spots where the receipts could have fallen. He poked around a few places but didn't find it.

Without a record of their largest delivery, the trip registered as a loss. Old Obie's death couldn't be considered a business expense, but that led to another question. Where did he keep track of his personal expenses?

So much needed to be done, starting with sorting through the things in Old Obie's cabin. He kept a room in Roma, but Ike couldn't do anything about that until they returned downriver. If possible, he would like to hire another pilot. Old Obie didn't entirely trust Pete at the helm, so Ike wouldn't either. The problem was, the best pilots were already employed or had retired.

Ike had promised Old Obie that he would make sure Blanche was provided for, and to help her obtain her pilot's license.

He had no idea how he would keep either promise.

Chapter 26

The hours on Sunday passed pleasantly. Blanche remained secluded in her cabin, refreshing body and soul. With her remaining sheets of stationery, she decided to record her short time with her father. Words spilled on page after page until she had filled front and back of each sheet. She wrote in the margin to finish the last sentence. Thoughts crowded to the front of her mind, wanting to find their way on paper. If there was time on Monday, she would buy more, or perhaps even a journal. She could think of so many things she wanted to say, things about her mother, even new things she had learned about herself.

Tears stained and blurred portions of almost every page, but by the end, her tears had dried.

The more she wrote, the more she realized how little she knew about her father. Despite her immersion in life aboard the *Cordelia* for the past two weeks, she remained so ignorant. She'd have to depend on Ike. Her father's insistence on his continued employment made total sense.

Blanche awoke on Monday morning refreshed, ready to make some preliminary decisions about her future. Her black suit needed laundering, so she set it aside for Dame Agatha. Instead, she reached for the deep purple dress her father had adored.

Effie turned over in her berth with a groan. "Would you like me to bring something back for you?" Blanche asked.

Effie flopped onto her back and yawned. "Maybe some toast and tea. I'm not all that hungry."

"I'll bring some." With honey and butter and jam and maybe some bananas and orange juice—anything to tempt Effie's taste buds. "I plan to meet with Ike about the business later this morning. I'd appreciate it if you could be there."

Effie's eyelids fluttered as if she were trying to see something through the curtain of her blindness. "I know very little about the business side of things. I wouldn't be any help."

Effie might not know dollars and cents, but she had her fingers on the pulse of the ship and crew. She would ask her opinion at a later time.

After a brief spell in front of the mirror, arranging her hair in a loose knot on top of her head, Blanche inched the door open. Smithers stood outside, his hand raised, ready to knock. "So you are joining us for breakfast." He sounded pleased.

"Yes."

"I will let Elaine know." He bowed and headed for the staircase.

Blanche followed. The floor undulated with minute dimensions, suggesting a wind was rustling the river beneath them. The first breakfast bell sounded, so she had time before beginning the day. She headed to the main deck. Wind whipped around the floorboards, whistling past the empty spaces where cargo had waited on the trip downriver. Voices called from the wharf, and she glanced at stevedores toting pallets to the ship. Somehow, business was continuing as usual.

The wind teased her hair out of the loose knot, but she was glad for the cooling breeze, not going downstairs until the final warning bell sounded. As she walked through the open door to the salon—quiet, without Effie's usual piano music—wide smiles broke out on several faces. A few brave souls applauded, but a frown from Smithers brought that to an end. Instead, he came forward to escort her to the captain's table. "It is good to see you this morning, Miss Lamar. We are most distressed about the captain's death."

Ike rose to his feet, and his smile helped ease the core of cold at her heart. When Elaine brought the food to the pass, everyone paused, waiting for the grace Blanche had instituted. If she tried to pray out loud, she doubted her voice would carry across the room.

Smithers—*Smithers?*—led in a simple, but effective prayer. The waiters brought out heaping platters. Elaine made a rare trip from the kitchen. "If there is anything special you wish to eat, just tell me and I will cook it for you."

Blanche shook her head, but Ike touched her arm. "Let her. She wants to help."

Blanche couldn't eat all the food already served, but she scrambled to think of something not on the table. "Maybe. . .some fried bananas? No, warm applesauce with cinnamon."

"Yes, Miss Lamar. I will get right to it." The cook's smile was as good as a bear hug.

No one had treated Blanche with such tender care in her entire life, not even after her mother died. She waited, expecting tears to well up and spill out of her eyes. But they didn't. Instead, tender gratitude held sway, filling her heart with peace. She'd like tea with cream and sugar. British style, Mother used to call it. "Elaine?"

The cook appeared at the window in an instant. "Yes?"

"I would like to have a cup of hot tea. Do you have a cozy?"

"Yes, ma'am. Right away."

Soon Blanche heard a teakettle whistling merrily and her insides warmed. She'd know she was truly better when the ice-cold spot at the center of her heart melted. For now she couldn't seem to get warm. Grits, that might be good. She shook her head. She had already given Elaine plenty of extra work.

Ike offered her the basket of biscuits first, and she took one. They both reached for the gravy boat at the same time. He pulled his hand away, gesturing for her to take it first.

"I've never seen you take gravy on your biscuits." He spooned eggs onto his plate.

"It sounds good this morning."

Elaine appeared with a teapot encased in a crocheted cozy and poured Blanche's cup mostly full. "Do you want more?"

Blanche shook her head. "That's perfect." She handed the gravy boat to Ike and added a spoon of sugar to the tea, then enough cream to fill the cup.

After she ate her biscuit, her hunger returned, and she ate bacon and eggs. When she had finished, she could almost see her reflection. Her mother used to say that. The memory brought a smile to her lips.

Ike smiled back. "You were hungry."

Blanche stared at her empty plate. "I feel like I haven't eaten for a week."

"You haven't done more than pick at your food since the accident." Ike brought the cup of coffee to his lips. "I speak for everyone here when I say I'm glad your appetite has returned."

Blanche finished a dish of warm applesauce then she settled back in her seat with a sigh.

"You know Effie better than I do. What will tempt her?" Blanche surveyed the choices.

"Biscuits." Ike wrapped the hot bread in a napkin inside the basket before adding butter and honey. "With sweet tea. I'll carry it for you." Together they headed down the stairs.

After delivering breakfast to Effie, Ike and Blanche returned to the salon. Logs and account books filled his arms; Blanche had to open the door. She brought pens and pencils, including a red one. Add "sensible and resourceful" to the list of qualities that described Blanche. His boss. He shook his head at the thought.

She poured herself a cup of coffee from the sideboard and added a dollop of cream. "I can't seem to stay warm this morning."

Summer heat bothered Ike as usual, but he nodded. "Do you want me to fetch a wrap from your cabin?"

"No, I'll be all right." She drank about half a cup, topped it off, and sat down at the table, keeping the cup away from the papers. "I was good with sums at school. I hope that will help."

Ike wondered if she intended to keep the account books now that she was the owner. Did that fall under daily operations? Or owner's prerogative? He wasn't ready to explain the special entertainment income.

He cocked his head at Blanche. "You've had a lot thrown at you at once. Where do you want to start?"

She picked up the coffee cup and blew across the top before taking a sip. "I want to know everything." She set the cup to the side. "But today, we need to decide our next actions. Are we ready to return to Roma? Roma *is* the *Cordelia's* home port, isn't it?"

"No, we're not ready. And yes, Roma is our home port." Ike hesitated then decided to mention what was on his mind. "Your father kept a room at the hotel in Roma. You'll want to go through his things when we get there. Or you may wish to keep the room, for yourself."

A lost look brushed across her face. "That sounds like a good idea. I don't have a place I can call home anymore."

"Yes, you do." Ike laid his hand on top of hers, where her trembling fingers held the red pencil. "The *Cordelia*, for as long as you want to stay."

"So I'm like Mrs. Noah, my home afloat on a sea of water. At least I don't have to take care of any animals." She brushed a stray curl behind her ear. "Only my ark won't come to rest on a mountaintop anytime soon."

"There are worse places."

She removed her hand from his and pointed to the stacks by Ike. "I recognize the captain's logs, but what are the other books?"

"Accounts. Sums, as you called them. Income and expenses

listed. Details of salaries. All the information needed to run Lamar Industries."

She nodded. "I will want to study those, I'm sure. But what do we need to do before we can leave? We already have cargo on deck. Are we expecting more? Or do you go from business to business, asking?"

"We could carry more cargo, but it's not too bad. I've posted notices in the hotels for passengers to contact us about a ride upriver."

Blanche nodded. "Do we have definite dates for the baseball trip with Mr. Ventura's team?"

Ike shrugged. "River travel is never that precise. The towns are expecting us, but they will announce the game after we arrive in town." He drummed the table with his fingers. "The main thing we are lacking is a pilot."

"What about Pete? I know my father did most of the work himself, but I always thought that was because he loved his work."

"He did." Ike nodded. "But he didn't completely trust the *Cordelia* with anyone else. Pete is an adequate pilot, but he doesn't have the feel for the river that Old Obie had. That you have, for that matter."

"Do you think I should apply for my pilot's license? Like my father suggested?"

The corners of Ike's lips quirked upward. "Absolutely. But we need someone to help us in the meantime."

Her eyes dancing, she challenged him. "Didn't I hear that you're a pilot yourself?"

He shook his head. "I'd be willing to take over for a few hours, in an emergency, but I'm less experienced than Pete. I don't want to risk our future with my hands on the wheel."

"Then what are our options?" She hit on the crux of the problem.

"I have a few ideas, but I have to warn you, there are reasons why none of the men I have in mind are on the river at the moment."

She grimaced. "Let's talk it over together."

"If we can coax him out of retirement, I'd like to get Captain Pettigrew. He helped teach Old Obie way back when."

Blanche absorbed that bit of news. "So he must be elderly by now."

"He quit the river about ten years ago when he decided to give up the fight against the railroads. I haven't seen him for a couple of years, but the last time I laid eyes on him, he was hale of body and sound of mind."

"And if he's not interested or available?" She left the question dangling.

"The others are either as old as Pettigrew or men who have lost the battle with booze." Ike didn't blunt the truth.

Her face paled, and she took a single swallow. "It's cooled off."

Standing, Ike reached for the coffeepot and refilled her cup. Satisfactory steam rose from the surface, and she gripped it gratefully. She closed her eyes, and her lips moved in silent words. When she opened them, determination shone from within. "Do you think Captain Pettigrew will be home this afternoon?"

That's my girl. Ike nodded. "So you want to come with me?"

"Of course."

The first luncheon bell rang. "I'll put these away."

Blanche tugged the account book toward her. "I want to study this one. Unless there are some figures you need to enter?"

"Not today." He wondered how long it would be before she began raising uncomfortable questions. If he was lucky, not on this trip. She'd be too busy studying the books, if he had anything to say about it.

Chapter 27

Blanche inched the door to her cabin open, in case Effie was asleep. She needn't have bothered. Her roommate was buttoning up a pretty apricot-colored dress, with square buttons. "Good morning, Blanche. Thank you for the breakfast."

"Elaine fixed a feast, with more to come." Pleasant aromas promised chili and cornbread for the noon meal.

"When Elaine is upset, she cooks. The captain said he always knew when something was on her mind." Tears filled Effie's eyes. "I promised myself I wasn't going to cry again."

"Oh, Effie." Blanche threw her arms around her friend's shoulders. "I've cried enough tears to make the Rio Grande flood its banks, if they had fallen in the river. No one expects you to have a smile on your face."

"Maybe not." She poured water into the bowl on her dressing table and dampened a washcloth. She dabbed it at her face, neck, hands, and then added a small amount of lotion below each ear. Blanche imitated her actions. Amazing how such a small gesture could offer so much refreshment.

"Are you ready?" Blanche gently encouraged her.

Effie nodded. Blanche laid down the account book and handed Effie her white cane. Arm in arm, they headed to the dining salon. Blanche explained about plans she had made with Ike to visit with Captain Pettigrew that afternoon.

"Captain Pettigrew." Effie smiled. "I remember him. He was funny. I loved listening to him exchange stories with Old Obie while I played with his cats."

"Would you like to come with us? I bet he still has cats."

Effie stopped mid-step. "No. I feel close to the captain as long as I'm aboard the *Cordelia*."

"I understand." And Blanche did. She had never seen her father any place other than onboard the *Cordelia*. She had a hard time imagining him in any other setting.

"You don't think I'm being silly?"

"Not at all." Whatever time Effie needed to grieve, Blanche would allow. She didn't want her friend's life turned upside down the way her own had been since her mother's death. Her first nineteen years in Roma, even the fellowship at Christ the King Community Church, seemed like they happened to another girl.

The earlier chill continued to cling to Blanche, and she would have welcomed a brisk walk, but Ike had arranged for a carriage. As they trundled past the wharves and the downtown district, toward the residential district, she recognized the wisdom. "Is he expecting us?"

"I sent a messenger to arrange the meeting."

"Thank you." Ike did so many things so efficiently.

Blanche studied the streets as they rode, noting the presence of more palm trees than she had seen upriver, with an occasional seagull diving for a morsel of food as they rode by. "Is the ocean close by?"

"Not far."

An impulse seized Blanche. "I want to see it. Can we go, after we meet with Captain Pettigrew?"

Ike twisted in his seat to face her more directly. "You've never been to the ocean? Of course not. I should have taken you before."

Her face turned downward, hoping to hide the heat in her cheeks. "As long as I am this close, I ought to see it. Don't you think so?"

"Absolutely. And here we are."

The house had to belong to someone who had spent his life on the water. Maybe she formed that impression from the narrow walk that circled the roof. What had she heard it called, a widow's walk? For the whalers' wives who waited at home? "Have you ever read *Moby Dick*?"

"That's the story about the crazy man who went after the whale, right? Great stuff. I'm surprised you read it, though. Didn't your mother think it was too harsh for your delicate mind?"

Laughter bubbled out of Blanche. "She didn't know everything I read. My reward for finishing my schoolwork early was to read, and my teacher kept me supplied in books. I fell in love with the idea of steamboats when I read Mark Twain's books."

"He got a lot of it right. Things have changed since his time, though." Ike helped her out of the carriage and opened the gate in the white picket fence. Flowers edged the length of the walkway, and rosebushes hugged the house. If her father was a different kind of man. . .if her mother were a different sort of woman. . .she might have grown up in a house like this. Blanche shook away the thought. Wishing couldn't change the past.

A man with a blue sailor's cap on his head and dressed in white came out on the front porch. She thought she had seen him at the funeral, but she wasn't sure. He waved them forward.

"Mr. Gallagher, Miss Lamar. I am honored that you would call on me in your time of grief." He came forward with an affable smile on his face.

"We appreciate you seeing us on such short notice." Blanche's nod felt stiff.

"I can guess what you came here to see me about." He flashed white teeth at her. "But first let me introduce you to my wife."

A kindly looking woman, a little plump, with a happy expression on her face, appeared at the front door at that moment, bearing a tray. "Do you mind if we take our refreshment on the porch?"

"That sounds lovely."

No one mentioned business as they made introductions and shared in sweet tea and pinwheel cookies. Blanche made an effort to finish the cookies Mrs. Pettigrew pressed on her. The affection between husband and wife was evident, a man comfortable in his retirement. She wondered if any inducement could convince him to leave the comforts of home to return to life on the river.

After they emptied the pitcher of tea and Mrs. Pettigrew disappeared inside, Captain Pettigrew grew serious. "As I said, I can guess why you're here. You need a pilot."

Beside her, Ike stirred but stayed silent. Perhaps he wanted her to approach Captain Pettigrew about the position. "From what I've heard, you're the best man for the job." She looked at him directly, refusing to drop her gaze.

"You're Obie's daughter, all right." Captain Pettigrew wiped at his eyes. "My wife stood by me all the years I spent on the river. I promised her before God that I would spend the last years of our lives at home."

"Are you a Christian?" Blanche couldn't keep the surprise out of her voice.

"Amen, sister." He winked at Ike. "Not all river men are heathen."

That statement sent heat rushing to Blanche's cheeks. She sipped her tea to give herself a moment to regain her composure. For once, Ike remained silent. He seemed to be enjoying her disquiet.

"We are not asking you to come out of retirement—not permanently." Blanche took a deep breath. "In fact, I am interested in securing a pilot's license for myself. My father—" She still stumbled over the word. "—felt I had an aptitude for it. And I have to confess, the idea intrigues me."

"But a woman pilot?" Captain Pettigrew left the question dangling.

Ike cleared his throat. "A woman on the Mississippi recently qualified as a riverboat pilot. Our Blanche plans to follow in her steps."

"Obie was a good judge of talent." Captain Pettigrew looked across the expanse of lawn. Standing, he went to the open door to the house and called for his wife. They conferred briefly in low voices then came out hand in hand.

"Is there room on your boat for my wife to travel with us?"

"Of course." Blanche smiled in relief.

"We have about an hour before the carriage will return." Ike held the gate open for Blanche to pass through. "You can see the ocean from here. We can spend a few minutes on the beach."

Blanche stood on tiptoe. "I can't see it."

"You can smell it, though." He took a deep breath. "All that salty air."

"Is that what it is?" Her nose wrinkled. "It reminded me of fish."

"That, too."

Palm fronds reached out to brush against them as they walked down the street, narrowing to a footpath about a hundred yards from the Pettigrews' house. Seagulls flew an elaborate dance overhead, demanding a tribute from the two intruders.

"Is that the ocean I hear?"

Ike stopped to listen. Ripple and swish. Not the roar of water tripping over rocks, such as he had experienced on a memorable trip to the headwaters of the Rio Grande, but the gentle wash of waves on sand. "Yes."

The boardwalk stopped about thirty yards shy of the high water mark. Blanche dipped a tentative toe into the sand, and her shoe sunk in the soft surface. Giggling, she pulled back. "Do I dare walk forward?"

"If you do, sand will cover your shoes. Anytime we went to the beach, we came home with sand in every possible crevice. Dame Agatha complained she couldn't get the sand out for two washings." The memory brought a smile to his face. "If you want to skirt the grass here, it shouldn't be bad. There's another boardwalk in that direction."

Blanche glanced at the sand then at Ike. "I'd like that." She kept turning to look at the ocean, mesmerized by the undulating waves. "I don't think I would ever get tired of watching the water. Each time the waves wash over the beach, they draw pictures in the sand."

The rather fanciful description suited the beach. "It's peaceful." Ahead of them, a family had spread out a blanket where gulls squatted, begging for leftovers. The father held a pair of binoculars to his eyes, and the mother glanced at a book between admonitions to their children. The young ones were busy filling a pail with sand. Pail-shaped mounds defined the outline of a sandcastle. Ike pointed it out.

"Oh, that looks like fun."

"Another time, perhaps."

"If I come back."

They needed to return to the Pettigrews' house to meet the carriage on time, but Ike hated for Blanche's time at the beach to end. The wave came up and washed away part of the castle.

"Oh dear." Blanche laughed. "That must be what the Lord meant when He talked about a house built on sand and a house built on rock. The house built on sand would be washed away."

"Temporary as sand, as eternal as the waves." Ike stood behind Blanche, and she leaned ever so briefly against his chest. He resisted the urge to put his arms around her and pull her closer.

Sighing, she said, "It's time to go back, isn't it?"

He nodded, and they turned in the direction of town.

The driver held a slip of paper in his hand and offered it to Ike after he assisted Blanche into the carriage. Ike read the message and nodded. Good. Today was turning into a lucky day, after the difficult times last week.

"What's that?" Faint pink appeared on Blanche's face. Ike hoped she wouldn't suffer from sunburn after their short time on the beach.

"Business." He smiled and patted her hand. "Nothing you need to worry your pretty head about."

She opened her mouth as if to protest then closed it without speaking. "Thank you for this lovely afternoon. I've been able to forget, for a few minutes, that I have lost both father and mother. God's reminder that life goes on and I won't be sad forever." Leaning back against the seat, she closed her eyes. When her head fell against his shoulder, he adjusted her wrap and let her rest. He sought to nap but stayed locked awake.

As soon as they finished supper, Blanche and Effie excused themselves. Blanche took the account book with her. "I hope you don't mind."

"I regret anything that takes you away from me." Eventually he would have to list the day's business in the books, but it could wait. "Until tomorrow then?"

She smiled, and the two women left.

Ike retired to his cabin and set up things, setting out the bottle of whiskey he had managed to purchase before Old Obie's death and opening a packet of cards. After full dark fell, he returned to the main deck and greeted Bart Ventura as he came down the wharf with a couple of business associates whom Ike had met.

"I've told my friends this is the best game in town. I'm glad you could accommodate us."

"Glad to oblige." He didn't host games in port very often—if he wanted a game, he sought one out on land—but he wouldn't refuse Ventura's request. They would discuss some business tonight, now that Ike had final details about the return trip to Roma.

The evening passed the midnight hour, with Ike stone-cold sober but his guests feeling the effects of multiple shots of whiskey, when a sharp knock rapped at the door. Ventura swept the cards off the table in a practiced gesture, and the men removed their markers. Only whiskey glasses remained as telltale signs of the night's activities.

"Who is it?" Ike spoke through the closed door.

"Police. Open the door or we'll break it down."

A swift glance at the table confirmed all signs of the game had disappeared. Half a dozen officers stood at the entrance, pistols in hand. With one hand pulling the door closed, he stood inches in front of the first officer.

"What can I do for the officers of the law?" Ike turned on his most convincing smile, the one smile that made women swoon and men agree to harebrained schemes. More than once, Old Obie had remarked that he was glad Ike was a reasonably honest man.

"Open that door." The officer—a captain, Ike guessed by his uniform—shoved a piece of paper in his face. "Here's the warrant."

"Certainly." Ike tried the door, pretending it was locked. "Silly me." He took his time fishing his key out of his pocket. Heavy breathing and the smell of sweat identified the cops as men on the hunt.

The door opened to three men sitting around the table, cigars burning in ash trays, which helped to mask the scent of whiskey. The drink, and the glasses, had disappeared, and all money had been put away. Ike allowed himself to relax. "How may I assist you this evening, Captain? As you can see, some friends of mine have gathered to offer their advice in this time of transition. You must have heard that our captain, J.O. Lamar, died last week."

"The police have an exhaustive history of this boat, Mr. Gallagher." He speared Ike with his glance while the officers pawed through his belongings. Ike bit his tongue to keep from asking what they were searching for.

"Here it is." One of the officers, a black-haired man who sounded like a Cajun from nearby Louisiana held up a decanter.

The police captain—Ike had determined his name was Mason— opened the decanter and sniffed. He tipped it and let a drop drip on his finger, which he licked. "You have been serving whiskey."

"What's going on?" A feminine voice pierced through the crowd of men. Wrapped in a dressing gown that covered her from neck to toe, Blanche appeared in the doorway like an avenging angel.

Chapter 28

The clamor of half a dozen feet stomping down the stairs and hallway had awakened Blanche from a sound sleep. Worried about some emergency onboard—a problem with the engine? A sandbar?—she had pulled on the dressing gown that covered her completely and followed the noise down the hall.

The hubbub centered in Ike's cabin. Policemen crawled through his belongings like ants covering an ant hill, together with several men she had never met—and Bart Ventura. She almost coughed on the miasma of cigar smoke and sweat-soaked bodies and something else she couldn't identify.

"Nothing you need to concern yourself with, ma'am."

Blanche wished she had taken the time to dress. It was hard to exert authority while wearing bedclothes. "Let me be the judge of that. You are?"

"Captain Benedict Mason, ma'am. There is no need to be alarmed.

I'll have one of my officers escort you back to your cabin."

When a dark-haired officer laid his hand on her arm, she shook him off. "If there is a problem with the boat, I want to know. I am the new owner."

Too late she caught Ike's frantic gestures.

Captain Mason's eyebrows rose. "You are?"

"Blanche Lamar. Captain Lamar's daughter."

The man's eyes darkened. "Were you aware that your—Mr. Gallagher was selling illegal whiskey to customers?"

Blanche looked at the decanter in the captain's hands. Whiskey must have been the odor she couldn't identify.

Ike pushed his way forward. "Captain, there is no need to distress Miss Lamar."

"No, I want to hear your answer." She wouldn't let Ike send her away.

"I brought a bottle to ease my friend in his time of grief. No money has changed hands." Mr. Ventura joined their circle.

Blanche reeled as the revelations poked more holes in her innocence in the ways of the world. "We don't have a license to sell liquor."

"No, you don't, which is why we were concerned when we received word about this evening's gathering." Captain Mason had toned down his belligerence.

A cry from one of the officers announced his discovery of a stack of money. He handed it to Captain Mason. His belligerence returned in full force. "If no money exchanged hands, why does this paper say 'IOU'?"

Gambling.

Mr. Ventura and Ike exchanged a long look. Ike gave an almost imperceptible shrug of his shoulders before speaking. "We were playing a friendly game of chance. I, um, wrote out the IOU until I can bring him the rest of the money. And that's not against the law." He cast an apologetic look in Blanche's direction.

The policeman shifting through Ike's trunk straightened. A shake of his head indicated he had found nothing.

The lines on Captain Mason's face deepened into a scowl. He turned on Blanche. "I'm surprised that a lady such as yourself would allow drinking and gambling aboard your boat."

Blanche slammed her mouth shut, jarring her teeth.

During the course of their conversation, two strangers had slipped through the door. Mr. Ventura stuck his right hand out and clasped Captain Mason's palm. "I wish we had met under different circumstances, but I trust there is no lasting ill will."

Did Blanche imagine it, or did he slip a bill to the captain?

"No." The word lacked the captain's earlier anger. "But the next time I board this boat, I trust I won't find any illegal refreshments?"

"No, you won't." Blanche took control. "I guarantee it." She decided to take it one step further. "And Mr. Ventura, I believe it's best if you make your future travel plans with a different company."

"Now wait a minute—" Ike barreled forward. "Bart, don't pay any attention to her."

"Do we have an understanding, Mr. Ventura?" Blanche extended her hand the way he had earlier.

He bowed over her hand, all of his earlier charm evident. "We will not be seeing each other again." Straightening, he shook Ike's hand. "It's been a pleasure." He wasted no time walking out the door.

Captain Mason bowed over Blanche's hand. "I wish you the best on this new venture." He nodded in Ike's direction. "Mr. Gallagher."

"Captain Mason."

They could have been two men about to walk six paces and duel at dawn. Ike walked him to the door and watched his departure. "They're gone." Grabbing a shot glass in his hand, he raised his arm as if he was going to throw it. Instead he placed it on a clear spot on his dresser. "Do you have any idea what you've just done?"

"Do you remember your promise?" she shot back.

"Ventura's one of our best customers. We have no way to make up for losing his business." Ike stalked the room. "There's a reason why the captain left me in charge of day-to-day operations. We *need* his business." He tossed things in his chest, not bothering to fold his clothes.

His actions reminded Blanche that she was alone with Ike in his cabin, wearing only her dressing gown. "This isn't over. We will discuss it"—she glanced at the clock in the corner—"in a few hours." Keeping her eyes dry and her back straight, she whirled around and headed back to her cabin.

Effie sat in the rocking chair, knitting needles clacking in the silence. "What happened?"

Effie would have to know sooner or later. "Police raided the boat." The words came out in clipped syllables. "They accused Ike of selling liquor without a license."

"Ike would never do that." Effie didn't appear in the least bit upset.

"There was liquor." Blanche still thought she might be physically ill. The smells in that room had overwhelmed her senses. Dry heaves shook her shoulders now. After a couple of unproductive bouts, she poured water into a basin and splashed her face.

"Ike doesn't drink. Maybe a glass every now and then. But he does provide refreshment for his guests."

Effie couldn't understand the effect of such simple words on Blanche. Her mother, her pastor, her church, were all teetotalers. Her background taught her a single drink always led to drunkenness. But that bothered her less than gambling—an activity she had expressly prohibited. "His marks. Isn't that the word they use? They were playing poker."

At those words, Effie's knitting needles stopped clacking. "I was afraid he would continue."

"He promised." Blanche choked on the words. "I thought I could trust him."

"Oh, Blanche." Effie folded the yarn back into the bag. "Come here." She patted the berth next to her chair.

"I can't sleep." Blanche plopped down on the pillow and unbuttoned her dressing gown. Even if she couldn't rest, she could be cool.

"You can trust Ike to do everything he considers in the best interest of the *Cordelia* and Lamar Industries and you."

"But he promised not to—"

"He promised not to do anything that would get you into trouble. Not the same thing." Effie lifted a single finger. "The police raid will weigh heavily on his conscience."

"He twisted my words." Blanche rang her hands. "You'll have to teach me how to knit. It might relax me." When she picked up a ball of yarn, it rolled across the floor. That brought a giggle to her lips.

"Maybe that's not a good idea. I never was all that good with thread and needle." The giggle turned weepy. She lay on the bed without climbing under the covers.

"There's nothing more we can do about it until tomorrow morning." Effie patted Blanche's shoulder before she climbed back into bed. "I'm praying about it."

Lately prayer felt like a wasted effort. Was prayer going to make up for the difference between Ike's promise and his betrayal? She had prayed and prayed and still had no clue what she should do for her future. Had she traded the sure friendship of the people of Roma for the passing regard of Effie and Ike? She never should have left home. She should have known nothing good would ever come of living on a steamboat.

If she had never boarded the *Cordelia*, she never would have met her father.

Once Effie's breathing had settled into a steady pattern, Blanche took her place in the rocking chair and stared at the door. Staying or leaving, she had to decide.

Ike didn't bother cleaning his cabin. He cleared off his bed and lay down. Guilt-plagued dreams that had police locking him in jail while he was awash in a river of whiskey troubled his sleep. After tossing and turning for a couple of hours, he awoke, his head splitting, leg sore where it dangled over the side of the bed.

The whiskey decanter stood on his table, taunting him, inviting him to drink a shot, to take the edge off the terrible day ahead. He had done what he must to protect Blanche's inheritance. That's why the captain had made him the director of daily operations. Wasn't it?

Ike had never used alcohol as a crutch and he wouldn't start now. No amount of alcohol or coffee would answer the central problem: would Blanche decide to direct Carver to sell the *Cordelia* and split the profits? Would his actions deprive himself and his sister of both a means of support and their home?

Whatever the day might hold, he would greet it with his usual savoir faire. A single glance in the mirror revealed dark stubble on his chin that made him look more sinister than daring, and dark circles emphasized the harshness of the night. Nothing could remove the dark circles, but he would allow himself the luxury of a hot shave. While he waited for the water to heat, he checked the suit that Dame Agatha had returned to him yesterday, freshly pressed. His hand wandered over his tie rack, settling on his red tie. Red always made him feel better.

Once he had his basin of hot water, he sudsed soap with his shaving brush and lathered his face. The bristles fell into the basin, and the brace of aftershave woke up his skin. He added pomade to his hair. Now he could face the day. With a tip of the hat he pretended he was wearing, he left the cabin with a swagger.

Soft piano music filtered from the salon as Ike approached. Effie must be doing better. The melodies flowed from one of Old Obie's favorites into another. Sentiment washed over Ike, causing a hitch in his step. When Effie began a new melody, Ike began whistling "Yankee Doodle Went to Town." The hand-clapping, happy song brimmed with the captain's larger-than-life personality. She must be doing better.

Taking courage from his sister's music, Ike pushed through the door. The room seemed empty, with only the crew and no passengers. Blanche wasn't at her usual seat at the captain's table. Relieved, he took another step into the room before he spotted the head of red hair at the long table with the rest of the crew. She talked and laughed as if nothing out of the ordinary had happened only a few hours earlier.

Two could play at that game. With a warm smile and a practiced air, he swept into the room. "Good morning, everyone."

Blanche's shoulders stiffened before she twisted in her seat. "Good morning, Mr. Gallagher."

Mr. Gallagher. That didn't sound friendly, not friendly at all. Ike headed for the opposite end of the table, but Blanche waved him back. "There's a seat across from me. We have some matters to discuss."

How did she sound so chipper? Ike took the seat she had indicated. Smithers poured a cup of coffee before he had a chance to say no. "I'll take a glass of milk as well."

Effie stopped playing and took the seat next to Ike. Blanche said grace over the meal. Conversation flowed around the three of them, sparing Ike the necessity of saying anything.

Under the cover of laughter, Effie's voice intruded on his thoughts. "How are you this morning?"

She knows. Of course she did. She knew everything that happened onboard. "I've had better nights." He kept a smile on his face for Blanche's benefit in case she happened to glance in his direction.

After the crew finished eating, Blanche stood to her feet. "I want to thank all of you for your patience and support through all that has happened in the past week. I'm sure some of you expected to be back in Roma by now."

A couple of the crew looked at each other and nodded.

"Captain Bruce Pettigrew has agreed to pilot the *Cordelia* until we make permanent arrangements. I'm sure you will make him as welcome as you have made me." She brought her hands together, and the others joined in clapping.

The salon emptied after she dismissed the crew. Ike tried to slip away, but Blanche motioned for him to stay. Effie remained as well. Elaine withdrew to the sink with the breakfast dishes. Blanche poured herself a fresh cup of coffee. "Let's change tables." She led them to a back corner, away from both the kitchen and the salon door.

"You're going ahead with the return to Roma." Ike decided to be direct. "So that means I'm coming with you."

"I have to get back to Roma. So do most of the crew. This is the most reasonable way to do it." Blanche's lips thinned, but her voice remained steady. "It will be a straight trip, no stops at any of the towns, and we're not carrying passengers. I trust that will limit your temptations of the games of chance you insist on playing."

"We'll lose money." He blurted the words out.

"Nevertheless, that is my decision."

Ike could swear she had tears in her eyes to match the wobble in her voice.

"I would rather be broke than be a stumbling block to others and take food out of the mouths of their families."

Ike didn't have a response to that. He hadn't left anyone penniless that he knew of. As far as he was concerned, that was their responsibility, not his.

Effie ran her fingers along the table, humming to herself, the way she did when she was thinking. "I have an idea about how we might increase profits."

Blanche widened her eyes and leaned forward. "Tell us."

Effie shook her head. "I need to think it through. I'll have something for you tomorrow."

"I'll look forward to it." Blanche settled back. "I'll be spending as much time as possible with Captain Pettigrew, once he arrives."

Ike started to speak, but she swept on. "In case I decide to stay, I will prepare to qualify as a pilot. I also want to look at the ship's accounts. Let's meet again tonight. In your cabin. It's too public in here."

"Is there anything you need me to do today?" He was prepared to crawl on the floor if she asked.

Blanche's mouth screwed in concentration. "Go through the captain's clothing. If there is anything that you can use, take it. Or if there are any personal mementos, set them aside to ask me. Effie, I need you to do the same thing."

At her dismissal, they each went their separate ways. He and Effie had a roof over their heads for a few more days. Ike felt light-headed with relief, a prisoner granted a stay of execution.

Chapter 29

"Y ou'll do well." Like Old Obie, Captain Pettigrew kept a light hand on the wheel and a sharp eye on the river. "Obadiah was right. You have a feel for the river."

Blanche glanced up from the compass she was studying. After the grueling session he had put her through, she didn't expect the compliment. "Truly?"

"Miss Lamar." The captain was painfully polite. "I have trained many pilots in my day. You already know as much as that wood-headed Ike Gallagher, even though he's spent a lifetime on the river." He tapped the wheel. "I refer of course to his ability to pilot the boat. He is an excellent businessman. You couldn't have a better partner."

Those words brought a cough to Blanche's lips. "That remains to be seen. This is all so new to me."

"The Bible says that when we are weak, that's when Christ shows His strength in us. He doesn't want a know-it-all. He wants men and women who will depend on Him for everything."

Blanche tried the compass one more time. For a second, she thought she had figured it out. Then her arm quivered and the needle turned before she had determined the direction. "My mother said the same thing. But everything that's happened since her death has tested me in ways I never experienced before."

"God puts us in new circumstances to test us. You don't have to know all the answers. You just need to know who to ask."

The sextant clattered as Blanche picked it up. Captain Pettigrew turned his attention on her for a second. "Call it a night. Tomorrow is another day."

Blanche rolled her shoulders, stretching her muscles. "That sounds wise." She stowed the compass and sextant. "I'll see you midmorning then. I have more material to cover with Ike and Effie." With a last glance at the river, she headed down the stairs as Ike was coming on deck. He looked impossibly handsome in his gray suit and natty red bow tie. A grin crossed his face when he spotted her.

"Blanche." He sprinted across the deck to join her. "I've gone through Old Obie's things, found a few things that might fit me. But I also found this." He held up a slender book. "His personal ledger." He gestured for Blanche to walk with him. On this return trip, the deck was only half loaded with cargo. They had a lot of space to walk.

"I hope you don't mind, but I looked at it. I was looking for clues about where Old Obie did his personal banking. His business account is with a bank in Brownsville, but he kept his personal account in Roma." He paused and opened the book to the front flap, which held a small bankbook.

Blanche's interest stirred at the idea of an account in Roma. Perhaps there was a little money to help tide all of them over until they found other paths in their lives.

"The thing is." Ike withdrew the bankbook and slid his finger between the first two pages. "There are two names on the account."

Not Ike, or he wouldn't be so surprised. Surely not. . .another wife? Bile rose in Blanche's throat.

"The first name is, of course, Jedidiah Obadiah Lamar. The second name. . .is Cordelia Adams Lamar."

Cordelia? "My mother?" Blanche wondered if her face paled as much as the patches of light wood beneath the places where pallets of cargo usually waited.

Ike nodded. "Regular deposits but no withdrawals that I see." He placed the book in Blanche's hands.

Blanche read the lists of credits and debits, deposits, but no withdrawals. She wobbled on her feet.

Ike led her to a stack of crates, the right height for her to sit on. Adjusting her skirts around her, she held the book out to Ike with trembling hands. "I had no idea he'd been sending money all along."

"It appears so, yes."

"Will the surprises never end?" Blanche looked over the side of boat without seeing anything on the riverbank. "Every time I think I have things figured out, I learn something new. My mother never did anything with this money. We lived on her income. I'm sure of it." Neither had sorting her mother's belongings revealed any hidden stashes of money.

"He always loved you, Blanche. And he continued to provide for your mother as well. He was an honorable man."

"So I'm learning." Blanche estimated the total amount of money withdrawn over the five-year span. Over five hundred dollars. "I wonder if there are earlier ledgers." Drawing a shaky breath, she added, "Thanks for showing this to me. Of course I'll split it among the three of us."

Ike just shook his head. The dinner bell sounded. "Ready?" At her nod, he extended his arm.

Music Blanche didn't recognize floated through the salon door.

"Effie's been in there most of the afternoon." Ike opened the door for Blanche. "She used to do that when she was upset. She said playing the piano helped her to feel better."

"I thought she was doing better." Blanche took a step in the direction of the piano then thought better of it. "It comes in waves, though. For all of us." The words brought renewed grief over her, for the father who had provided for his daughter, sight unseen.

At their entrance, Effie turned around and smiled. "Look who's here."

She stepped away from the piano bench and touched the back of each chair as she moved toward the center of the long table. "It's nice when we can all eat together, isn't it?"

Whatever emotions she had processed while playing the piano, Effie seemed in good spirits now. "I made good progress this afternoon." Her voice held a hint of breathless excitement. "How has your day gone?"

"Interesting." Blanche left it at that. She wanted to tease Effie's secret from her, but she doubted she would succeed. Instead, she'd enjoy this meal without all the worries and secrets and uncertainties that had dominated the past few days. At least she would try.

Ike awoke on Wednesday morning with two things on his mind: curiosity about Effie's plan—and a determination to make things right with Blanche.

Effie only stayed in the dining salon long enough to wolf down a soft-boiled egg and a couple of slices of toast before she excused herself. "Come ahead to the theater when you are ready."

Her departure left Blanche and Ike in a cocoon. Around them, the crew laughed and chattered. He broke a strawberry muffin in half and buttered it. After he took a bite, butter chased the tasty crumbs down his throat. Clearing his throat, he leaned forward. "I need to ask your forgiveness for what I did the other night."

Her eyes flashed. "You mean, the. . ."

He nodded. "For everything. I still disagree with your decision, but I was wrong to go ahead when you believed I would stop." Now came the last part, the hardest part. "I promise it won't happen again."

Hope flickered in her eyes then disappeared. *She doesn't believe me.* Why should she? Ike would earn her trust day by day, week by week, by behaving in an honorable manner. If she let him have that long.

Warmth just shy of trust shone in her eyes. "Thank you for saying that to me. I know it was difficult for you. 'I'm sorry' is always hard to say, so thank you."

The chatter flowing around them slowed, and they ceased their personal conversation. Blanche drank a cup of coffee with evident relish. "Are you ready to learn what Effie has for us? She seems very excited."

As they neared the theater, more of the unknown music piped through the open door. Effie repeated the same section several times, and Ike wondered if she was trying to commit it to memory.

Blanche approached Effie. "I like that song. What are the words? Or are there words?" She hummed the melody Effie had been playing.

"There are." Effie's smile widened. "Let me explain what I have in mind." She swiveled around the piano bench, her face alight with enthusiasm. "I've had the most marvelous idea. Blanche, you are committed to stopping the gambling; and Ike, you're worried about how to make up the difference in income."

Ike and Blanche exchanged an uneasy glance. "I've promised I won't do it again."

"But you are still worried." Blanche laid a gentle hand on his arm. "I know you have the best intentions, but I just can't allow it. What do you have in mind, Effie?"

"Instead of offering gambling to a handful of guests, why not invite the people of Roma to come to dinner and a play aboard the boat, the nights that we are in town? Elaine thrives on cooking for banquets. We can easily fit one hundred fifty people in here. If we hold four performances in a weekend—we could do five or even six if we gave performances on Sunday as well, but I know you would object—we could make quite a bit of money."

Blanche looked at Ike, neither one of them having any idea how to respond. "And the music?"

"An idea I have for the first show. A musicale, about Noah and the ark. Perfect for a boat setting." Her laughter delighted his ears.

Intrigued, Ike said, "Sing the words."

Effie ran through several songs. One recorded Noah's argument with God. "Build me an ark of gopher wood. But God, what is this rain You're talking about? Build me an ark." Another reminded Ike of the children's song about Old MacDonald's farm, one that imitated the animal sounds. A piano solo echoed rain pounding on the wood of the boat, the roof, the walls, the surface of the river.

"I didn't know you were so talented." Blanche clapped her hands together. "I love it, but I don't have any experience with plays—not unless you count nativity plays at church. Do either of you? Would we have to hire actors? Or do any members of the crew have unexpected talents?"

Effie waved her concerns away. "You and Ike would play the title roles. You might not have heard him sing, Blanche, but my brother has a good voice."

Ike shut his mouth. "I didn't volunteer."

"I'm your sister." Effie wasn't concerned. "I've drafted you. We could hold auditions for the other parts; and I wondered if Captain Pettigrew would be willing to do God's voice in the play."

"He certainly has a lovely, deep voice." Blanche leaned forward. "But I told you. I don't know a thing about theater."

"You'll learn. I wondered if we could prepare the play for a premiere when we arrive in Roma. I know that's only a few days away, but I believe we can do it if we start right away."

"With a small cast, we could offer the performance at other towns on the river route." Blanche looked thoughtful. Her eyes were completely serious as she turned to Ike. "How do you feel about playing Noah?" She held up a hand. "I'm not criticizing you. But such a play has spiritual implications." She let out a self-deprecating laugh. "If you don't believe the truth, can you at least act well enough to convince everyone else?"

The words Effie had spoken echoed in his head. "Build me an ark of gopher wood, Noah. But God. . ." Ike was stuck in the "but God" phase. "I can try. You will have to be the judge of how effective I am."

"Then will you announce auditions at luncheon today? For anyone who is interested to come to the theater after dinner tonight? And I'll need your help, Blanche, in writing the scripts I've written in my head."

"Yes."

Effie's crazy idea gave both women purpose for the day. He consulted with them about set construction. His sister's requests for simple animal pens would provide a pleasant diversion of his other duties. "I'll determine ticket prices. Is that acceptable?"

"It sounds like a good idea," Blanche said, and Ike left them to writing the script.

Blanche's nerves tripled as she climbed the steps to the pilothouse. Effie's idea, which seemed so brilliant in the indoor theater, faded as she walked into the light of day. She and Effie agreed Captain Pettigrew would be perfect for God's voice, but she hated to ask even more from him.

"You've neglected me today, Miss Lamar." His voice teased her as she entered.

She edged into the room.

"What is it?" The man seemed to have eyes in the back of his head, much like her father had. Maybe she would acquire the same skill, in time.

"Effie has come up with a wonderful idea to make money for the boat. Dinner and a play, a musicale, based on the story of Noah."

From the side, she saw the captain's left eyebrow rise high. "A play, hmm. Interesting idea. Aboard a steamboat—maybe churn a few miles up and down the river—could be an attractive proposition."

"We would like for you to take part in the play, Captain." She held her breath.

"Me? I have no theater experience."

"You wouldn't even appear on stage. We just want to take advantage of your marvelous bass voice." Blanche smiled and used her most persuasive voice. "You see, God and Noah have an argument when God tells Noah to build an ark."

Captain Pettigrew threw his head back and laughed. "That would have been quite an argument. Who's playing Noah?"

Blanche hesitated. "Effie, um, suggested Ike."

"Ike." The captain stared straight ahead at the river. "If he plays the part of a man of faith—especially one who was willing to argue with God about it—he might think about what it means to him personally. I like it, a lot." He winked at Blanche. "Where do I show up?"

"Ike suggested we hold the rehearsals for your scenes together up here. The performances will be given Thursday, Friday, and Saturday, after we arrive in Roma."

With the major roles covered, Blanche wondered who else

would be interested in participating. Effie said they could use everyone who expressed interest. They needed neighbors, Noah's three sons and their wives, even animals. If no one showed up, the four of them would have to manage.

They needn't have worried. Every member of the crew came through the theater at some point. Either they auditioned, or they sat in the audience and applauded. Smithers proved the surprise of the evening, handling some of the humorous dialogue with a skill unexpected of him. Blanche thought he would be perfect for the role of the officious mayor who refused to listen to Noah's warnings. Even Dame Agatha offered to create costumes from scraps of leftover material.

At the end of the evening, Effie faced the group. "Thank you all for coming this evening. We will announce the cast at breakfast in the morning. We'll also schedule rehearsals around your work schedules and plan for the entire cast to join together in the evenings."

Blanche stood next. "I know this is extra work for all of you. Thank you so much for coming out! We have a lot of work ahead of us in the next few days, but I believe the people of Roma will enjoy our production. And now, I will pray and ask God's blessing on us as we seek to communicate His eternal truth."

Peace permeated the corners of the room after her amen.

God was doing something unexpected, something unexpected indeed.

Chapter 30

The bow shall be in the cloud; and I will look upon it, that I may remember the everlasting covenant between God and every living creature of all flesh that is upon the earth."

Even though Captain Pettigrew repeated the familiar words offstage, Blanche felt as though God Himself was speaking the words of eternal promise. A solemn hush fell over the theater until one brave soul clapped, and then the room rang with applause. The actors who had played the townspeople, including Smithers, walked onto the stage and took a bow. Next the actors who played Shem, Ham, and Japheth, Noah's sons, and their wives, entered to louder applause. Last of all Ike took her hand and swept her onto the stage. The audience stood to their feet, clapping. "Encore!" someone shouted.

They had debated whether Captain Pettigrew should also take a bow; but he had demurred, saying he didn't want to detract from the holiness of God's covenant. In the end his argument won out, although he was mentioned in the credits of the programs they had distributed among the audience.

As the cries for an encore continued, Effie played the introduction to "Build Me a Boat." The chorus and cast joined Blanche and Ike in singing it one more time.

When the applause at last died down, Blanche took her place at the front of room. Although her stomach roiled with butterflies, she focused on first one smiling face then another. Toward the back, she saw the Davenports from Christ the King Community Church. Their facial expressions remained neutral, and Blanche's insides tensed. Once she passed on to the next smiling face, her nerves settled. "Let's offer another round of applause for the composer of tonight's musicale, Miss Effie Gallagher."

Effie stiffened at the piano.

"Take a bow, Effie."

Effie swung around on her piano stool and stood, shock and surprise on her face. When the audience noticed the cane by her right hand, applause grew louder. She bowed and sat back down.

"We will have a repeat performance tomorrow evening and twice on Saturday. Please tell your friends and family." Nods and whispered conversations encouraged Blanche that they would spread the word. After her dismissal, she resisted the temptation to slip out the side door, but instead remained at the front. A few people pushed forward, including the Davenports. The expressions on their faces told her nothing, and she struggled to focus on the person in front of her.

"We'll be back Saturday afternoon, with our children," a matron dressed in a suit in a colorful blue with gray piping gushed. "We wanted to check it out first. It gave me several things to think about. It's not always easy to trust God."

Blanche thought back to the day when Effie had asked, "What will you do when God doesn't seem to come through for you?" Noah might have wondered the same thing, fearing if he would ever get to leave the ark.

The Davenports were next to last in line. Mrs. Davenport embraced her briefly before stepping back.

"I must confess I was surprised when I heard about this performance," Reverend Davenport's voice rumbled.

"I told him, there must be some mistake. Cordelia's daughter wouldn't be involved with anything so worldly."

The joy drained from Blanche.

"I was pleasantly surprised that there were a few redeeming qualities in the play. I will not speak against it." Reverend Davenport nodded his head as if his lack of condemnation should please Blanche, but her heart ached for more.

"Miss Gallagher did an excellent job in capturing the spirit of the biblical account." Captain Pettigrew entered from the wings, now that the audience had wandered out. "I had misgivings myself, until I read the script."

The man behind the Davenports—dressed in a somber dark suit but with a welcoming smile—stepped forward. "I have to agree. 'Build Me a Boat.' Pa-rum-pa-pa-pum." He hummed the melody. "I believe I'll be singing that tune the next time I have to hammer something together. My compliments to Miss Gallagher." He bent in her direction then took her hand and kissed it. Effie giggled.

"I am Ronald Sanders. Former gentleman of the stage and now a preacher for the Lord." He sounded more like an actor than a preacher like Reverend Davenport. "I have often despaired that God could use anything from my former life, but you have shown me differently."

Blanche looked from Sanders to the Davenports to Captain Pettigrew. The differences of opinions didn't help clarify the decision she must make.

Mr. Sanders said it had helped him. Despite his old-fashioned hairstyle, bushy eyebrows, and long sideburns, kindness shone from his eyes, the love and joy of Christ. "I'm glad our little play helped you, Mr. Sanders. Are you pastoring a church in Roma?" She didn't think she had met him before, but she didn't know much about the churches of Roma outside of her home fellowship.

Reverend Davenport's frown indicated he hadn't either, and Mr. Sanders confirmed that by shaking his head. "God told me to come to Roma, that someone here needed my help." He winked at her. "Now I am wondering if that person might be you, Miss Lamar. Do you have need of a chaplain? Or perhaps a theater director?"

Mrs. Davenport drew back. "You must have a lot to do. Come see us, if we can help you with anything." She embraced Blanche one last time and left without a backward look.

Blanche wanted to run after them, to chase that expression of disapproval from their faces. But nothing she did now could undo their disappointment in the play.

Blanche shook aside the distraction. "Mr. Sanders, I'd love to discuss your ideas with you. Tomorrow morning? Say, at eleven o'clock?"

"I'll be here, eleven on the dot. It's been a pleasure." With a sweeping bow, he took his departure.

"Don't worry about anything Reverend Davenport has to say. That play of my sister's gave me plenty to think about. It's a different kind of sermon. One that settles on a listener's ear easier than sitting in a church listening to someone drone on in a monotone."

He mimicked Reverend Davenport's tone so perfectly that Blanche couldn't quite stifle her giggle. "It's not that bad." She wouldn't admit how often she had to fight a desire to nap about halfway through his sermons.

"Whatever else Mr. Sanders might be, I doubt he ever speaks in a monotone."

"No, I doubt that." Ike's words had helped restore her good humor. "This idea of Effie's seems to be working. Do you think people downriver would like to see the play?"

"Positively. Does that mean—?"

She nodded. "We'll make one more trip to Brownsville and back."

Ike woke early on Sunday morning. Amazing how much more sleep he was getting since he stopped gambling. If he had any intentions of continuing on the sly, he couldn't have. Either Blanche or Effie stopped by every night, checking on him.

Life aboard the *Cordelia* ran to a different rhythm now—prayers at meals, Sunday services, a mid-week Bible study as well. Blanche had even provided a multivolumed Braille Bible that Effie spent hours reading. The latest volume remained propped open on a corner table in the dining salon. Musicales, plays, and recitations had taken the place of gambling for entertainment. In the week since they had left Roma, they had performed "Build a Boat, Noah" to sold-out crowds every night and enthusiastic requests for a repeat performance when next they came to town. In fact, they made as much money through the plays as he had expected from sponsoring the Bats' exhibition baseball games.

Then again, their expenses had increased; they were paying two additional salaries, for Captain Pettigrew and Mr. Sanders. In addition to serving as ship's chaplain, Sanders took over the role of Noah in the play. The reprieve gave Ike additional time to drum up shipping business.

All in all, business was faring better than he'd feared, but not as well as they needed. On this Sunday morning, he decided to check out the worship service. He chose one of his darker gray suits with a white shirt. Not his favorite, but he thought Blanche would approve.

As he reached the head of the stairs, he encountered Captain Pettigrew headed in the same direction. "Good morning. I thought you gave these Sunday services a miss." Pettigrew had made no work Sundays a condition of his employment, and Blanche had gladly complied.

"I don't have anything better to do." He noticed the Bible in the captain's hand. He hadn't given it a thought. "Go on ahead. I'll join you in a moment." He peeled away from Pettigrew and headed for Old Obie's cabin.

One of the surprises that had come from sorting through

Old Obie's things was the discovery of a worn Bible among his possessions. Ike intended to give it to Blanche; he'd do it after the morning service. A glance at the clock told him he'd miss the first few minutes of the service. He'd bet—not that Blanche would allow him to bet—that she would be happy to see him, late or not.

Music streamed through the open door. One of the young maids scurried down the hall ahead of him and headed into the theater. Had a church service ever been held in a stranger location? Half the congregation was dressed for work, ready to return to the business of the day once the final amen sounded. Most of the passengers attended—that would please Blanche. For the most part, they had dressed in their Sunday best. Theater backdrops remained on the stage. Plush chairs rather than padded pews formed rows for the congregation. Ike slipped onto the last available seat, next to one of the single male passengers, Robert Albertson. Someone he would have recruited for a hand of poker, and here he was attending church.

When they finished the hymn they were singing, Blanche glanced at Ike and smiled. "Next we will sing 'Blessed Be the Tie That Binds.' In my short time aboard the *Cordelia*, I have met many wonderful Christians. The tie that binds us together is indeed a blessing."

Albertson held a hymnal where Ike could see. Hymnals? Where had they come from? No one kept him informed of developments in this Christian business, but things appeared to be going well.

With the presence of Sanders, Ike expected to endure an hour-long sermon. He kept his remarks short, directing their attention to the biblical account of Noah. Even though Ike didn't know much about the Bible, he did know Genesis was the first book. He found the sixth chapter without much trouble.

As Sanders read the verses like the Shakespearean actor he had once been, Ike remembered another reason why he hadn't read the Bible all that often. Full of *thees* and *thous* and *shalts* and verbs ending with *eth*. He preferred plain speaking. A glance around indicated a few others felt the same way.

Then Sanders set down his Bible and began speaking. Preaching, Ike supposed you could call it, but it was neither like the rantings he had heard from some tent evangelists nor the monotone of preachers like Davenport. Nor was it melodramatic posing—what Ike might have expected. No, Sanders spoke as he might to a table of close friends. Humming, he started in on a few words of "Build Me a Boat, Noah." He began clapping; Effie joined him, then Blanche, then Ike as well as everyone else in the back row. Soon everyone was clapping and singing. The place rang with enthusiasm and felt nothing like any church service Ike had ever attended.

Sanders cut them off. He spoke the words of the song. " 'Build Me a boat, Noah.' But Noah didn't have any idea what a boat was. It had never rained before. But God gave him a blueprint, and Noah started building. And *building*."

He laughed. "Now, I know people lived longer in those days than they do today, but even back then, a hundred years was a long time. And that's how long it took Noah to build the ark. A hundred years."

Sanders kept going through the story, singing different parts of the music, pointing out how time after time it wasn't easy for Noah to trust God. "And how about all those months they lived on the boat? With all those animals?" He chuckled. "I've only lived on a boat for one week and my feet are already itching for dry land. I can't imagine what it was like for Noah."

Laughter rippled around the room.

Sanders made it clear that Noah had plenty of reasons to doubt and complain. But he trusted God, no matter how bad everything got. His reward? Rescuing all of his family, not to mention all mankind.

Nothing that had ever happened to Ike could compare to what happened to Noah. The light shining from Blanche's face made sense to him in a way it never had before. Nothing he had ever done, or could ever do, would bring that expression to her face. He couldn't compete with her faith—but could he share it?

He found himself fidgeting in his chair and biting his lip. Not because he was bored—but because he wasn't. He wanted to put his fingers in his ears, to stop the words cascading down his eardrums to his heart. Surveying the theater for needed improvements helped pass the time. The sound of shuffling feet, Effie moving to the piano, broke into his attention and he noticed everyone around him was bowing their heads. Sanders finished his final prayer with a loud "amen," not a moment too soon.

Ike stood with the others and slipped through the door, unnoticed. The always-moving, unpredictable but at least familiar, river would restore him to balance.

Blanche hoped to greet Ike, but he disappeared before she could reach him. Something in his face tugged at her heart, as if he was taking a good look at his soul for the first time. But he left before she had made her way past the first row. With a final glance at the door, she approached the preacher. "That was an excellent sermon, Reverend Sanders. When I think about what Noah had to face, and the comparatively minor problems I have encountered, I am put to shame."

"We all feel that way. He's an example, a demonstration of what faith in God looks like." He gestured with his hands then clapped them together. "I'll stop before I start preaching again."

The people around them laughed. Blanche said good-bye to the gathering and went in search of Ike. No sign of him lingered in the hallway or the dining salon. Her footsteps led to his cabin, but she left without knocking. If he was there, she didn't want to disturb him. She headed on deck. He might be up in the pilothouse, or perhaps in what she had come to call his thinking spot. Only one silhouette appeared in the pilothouse, so she headed for the prow of the ship.

She took two, three, half a dozen steps in his direction, her shoes making soft clipping sounds on the floor. His shoulders stiffened but he didn't turn around.

When only a yard separated them, she stopped. "Ike?"

He kept his gaze on the sky. "Looks like we're in for a bad storm. What happens if we have a Noah-sized rain?"

Chapter 31

Gray clouds scudded across the sky, whipped into a frenzy by lightning striking the earth to the east. "It looks bad." Blanche heard the thread of fear in her voice. "What are storms like on the river?"

"The boat will rock a little bit. If it gets bad, we can stop forward progress and drop an anchor."

"Is that what my father would have done?"

She felt the shrug through his suit jacket. "Probably not. But he had a lifetime of experience on the river. And he did shut down the engines once or twice."

An overnight stop now would mean a day's delay in their arrival in Brownsville. Three more meals. Another day's expenses. The time she had spent pouring over the account books had revealed how close to the bone the boat ran. "Captain Pettigrew is a good pilot. We'll continue running unless he decides it is dangerous. I'll ask him to take over at the helm after dinner. Before, if the weather deteriorates."

"Wise course." The corner of Ike's lips lifted in a smirk. "Why not go full steam ahead and trust God to keep us all safe?"

His eyes expressionless, she couldn't tell if he was serious or joking. "Trusting God doesn't mean being foolish."

"I don't know. From what Sanders said today, it sounds like it was pretty foolish for Noah to build that boat."

A definite challenge. "That was different. God spoke to Noah directly."

"So God doesn't speak to you today?"

Blanche bit her lip. *Give me wisdom. And patience.* "Not in the same way. We have the Bible." A bit of humor wouldn't hurt. "And I have never read in the Bible about steamboats or the Rio Grande River or even the great state of Texas."

"Touché." He smiled that strange half-grin again. "Would you like for me to quiz you on the pilot's test after we eat?" Captain Pettigrew had agreed to work a maximum of three months; she dedicated time each day to earning her license before he left.

Blanche gave thought to the safety of her cabin, but life as the owner didn't allow for self-indulgence, at least not on a day with a looming thunderstorm. "Yes." A single drop of rain fell on her face. "Perhaps I can take the wheel for a few minutes before the weather gets too bad." She laughed nervously. "I have to learn how to manage the boat in all kinds of circumstances."

Three hours later, she debated the wisdom of that decision. Pete was more than happy to let her take his shift at the helm. Since Ike was a licensed pilot, although he seldom worked in that role, he could supervise Blanche. She stood on a crate, an adaptation her father had recommended to make up for her short stature. The additional height didn't make up for the cascading rain. She found herself trying to look between raindrops—an impossible task. "I'm afraid I'm going to miss changes in the river."

"Want to quit?" Ike lifted an eyebrow.

"Captain Pettigrew said he would come up if he felt it got too bad." She took a shaky breath. "But if this isn't bad, I don't know what is."

"Your faith in God isn't up to the task?"

Leave God out of it. Squinting, she didn't respond.

Ike put his hands on her shoulders and rubbed her sore muscles. "Relax. Look at the whole tree, not the leaves."

"I'll try."

After that, Ike remained quiet. Blanche's shoulders kept rising, tensing her entire body until a soft touch of his hand reminded her to relax. Even so, her muscles would feel sore in the morning. She'd resort to willow bark tea and soak in hot water. Rain lashed against the front window, giving both sky and river a rippled effect. The sun disappeared from view, melding white sky to gray horizon that gradually darkened to the same shade.

After half an hour by the hourglass, the pattern of the rain changed, and she called for an increase of power. The *Cordelia* plowed her way through the spot, and Blanche called for a return to normal speed.

"Well done." Ike clapped twice. "Old Obie was right, you know. You have a real feel for the river."

She rolled her shoulders. "Thank you."

After that, she felt more comfortable as she made small adjustments in direction or power. The dinner bell sounded.

"Do you want me to call Captain Pettigrew when I go to dinner?"

Blanche stared out the window, debating how much time remained before the sky turned a blinding black. "I can wait until after he eats."

When the captain arrived after dinner, Blanche accepted his hand in getting down from the crate. Her legs trembled more than she liked, but she felt exhilarated.

"You go get a bite to eat, warm up some." Captain Pettigrew stood behind the wheel as if the rain didn't bother him in the least. "Do you want to keep watch with me tonight?"

Blanche blinked. "That sounds good. I've only been here one other night."

"I'll see you later then." He crammed his captain's hat on his head and nodded, turning his full attention out the front window.

"How do you feel?" Ike welcomed her to the dining salon.

"Tired enough to sleep for a week." She thought about it a bit more. "And excited enough to stay awake until Christmas morning."

That earned a laugh. "I know the feeling."

The smell of chicken soup drew Blanche like a magnet. Ike brought out two steaming bowls with a plate of crusty rolls. Elaine came to the window. "What can I get you to drink?"

Blanche was about to ask for a glass of cold milk, but then thought about the long night ahead of her. "Better make that black coffee. I want to stay awake and alert tonight."

She breathed in the steam from the soup. "It smells wonderful."

She spooned it quickly and cleaned the bottom of the bowl with a roll.

When she finished her first bowl, he exchanged it for a fresh serving. Ashamed by the speed with which she ate a single bowl of soup, ordinarily enough for an entire meal, heat slammed into her cheeks. She ate the second with more ladylike decorum.

Ike studied her with undisguised humor. "Do you want to rest before you go back to the pilothouse?"

Blanche considered. "I'm afraid that if I lie down, I won't get up again before morning." She poured another cup of coffee, her third, and drained it before wrapping a couple of rolls in a napkin. "I'll chew on these if I get sleepy."

"Do you want me to come with you?" Hands square on the table, eyes level with hers, Ike gave no hint of his preference.

She should leave him alone and let the Holy Spirit do His work. "That's not necessary. I'm just there to watch, and Captain Pettigrew will answer any questions that I have."

Ike started to object, but Blanche raised a hand. "If it's a question about the *Cordelia* that only you can answer, we'll get you right away. Or if possible, I'll ask you tomorrow. Take the rest of the day off. And thank you for all the ways you've helped me today."

Smiling, he held on to her hands. Then he leaned forward and kissed her briefly on the cheek. He withdrew, sketched a wave, and walked toward the staircase leading to the cabin level.

Blanche stared after him, her hand cupping her cheek where he had kissed it. *Oh, Ike.* Her prayers for him doubled, but it seemed as if the overcast sky held her thoughts earthbound.

Once she joined Captain Pettigrew in the pilothouse, she

focused on the worsening weather. Thunderstorms had never bothered Blanche. Before now. Before she was on the water. Before each strike of lightning felt like it would break the glass and knock them down. Before the wind rocked the room at the top of the boat in a constant seesaw.

"Should we stop the engines?" She had to shout to make herself heard.

He shook his head. "That would create more problems than it would solve. It's better if we run with the wind and steer clear of any problems with the river." He flashed white teeth at her in a blast of lightning. "And pray with your eyes open."

"I'm already doing that." She hadn't stopped praying since she arrived on deck. Crossing the few feet from the indoor stairway to the door to the pilothouse had left her soaked to her unmentionables. If she hadn't memorized the route from previous trips, she doubted she could have found the door. Rain pounded her skin, causing her to close her eyes against the onslaught.

Wind whistled overhead, rattling the ceiling and windows. "Will the glass break?"

"It might." Pettigrew pulled the bell, alerting the engine room to a slight change in speed. "Can't worry about that now."

Blanche spared a thought for the danger broken glass would pose. But she was here to learn, not to tremble in fear. "Why did you tell them to decrease speed?"

"Wind is pushing us along. We need less steam to keep the boat moving at the same speed." He tugged the wheel one spoke to the right. "If we were going in the other direction, we'd increase power instead."

Lightning crashed and thunder sounded immediately. A lack of power wasn't the problem on this evening.

In the wake of that spontaneous, spectacular kiss, Ike stumbled on the first step. He straightened himself, but he couldn't do anything about the silly grin on his face. He had kissed women before, several of them, but none of them made him feel like that innocent caress of Blanche's cheek. He lifted his foot to take the second step when the boat rolled underneath him. The storm had risen another notch. He skipped down the steps two at a time to reach the bottom as quickly as possible.

At the bottom step, the boat lurched again, throwing him to the floor. Down the corridor, Effie opened the door to the girls' cabin. "Is everyone okay?"

Ike stood and dusted himself off. "It's just me."

A frown creased Effie's face. "I thought I heard something fall down. The rocking motion is tossing things around my cabin. I've put a few things in my dresser drawers."

"It's pitching badly." This time when the boat swung, he braced himself against the wall. "Anything broken?"

"Not yet. Isn't Blanche with you?"

"Captain Pettigrew asked her to stay with him during the storm. She wants to learn how to pilot the boat in all kinds of weather."

"Oh." Effie's shoulders slumped. "I might as well go to bed. If the wind doesn't toss me out of my berth." For a moment, she reminded him of the little girl who was scared of staying alone for the first six months they lived aboard the boat.

"Would you like me to stay with you for a while?"

"Would you mind?" Her words offered an out, but she was already opening the door to let him in.

Her bag of knitting sat tucked under her chair. "I tried working on the sweater, but after I jabbed myself once and lost stitches twice, I decided I better put it away."

"And on the desk, is that the Bible Blanche got for you?"

"Yes. I was reading the story of Noah again. And it was a little frightening, with the storm tonight."

Thunder rumbled through the deckboards overhead, and she shrank away.

"Stop reading before you give yourself nightmares."

"If that happens, I'll come running to my big brother."

Thunder, or perhaps waves, shook the cabin, and Effie trembled. Ike planted himself behind Effie and placed his arms around her shoulders. "Shh, I've got you."

Her shivering continued. After the next crash of thunder subsided, she asked, "Ike, would you pray? For our safety?"

Her simple request yanked him back by fifteen years. Their mother lay dying in another room, and she asked him to pray. When God didn't answer that prayer, he had stopped praying.

"For you, Effie, anything." At church, people bowed their heads and closed their eyes when they prayed, but Ike felt more natural speaking with his eyes open. He looked at the ceiling, where thunder crashed and the boat shook.

"God. According to the Bible, it'll never rain for forty days and nights again. I guess I should thank You for that. But even shorter storms can turn deadly, and You didn't say anything about them. So I ask You first of all for the lives of the people on this boat."

"Amen." Effie whispered.

"And I suppose I should ask You for anybody else crazy enough to be on this river tonight. Or on the riverbanks, if it floods.

"Then I guess my mind rushes to things. Does that make me selfish? I don't care, not a lot. We need to deliver our cargo safely to make a profit. We need to make a profit for us not to run a gambling game. And You want us to work for our food, right? Well, if we lose the cargo, that's going to be hard. So I ask that things won't get broken or wash overboard."

Effie reached up and patted his hand, as if reassuring him that his prayer was acceptable.

"And I pray for Captain Pettigrew and Blanche. Effie, too. I know she's scared. So I ask that You will take away that fear."

He paused. "I guess I can't think of anything else. So, how do I say good-bye? I guess Amen."

"Amen," Effie echoed, a sob breaking the word.

Ike's arms tightened around her. "What's the matter?"

"You prayed." Tears moistened his shirt sleeves. "Oh, Ike, are you ready to trust God with your life?"

Ike didn't move or speak. "I think I am. Who would have believed it?"

"Me. God. Blanche. Mr. Sanders. Lots of people." She laughed through her tears. "No time like the present to ask Him to save you."

He couldn't fight it any longer. He and God had been waging war ever since he first saw Blanche at Christ the King Church, and

God had won. He stifled the desire to fold his hands and bow his head. Now if ever he wanted to face God like a man. Raising his face to heaven and lifting empty hands to accept God's gift, he reopened his dialogue with God.

"God, I know I'm a sinner. I never pretended to be anything else. Not the worst, but I'm not a good person either, and besides, I hear that doesn't matter to You. You sent Your Son to die for me. Will You forgive me for all the things I've done wrong, please?"

He squeezed Effie's shoulder. "Is there anything else I should say?"

"God sees your heart. There are no perfect words."

"Well then, I guess that's it. Again. So. . .amen."

Thunder crashed again, and Effie laughed. Ike joined her.

"I guess that's God's answer."

"What, a big no?"

"No, silly. Amen! Exclamation point!"

A big grin split Ike's face to the breaking point. "Exclamation point! I like that." He jumped to his feet.

"Careful, now." Effie's tears had stopped, her fears at bay. "I don't know if that prayer will protect you from sheer foolishness."

The ship pitched, slamming him against the wall. The loudest crack of the night sent shudders through the ship. The nightstand tilted, throwing the lantern off. Ike caught it with his hands, heart in his mouth. *Fire.* He blew it out, the sudden darkness disorienting him. A sharp crack ripped through the air.

"Effie."

"I know. You have to go."

"I have to find out what happened."

He took a lantern in his hands and doused each lamp as he went down the hallway. He knocked on the doors. "Anyone hurt? Turn out the lights." His heart urged him to get up to the pilothouse, to Blanche, but the danger of fire couldn't be overlooked.

God, if ever we needed help, it's now.

Chapter 32

Lightning shimmered off the water and raced to the boat. Shivering, Blanche couldn't manage much of a prayer beyond *I'm scared, God.* The fear didn't go away, but she gained control of it, trusting God to look over the boat and all its inhabitants. Short breaths interspersed with quick glances out the window. The boat headed straight into the heart of the storm. Lightning traveled through water, didn't it? That meant she was more in danger from the storm on the boat than on land.

When Blanche was a little girl, a tornado had ripped through Roma. Wind whipped sand in the air as they rushed to the storm cellar. Below ground she could hear but not see the wind devastating the town.

Tonight she could both see and hear the wind. The mixture of wind and water could turn over this sturdy boat as easy as a house made of matchsticks.

Lightning struck so close that it blinded her. The boat heaved to one side, sending her into the wheel. Captain Pettigrew groaned, and she heard the sound of him hitting the floor. Hearing replaced sight as thunder crashed and a loud crack suggested something had broken.

Grasping the wheel, she pulled herself upright and sight returned. Miraculously, the windows remained intact; and the boat appeared headed on a straight course. She turned, expecting Pettigrew to take charge of the wheel.

He lay slumped against the captain's table, blood seeping from his forehead, his eyes closed. "Captain! Captain!" Panic laced her voice.

A moan greeted her cry. *He's alive.*

The need to keep her eyes on the river battled with the need to attend to the man lying on the floor. Deciding she'd have to chance it, she knelt down. "Captain?"

His eyes fluttered open. "Can't. . .move. . .my arm. You have to pilot the boat."

"Me?" Blanche's stomach flipped. Piloting the boat on a calm sunny day was one thing. A night when storm filled the skies was another matter indeed. "I haven't even taken the test yet."

"Noah didn't need a test when God called him to pilot the ark."

With a pleading eye on Captain Pettigrew, Blanche dragged the crate behind the wheel.

"Keep your eye sharp out there. Don't worry about me." He grunted, a cry of pain, and Blanche jerked her head to keep from turning around to see what had happened.

"It's my job to pray while you man the helm. Remember what

I told you. Keep to the middle of the river. If the wind dies down, slow the engines."

Unwilling to trust her voice, she nodded. *I'm not ready for this.* "You need medical attention."

Pettigrew chuckled. "Have you hired a doctor recently? Ike will know who takes care of minor injuries while you're on the river. But you can't leave the wheel and I can't get down there on my own power." Another chuckle. "Besides, I'll be right here if you need to ask me a question." The words stopped, and his breathing rasped.

Lightning flashed again, farther away this time. *Praise God.* The captain cupped his right arm with his left, his face twisted in pain, his eyes closed. The thunder drowned out his breathing.

God, why this? Why tonight, before I'm ready? She channeled her fear into angry questions that helped strengthen her shivering limbs. *You gave Noah one hundred years. I haven't even had a month. Is this all some kind of punishment? Or maybe You're testing me, to see if I'm worthy?*

Her internal argument with God continued unabated while she kept her eyes fixed out the window, when the crate fishtailed beneath her and she had to climb off and reset it behind the wheel again. In between flashes of lightning, she snuck glances at Captain Pettigrew. Despite his brave words, he was in no condition to answer her questions. Had the wind lessened? Was it time to decrease the speed? Not yet.

Blanche needed to get a message to Pete and Ike, but she couldn't leave. They hadn't considered this possibility when they planned the schedule.

I suppose You planned that, too, God.

Where was Ike? She hadn't asked him to come to the bridge tonight, but she missed the security of his presence. *God, send him here tonight.*

She thought she heard the stairs creaking, but when no one came into the pilothouse, she decided it was only the deck shifting in the wind.

So I guess it's just You and me tonight, God.

Another clap of thunder followed, as if God was saying *I'm right here.* What had Reverend Sanders said about Noah's argument with God? That you have to believe in God to argue with Him? She looked at the clouds racing alongside the boat, the lightning striking on the Mexican side of the river. "You are here. Right here with me."

Her grip on the wheel remained strong and steady, but her heart stopped racing as fast as the boat. God was here. She could trust Him.

Ike stood still in the center of the hallway, gauging the motion of the boat. She rocked a little as it might at sea, but nothing felt broken beyond repair. Up until now, he had stayed busy taking care of passengers. People ran in and out of cabins, screaming questions and fighting small fires.

The storm had decreased in power, and he finished his inspection of the cabins. Next he would check the communal areas. In the kitchen he ran into Elaine, her round face gray by lantern light. "I turned off the ovens. It'll be a cold breakfast in the morning."

Ike nodded. "Smart move." Elaine was a veteran of storms on

the river. After the kitchen, he toured the theater. Aside from a few repairs to stage props, the room remained undamaged.

When he put his foot on the staircase leading to the main deck, wind carrying raindrops whistled down the hole. Frowning, he considered going back to his room for a rain slicker. *No.* Someone might interrupt him with another problem. He wanted to check on Blanche and Captain Pettigrew, to reassure himself that the storm had left them unscathed. He hadn't hurried before now because the boat continued to run smoothly.

As he crossed the deck, lightning revealed pieces of a broken crate and other items scattered across the deck. In the pilothouse, a slight, feminine figure stood at the helm. Dark and rain descended again, and he couldn't see where Pettigrew was located.

What the fool was the man doing allowing Blanche to take the helm in weather like this? Keeping the lantern aloft so he could spot obstacles underfoot, he ran up the stairs.

Turning the corner into the room, he almost stumbled over Pettigrew's prone body. For a quick, frightening moment, he wondered if the man had died. Then the captain's chest heaved and a moan came from between his lips.

"Ike?"

Blanche turned her face, white in the bright flash of lightning, a hint of lines at her eyes suggesting she had peered into the heart of the darkness of the sky. He also thought he saw a hint of excitement.

It's the Lord. What would Blanche think if he said that? She might faint alongside Pettigrew, and what a mess that would make of things. "What happened?"

"Captain Pettigrew fell and broke his arm. Since someone had to stay at the helm. . ." She risked a quick glance at Ike then returned her attention to the front window. "I had to take over."

"She's doing a fine job of it, too." A weak voice spoke from the floor.

"You're awake." Blanche shifted her feet beneath her. "I was getting worried about you. Ike, is there someone in the crew who sets bones and such?"

"One of the valets."

"Good. Get him to look after Captain Pettigrew."

Ike hesitated. He had come to offer them his help and support, and she was sending him away?

"Unless you want to take the helm?" She didn't turn around.

"Not him. You. You're doing a good job," Pettigrew said.

"Old Obie would be proud." Ike draped Pettigrew's good arm over his shoulder and helped him to his feet. His right arm dangled at his side, the elbow jutting out at an odd angle.

Ike speared Blanche with his eyes. "I don't like leaving you here alone."

"I'm not alone." Her voice shook the slightest bit.

Ike glanced around the pilothouse. *Who?*

"God." She answered his unasked question. "God reminded me that He is always with me."

Of course. A smile came to his face. He couldn't wait to tell her about his decision, but now wasn't the time. He took her words to his heart.

"Now go. Send Pete up here once you leave the captain with the valet."

Lightning flashed in the distance, accenting her words. "The storm is moving away. I'll be fine."

Ike and Pettigrew had already taken a step down the stairs. She was wrong about one thing; he would come back himself rather than send relief. Until the crisis had passed, he wanted to stay by her side. In good times and bad. The two of them had a lot to talk about.

Somewhere, in the long stretches of the night, Blanche's argument with God turned to praise. With each shift of the wheel, each tug of the bell pull to the engine room, she felt His presence stronger and stronger. Every time lightning illuminated the sky, she remembered lessons her father had taught her. If she could get through this storm without harm to vessel or personnel, she could pass the pilot test with ease.

Lightning flashed to her far left, and she held her breath while she counted under her breath. One Mississippi, two Mississippi. . . She got as far as ten Mississippi before thunder followed. The storm was falling behind them. She pulled the bell to slow the engines.

Ike was sweet, the way he didn't want to leave her to face the big bad storm alone. He hadn't even teased her when she said God was with her. Was it possible? No. God had given them one miracle in bringing her through this storm. She couldn't expect Ike to change his soul-deep beliefs after such a short time.

She jerked her mind back from the subject, rejecting the distraction. What she needed was a cup of coffee. Weariness warred with her stamina. When Captain Pettigrew and Ike were in the room, she could carry on a conversation. Of course she could talk with God, but it wasn't the same.

Sing. That worked in the past when she needed help focusing. She envisioned the hymnal from Christ the King church. Starting with the front piece, she sang the doxology. "Praise Father, Son, and Holy Ghost." Also inside the front cover she envisioned the Apostles' Creed and the Nicene Creed. She scrunched her eyes in concentration then forced them open to keep her eyes on the river.

The first hymn, "Holy, Holy, Holy," repeated the cry of the angels in front of the emerald throne from Revelation. She sang through hymns of praise, sometimes singing one verse, sometimes all of them, humming when she couldn't remember the words. With each song, the time between lightning and thunder grew further apart. By the time she got to "Praise to the Lord, the Almighty!" she realized she hadn't seen any lightning for a few minutes, and she caught a glimpse of the moon as the wind blew the clouds away.

Praise the Lord. They had survived.

Chapter 33

The back of Ike's eyes felt like sandpaper, but his heart was as soft as cotton. The night had ended and the storm had passed. He and Blanche planned to walk the ship from stem to stern, to determine what damages the *Cordelia* had sustained. Elaine had changed her mind and relit the oven for a hot breakfast. Never had grits, crisp bacon, and orange juice tasted so good skipping down his throat.

"We should get going." Blanche wore her old, sensible black traveling suit, but Ike didn't blame her. He had donned Levi's himself. Water, mud, splinters—he suspected they would find all of that, and more, from what the watery moonlight revealed last night.

"We have time to finish another cup of coffee." Ike poured them each a fresh cup and grabbed a couple of peach muffins for good measure. "I asked Effie to join us."

Blanche blinked. "I thought you would want to check everything right away." She made no effort to leave the table.

"I do, but I have something I need to tell you first. And here's Effie." The door opened and Effie took a seat at the table. "I have coffee and muffins for us to celebrate."

Blanche stirred cream into her coffee. "What are we celebrating? Surviving the storm?"

"That's part of it." Effie nudged Ike in the side. "Tell her."

Blanche set the spoon back on the napkin. "What is it?"

Ike couldn't keep the scowl on his face, and a smile broke out. "Effie asked me to pray during the storm."

"And he did."

A smile as brilliant as sunshine lit Blanche's face. "That's wonderful. Amazing!" She grabbed one of the muffins and split it open.

Another nudge poked him in the ribs.

"And then I realized—with Effie's help, of course"—he patted her hand—"if I believed in God enough to think He'd care about us in the middle of a storm, and if I believed He had enough power to do something about it. . .then I must believe the rest of it, too."

Blanche slowly spread butter on her muffin that melted into the surface while her smile grew even bigger. "You mean. . ."

"I asked Jesus to be my Savior. I've joined the good guys, or I guess, God made me one."

The butter knife slipped from Blanche's hand and clanged against the plate as she clapped her hands. Her cheeks grew fever pink, and her breath came in little gasps. She swallowed a couple of times and drank from her water glass. When she finally spoke, her voice came out in a whisper. "Praise God. Oh, praise God." Tears sparkled in her eyes. "I doubted God." Her laugh came out as a hiccup. "You seemed, well, different, last night, and I wondered if something had happened."

"But you didn't think I would ever change my mind?" Ike didn't blame her. "I didn't think so, either."

This time the tears slid from her eyes down her cheeks. "I told God He had performed one miracle already, helping me pilot the boat. I didn't want to be greedy and expect two miracles in one night. But He was, He is always, gracious and compassionate and giving. He gives more than we can ask or think."

Standing, Blanche put an arm around Effie and then Ike. "I had no idea why God brought me to this boat. I felt so alone. But when Effie came back to the Lord, He gave me a sister. . ." She squeezed Effie's shoulder as she said the words. "And then a father." She sniffed back a tear. "And now a brother."

Ike forced a smile as his heart sank. Her *brother*?

"The family of God," Effie said.

"Adopted by the Father and coheirs with Christ. This *does* call for a celebration." She sat back down and ate the muffin in tiny bites. "Do you have a Bible?"

"I found a Bible in Old Obie's cabin. I thought I could borrow it, if you don't mind."

Blanche nodded. "That's a good idea. Effie and I are studying the Bible together at night, some basic information new believers need to know. Do you want to join us?"

"An instruction course in how to be a Christian?"

"Nothing that fancy." Blanche laughed. "But a lot of people get bogged down if they start in Genesis and try to read through the Bible. Or maybe you should meet with Mr. Sanders."

"Or both?" He grinned.

"Good idea."

They finished the muffins and polished off the pitcher of coffee. Effie stacked their plates and headed for the kitchen. "What do you think about holding a service this evening, thanking God for bringing us safe through the storm?"

"Of course." Blanche giggled. "And Ike, you'll even want to come."

"Amen." Ike used his best actor's voice. With a chuckle, he said, "Can you believe it?"

"I'll get together with Reverend Sanders then." Effie stood. "And I have some ideas for a new play that I want to think about."

"My little sister." Ike shook his head. "You are amazing." He offered his arm to Blanche. "Shall we?"

Blanche leaned on his arm as they walked out of the dining salon. "I want to check on Captain Pettigrew first. And we need to come up with a schedule to pilot the boat until we arrive in Brownsville." She paused, her hand on his arm holding him back. "Do you think I'm ready to take the test for my pilot's license?"

Ike threw back his head and laughed. "I'd say anybody who brought the boat through that storm already passed the real test. You're more than ready."

"I want to arrange for it as soon as possible then. Captain Pettigrew can't work until his arm heals. We're back where we were before we hired him. We need another pilot."

"We'll have to stop at night until we take care of that." Ike nodded. "I've thought of that. It's a good thing we're only a couple of days away from the mouth of the river."

The sling on Pettigrew's arm couldn't hide his pain. "I'm sorry to leave you in a lurch."

"And I feel terrible about your broken arm." Blanche took the chair next to the berth.

"Don't worry about that." With his good arm, Pettigrew waved away her concern. "God will work it all out."

"For both of us." After they said their good-byes, Ike and Blanche stopped by each cabin. The furniture had been tossed about, but nothing had broken except a few cracked lanterns, and no one was injured.

Ike made a mental list of needed repairs below deck. "I've seen a lot worse damage in other storms."

He glanced at Blanche, and they spoke at the same time. "God."

Next they headed for the main deck. Fresh cedar scent washed through the air, carrying a refreshing after-rain smell. Blanche drew a deep breath. "I bet the earth smelled like this after the flood."

"And required a lot more cleanup." Ike took her hand and led her toward the cargo hold. A mixed mess greeted them. Most of the heavy crates, tied in place with heavy rope, hadn't budged, but the wind had moved some of the empty pallets. Water stained heavy burlap sacks of flour, sugar, and cornmeal.

"Can we salvage the flour?" Wheat flour didn't grow easily in Texas. Of the different consumables, it was worth the most money.

"I. . .doubt it." She lowered her face and closed her eyes as if in prayer.

Ike also sent up a silent prayer. He supposed God could listen to more than one prayer at a time. Add that question to the list of things he didn't know.

Opening her eyes, Blanche took a resolute step forward. "We'll get someone up here to get a count. Let's see what other damage we're faced with."

A couple of the smaller crates had broken open, but the straw packing had protected most of it. "The foreman can check the number of crates, but it doesn't look like we've lost much. I think the food stuffs is the worst of it." Grimacing, he shrugged his shoulders. "It could be worse." A night or two of cards with Ventura and his friends would make up the difference.

"Thinking about the gambling you gave up?"

Could she read his mind? "I wish I could say no. I don't have a handle on this faith thing."

"None of us do. Even Paul said, 'Not as though I had already attained, either were already perfect.' And Paul had more faith than anyone else in the entire New Testament." She gave a shaky laugh. "So what if we don't have hot bread for a few days? And besides, the plays are bringing in more money than we expected." Turning, she looked Ike straight in the eyes. "Being a Christian doesn't mean everything is easy. But it does mean God is with us through everything that happens."

Ike thought about that. No one could call Blanche's life easy, but her faith in God grew stronger with each challenge. "It will be interesting to hear what everyone has to say at the service tonight. I'm sure we'll hear some tall tales."

Blanche enjoyed listening to the testimonies. More than any time since she had arrived aboard the *Cordelia*, she felt at ease with the members of her crew.

The stories varied from childhood memories of running to her father's lap when she was a little girl—a surprising revelation from the imposing Dame Agatha—to playing baseball during a rainstorm when lightning hit the field—an equally surprising revelation by Smithers.

After everyone who wanted to had shared—only one extremely shy server and a couple of the gruffer stevedores demurred—Ike rose to his feet. "I had a life-changing experience during this storm."

He glanced at Blanche, and she nodded, smiling to encourage him to go forward. He looked handsome as always, dressed in his beige linen suit, a gold brocade vest, and an olive green shirt. Perfect match with his bright blue eyes. Yesterday she had called him her brother, but if she was honest with herself, the feelings growing in heart differed from those for a brother.

"When the storm started last night, I prayed for the first time in a long time. I'm not sure why." Shrugging a single shoulder, he flashed that amazing grin. "Those of you who have been with us on the river for a while know we have these storms from time to time. And I haven't prayed before. But yesterday I did.

"And then I realized that if I trusted God enough to ask Him to save us from the storm, I could trust Him with the rest of my life. And so I did. I asked Jesus to be my Savior."

"Praise the Lawd," Reverend Sanders called out. Around the circle, several people clapped and others added a quiet "amen." Some of the engineers and stevedores exchanged covert looks, probably wondering how life aboard the *Cordelia* would change.

"And I guess. . .that's all." He bowed to another burst of spontaneous applause and sat down.

"I'll share next." Effie rose to her feet with a quiet rustle of fabric. "When the storm kept raging and it became clear we wouldn't get much sleep last night, I made my way to the dining salon. When I felt bad when I was a little girl, I played the piano. I still do." She walked in the direction of the piano. "So last night, I remembered a hymn I heard at a revival service about a year ago." She sat on the stool and began to sing "It Is Well with my Soul." When she reached the chorus, Blanche added the echoing "It is well" in the alto voice, to Effie's strong soprano. Her heart beat strong. *It is well with my soul.* They sang all three verses, ending with the resounding excitement of "Haste the day when my faith shall be sight." They'd have to teach Ike one of the men's parts and sing it at their next Sunday service.

After the resounding amen at the end of the hymn, Effie turned around on the piano stool. "I knew it was a special song as soon as I heard it, but the story is even better. Horatio Spofford had already suffered the loss of a son and of a fortune when his four daughters died in a shipwreck. Only his wife survived. When he said 'when sorrows like sea billows roll,' he was speaking the literal truth." Lowering her head, she dabbed at her eyes. "I have to confess I couldn't have said 'it is well with my soul' or written such beautiful music after I lost my parents, or after Captain Lamar died. But this man did. So last night, while the thunder continued crashing and crates rattled around overhead, I sang Mr. Spofford's song. It is well with my soul, because God is always with me. In the worst storm or on the hottest summer day. In the dining salon or aboard Noah's ark." Twirling the piano seat back to the correct position, Effie made her way back to the congregation.

The crew turned their attention to Blanche. This part of her inheritance still caught her in unexpected ways. Nothing in her life had prepared her to lead a company, but she enjoyed it more than she thought she would.

The closest thing in her past was singing in front of an audience, but it didn't feel the same. The people waiting before her were both employees and her new family, people to whom she was bound by chords of responsibility, concern, and affection. She looked around the room, engaging each pair of eyes for a brief second before moving on. "After everything that's been said, I don't have much to add. I love that hymn. It is well with my soul. I didn't know if I would ever feel that way again after my mother died. I was scared when I first arrived onboard. I didn't know anyone. Even worse, I didn't know if I could trust anyone. But God." To her surprise, tears clogged her throat, and she coughed to clear her throat.

"But God had other plans." Blanche reviewed some of the highlights of her time aboard the *Cordelia*. She found something to say about everyone, although Ike dominated her thoughts.

"Now I hope to become an official pilot. For as long as God permits us to make a living, I look forward to life aboard the *Cordelia*." She sat down amidst enthusiastic applause, and realized she had announced a decision that she wasn't consciously aware she had reached.

Everything was well with her soul, aboard the steamboat *Cordelia*.

God was good.

Chapter 34

One month later

Blanche sat next to Effie at the piano, making a stab at noting the melodies from the new musical on music graph paper.

"Dum, de-dum, dum," Blanche hummed. "Sorry this is taking me so long."

"I'm thrilled someone can write it down." Effie's hand riffled over the keyboard. "I don't think anyone has come up with Braille for music yet."

Blanche giggled. "I'm picturing someone trying to read Braille music and play the piano at the same time."

"That might be hard." Effie repeated the first line again. "I'm glad Mr. Sanders suggested the story of the Israelites crossing the Jordan River and the fall of Jericho for this musical."

"He's preparing a list of all the stories that take place on a river or the sea. We won't run out of ideas for a while."

"Moses in the bulrushes—"

"Jesus calming the storm—"

"Paul's shipwreck—"

"But the walls of Jericho is an exciting story to start with. I can't believe I'm going to be Rahab." Blanche draped a pillowcase across her face like a veil and giggled.

"With Ike as Salmon." Effie kept a straight face. "Rahab's future husband."

Blanche cheeks heated, and she was thankful Effie couldn't see her face. There were times that Effie's blindness was a blessing. "And I can't believe Dame Agatha has offered to make all the costumes we need, so everyone who wants to can march around Jericho."

She wanted to hug herself. God had blessed their showboat drama program so that their financial problems had disappeared for the moment. "We're not getting anything done this way. Go on."

They had already finished the marching song, with the chorus they repeated seven times. This song occurred earlier in the story, when the spies told Rahab about the one true God. Effie had written a haunting melody with memorable harmonies, but Blanche struggled to get them on paper. Half an hour later, she had managed the three voices. "I'll work on the piano part later. If we run out of other things to do."

The first lunch bell rang. "That's all we'll get to today. I'm going to be in the pilothouse this afternoon." Work filled Blanche's days from morning to night, and she loved every minute of it.

Outside the theater door, the thrum of footfalls raced down the hall. Blanche frowned. "Who is making all that noise? There aren't any children onboard this trip."

"Give me a minute to clean up. Then we can go see."

Blanche wanted to go remind—whoever it was—that crew didn't run in the halls. But she wouldn't run out on her friend. Minutes ticked by, the halls grew quiet, and the last warning bell rang.

"I'm ready to go now. Sorry it took me so long today." Even with those words, Effie leisurely stacked papers on top of the piano and took up her cane. If they didn't get to the salon soon, they would delay the meal for everyone else.

Blanche matched Effie's speed as they made their way down the hall to the dining salon. The aroma of saucy beans greeted her nose. She loved beans and cornbread for lunch. Her stomach growled.

Through the door—closed, not propped open the way Blanche had instructed—she heard low murmurs, as if the room was crowded. "I'm afraid we're really late."

"I don't think Elaine will mind." Effie's voice held a hint of laughter as Blanche swung the door open.

"Surprise!"

Every member of the crew not on duty stood in a loose circle around the room. Someone had draped a banner reading "Congratulations, Captain Lamar!" in gigantic red letters across the kitchen window.

"You—you. . ." Blanche stammered.

Ike stepped forward. "I ran into Mr. Roberts from the Board of Examiners when we were in Brownsville the last time, and he told me the news."

Smithers exited the kitchen, bearing a shining silver platter with a thin envelope. Elaine and one of her assistants followed, balancing a cake between them. A single white candle burned brightly in the center.

"Here is your mail, Captain." Smithers smiled. He *smiled*. With the envelope between two thin fingers, he extended it to Blanche.

Two dozen pairs of eyes trained on her. What if. . . Blanche couldn't stand waiting any longer. Grasping the letter opener, she slit the end of the envelope and pulled out a thin sheet of paper. "It's from the Board of Examiners." Blanche read the return address.

"What does it say?" Effie's smile told her she had known about the celebration.

"We are pleased to inform you. . .you are now qualified to pilot a boat on any of the waterways in the state of Texas." The letter dropped from Blanche's hand, her arms, her legs, her shoulders trembling beyond her control. "I'm a pilot." Her voice came out as a squeak.

The room rang with applause.

"Ahoy, Captain."

"Aye, aye, Captain!"

Different calls erupted across the room.

Elaine had positioned the cake on the table. "Blow out the candle." She gestured to the fantastic concoction of flowery frosting and "Captain Lamar" written in blue and red letters. "I know it's not your birthday, but it seemed right."

Heat rushing into her cheeks, Blanche leaned over the center of the table and blew. As nervous as she was, she didn't know if she could expel enough breath to blow out the flame. It flickered and went out.

With a sparkle in his eye, Ike handed her a knife. "Go ahead and cut the cake."

With the knife as long as her forearm, Blanche cut a two-inch corner piece. "You take the first piece." Ike took over with the server.

Each crew member stopped by to say a few words, so Blanche ate the cake very slowly.

"Well done, Miss Lamar." Dame Agatha came about midway through the line. "I have asked Mr. Gallagher to buy some material to make you a captain's uniform."

"Why, thank you, D—Agatha."

Some of the crew ate quickly then slipped out. Others came when they left. "Sorry I couldn't be here earlier," McDonald said. "I stayed downstairs so Jose and Tomas could be here at the start. Congratulations, Captain!"

"Thank you for coming." Tears came into her eyes. Her crew had done so much to make this day special.

She eventually finished that first piece of cake and eyed a second piece. Ike slid a corner piece onto a plate and handed it to her. "I saved this piece for you."

One of the younger maids approached, and Blanche asked Ike to set it aside for later.

Alice, the maid, approached. "I just wanted to say, ma'am, how very pleased and proud we all are of your passing your pilot's test. I can't believe as how they let a woman do that. It makes me think maybe someday women will be able to do anything they want to. Maybe even vote." The timid girl's eyes blazed.

"Who knows what the future holds?" Blanche hugged the girl. "Whatever dreams God gives you, pursue them with all your heart."

Elaine disappeared to the back of the kitchen, and Blanche glanced at the clock. When had it grown so late? Soon the dinner bell would ring. "I hate to say it, but. . ."

". . .We have a show to put on tonight. Don't worry. Several of the crew members are in the theater getting everything ready. You should rest."

"I'm supposed to be in the pilothouse!" Blanche's hand flew to her mouth.

Ike and Effie laughed. "We've been anchored at the wharf for the past two hours. Pete decided he should rest, since he knows we'll want to leave as soon as we clear out from tonight's performance. He sends his congratulations, by the way."

"I'm a pilot." She whispered the words. Butterflies fluttered in her stomach, and she had no room for the second piece of cake. "Save it for me, Elaine. I'll eat it later."

"I'm going to rest until supper." Effie headed for the door. "Are you coming with me?"

Blanche circled, taking in the banner, the remains of the cake sitting on the table, with the single white candle in the middle. She picked up the letter from the board and raised it to her lips. "Not this afternoon. I'll take a turn around the deck."

"May I join you?" Ike held his hands behind his back.

"Of course." They walked toward the door.

"Congratulations. Again. I am so proud of you." With a flash of his hands, he brought a single red rose from behind his back. "For you."

"How beautiful." She brought the rose to her nose as he opened the door. "But how did you. . . When did you. . ."

"I dashed into town as soon as we received the mail and begged the rose from someone with a rosebush in her front yard." His eyes darkened to the midnight blue. "I told her it was for a special occasion for a special woman."

How should she respond to that? "Thank you."

They promenaded around the perimeter until they reached the prow. The boat split the water, causing small waves to stream backward.

"I can't ever decide what I like better. Watching the water spill over the stern wheel or watching the prow split the river." Blanche kept the rose close to her nose. The velvety soft petals brushed against her cheeks.

"Isn't there a verse that warns against looking at what lies behind?" Ike picked up a small piece of wood and tossed it over the side. "But I know this: I am looking forward to the future."

"That's good. So am I."

"So you should, Captain Lamar."

They didn't speak for a few minutes. Blanche felt long fingers wrap her free hand in his, and she turned to look at Ike.

"I can't predict the future, but one thing I know for sure." Ike spoke in a low, warm voice. "I love you, Blanche Marie Lamar, and I can't imagine a future without you."

Blanche's gaze slowly traveled from the spot where their hands joined, to his shoulders, to his strong chin, at last allowing herself to gaze into his clear blue eyes. She reached a hesitant hand to caress his cheek. "Oh, Ike."

"I know that I have a lot to learn, to be ready to be the kind of husband God wants me to be."

"Ike—"

"Let me finish." He took a deep breath. "All I can ask you for now is if you are willing to wait for me, until I *am* that man, and

I feel qualified to ask you to share my life." His eyes stayed as sharply focused, but had turned to a lighter shade of blue, more like the color of fragile china.

"Ike. Oh, Ike." She leaned forward and kissed him on the lips then stepped back, shocked at her boldness. "I don't expect perfection."

Ike stepped forward, closing the gap between them. "Then?"

"I will gladly wait." She blinked through the happy tears. "As long as you don't take too long."

This time Ike leaned in and sealed her promise with a kiss.

Christmas Sunday, 1894

Blanche had never worn such a fancy gown, although Dame Agatha insisted the lack of puffed sleeves made it plain. The skirt fell in unbroken folds of winter white brocade. White tulle trailed from her veil down her back. The hairdresser Dame Agatha had recruited from Roma was weaving strings of pearls as well as orange blossoms into the soft curls on top of her head. Blanche could never have managed such an elaborate coiffure on her own.

The red roses of her bouquet were a different matter. Blanche had approached the same lady who provided the rose from her garden and asked for a posy. She had agreed and fashioned a beautiful bouquet.

"I don't often mind being blind, but I wish I could see you in your dress." Effie herself looked beautiful in her Christmassy dark green dress.

When planning the wedding, they had debated whether Effie should play the piano—her preference—or be her maid of honor—what Blanche wanted. When the Davenports heard about the impending nuptials, Mrs. Davenport graciously offered to play the piano for the wedding. Reverend Davenport and Mr. Sanders would both officiate.

"I will tell Mrs. Davenport to start Lohengrin's 'Bridal March'." Agatha dipped in what could have passed as a curtsy. "You are truly beautiful."

Ike and Blanche had given brief consideration to holding the wedding at Christ the King Church but decided the best place for the wedding was aboard the *Cordelia*. She had dressed in Dame Agatha's room, since the laundry was on the same deck as the theater. Various members of the crew had decorated the theater like a chapel; half the town of Roma was invited.

Even now Ike was making his way into the theater. A thrill ran up Blanche's spine as she considered him waiting for her, dressed in a black tuxedo. After his salvation, he had devoured the Bible, reading all the way through it twice, and had become as committed to following the Lord as he had pushed Him away earlier. So when Ike asked for her hand at Thanksgiving, Blanche had gladly accepted.

Captain Pettigrew appeared at the door. "Is the bride ready?"

Blanche blinked away the happy tears. She imagined Old Obie watching from heaven.

"Yes." She accepted his arm.

"You are breathtaking, my dear. And so are you, Miss Effie."

Music streamed through the open doors of the salon. Effie had decided not to use her cane since she knew the boat like the back of her hand. She took half a dozen steps, turned at the entrance to the salon, and walked through.

At the first chords of the "Wedding March," Captain Pettigrew drew Blanche gently forward. When she crossed the threshold, Ike filled her vision. He smiled, and her face widened in answer.

When she reached her groom, the "Wedding March" ended, and Effie began singing. "When peace like a river attendeth my way. . ."

It is well; it is well with my soul.

Award-winning author and speaker DARLENE FRANKLIN recently returned to cowboy country—Oklahoma. The move was prompted by her desire to be close to her son's family; her daughter Jolene has preceded her into glory.

Darlene loves music, needlework, reading, and reality TV. Talia, a Lynx point Siamese cat, proudly claims Darlene as her person.

Darlene has published several titles with Barbour Publishing.

To learn more about Darlene and her work, check out her blog at http://darlenefranklinwrites.blogspot.com/

Check out these other great
Destination Romances from
Barbour Publishing

A Wedding Transpires on
Mackinac Island
978-1-61626-535-9

A Bride's Dilemma in
Friendship, Tennessee
978-1-61626-571-7

A Wedding Song in
Lexington, Kentucky
978-1-61626-573-1

A Bride Opens Shop in
El Dorado, California
978-1-61626-583-0